Alexandre Dumas (24 July 1802 – 5 December 1870), also known as Alexandre Dumas père (French for 'father'), was a French writer. His works have been translated into many languages, and he is one of the most widely read French authors. Many of his historical novels of high adventure were originally published as serials, including The Count of Monte Cristo, The Three Musketeers, Twenty Years After, and The Vicomte of Bragelonne: Ten Years Later. His novels have been adapted since the early twentieth century for nearly 200 films. Dumas' last novel, The Knight of Sainte-Hermine, unfinished at his death, was completed by scholar Claude Schopp and published in 2005. It was published in English in 2008 as The Last Cavalier. Prolific in several genres, Dumas began his career by writing plays, which were successfully produced from the first. He also wrote numerous magazine articles and travel books; his published works totalled 100,000 pages. In the 1840s, Dumas founded the Théâtre Historique in Paris. (Source: Wikipedia)

Literary works:
The Three Musketeers
Twenty Years After
The Vicomte of Bragelonne
Ten Years Later
Louise de la Valliere
The Man in the Iron Mask
The Count of Monte Cristo
The Women's War
The Pale Lady
The Black Tulip
Olympe de Cleves
Isaac Laquedem
Catherine Blum
Georges
Amaury

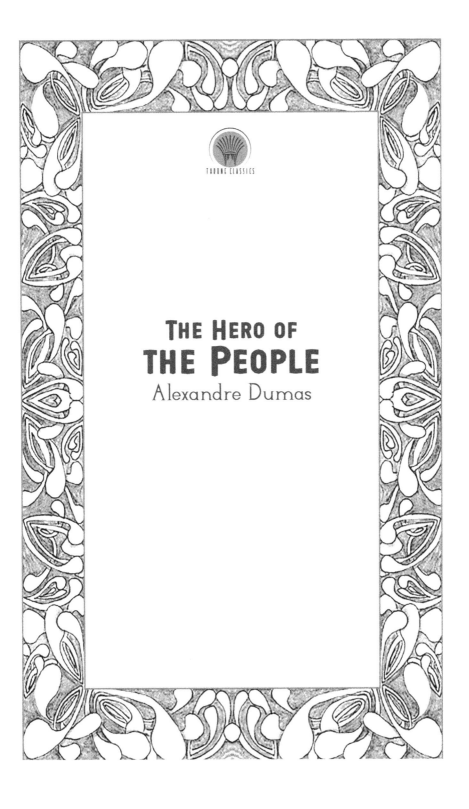

THE HERO OF
THE PEOPLE
Alexandre Dumas

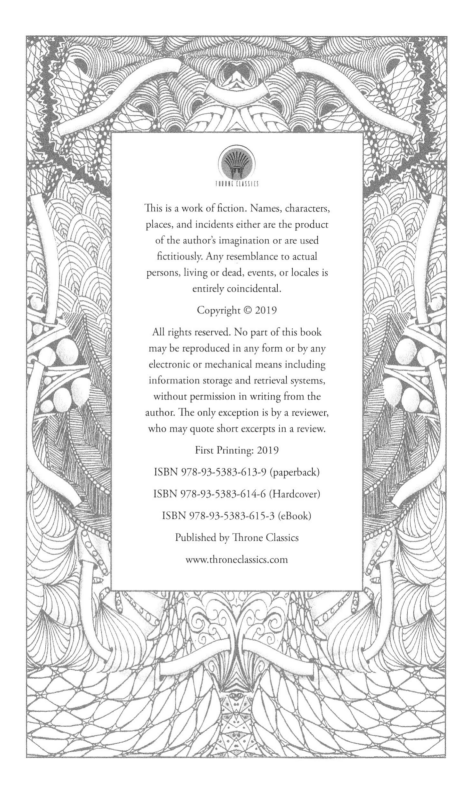

THRONE CLASSICS

Copyright © 2019

First Printing: 2019

ISBN 978-93-5383-613-9 (paperback)

ISBN 978-93-5383-614-6 (Hardcover)

ISBN 978-93-5383-615-3 (eBook)

Published by Throne Classics

www.throneclassics.com

Contents

THE HERO OF
THE PEOPLE

CHAPTER I. LOCKSMITH AND GUNSMITH.

THE French Revolution had begun by the Taking of the Bastile by the people of Paris on the Fourteenth of July, 1789, but it seemed to have reached the high tide by King Louis XVI, with his Queen Marie Antoinette and others of the Royal Family, leaving Versailles, after some sanguinary rioting, for the Capital, Paris.

But those who think, in such lulls of popular tempests, that all the mischief has blown over, make a mistake.

Behind the men who make the first onset, are those who planned it and who wait for the rush to be made and, then, while others are tried or satisfied, glide into the crowds to stir them up.

Mysterious agents of secret, fatal passions, they push on the movement from where it paused, and having urged it to its farthest limit, those who opened the way are horrified, at awakening to see that others attained the end.

At the doorway of a wine saloon at Sevres by the bridge, over the Seine, a man was standing who had played the main part, though unseen, in the riots which compelled the Royal Family to renounce an attempt to escape out of the kingdom like many of their sycophants, and go from Versailles Palace to the Tuileries.

This man was in the prime of life: he was dressed like a workingman, wearing velveteen breeches shielded by a leather apron with pockets such as shinglers wear to carry nailes in, or blacksmith-farriers or locksmiths. His stockings were grey, and his shoes had brass buckles; on his head was a fur cap like a grenadier's cut in half or what is called nowadays an artillerist's busby. Grey locks came straggling from under its hair and mingled with shaggy eyebrows; they shaded large bulging eyes, keen and sharp, quick, with such rapid changes that it was hard to tell their true color. His nose was rather thick than medium, the lips full, the teeth white, and his complexion sunburnt.

.

Without being largely built, this man was well formed: his joints were not course and his hands were small and might have seemed delicate but for their being swart like those of workers in metal.

Despite the vigor of the biceps muscle shown from his having rolled up his shirt sleeves, the skin was remarkable for its whiteness, and almost aristocratically fine.

Within his reach was a richly gold-inlaid double-barrelled fowling piece, branded with the name of Leclere, the fashionable gunsmith of Paris. You may ask how could such a costly firearm come into the hands of a common artisan? In times of riot it is not always the whitest hands which grasp the finest weapons.

This man had only arrived from Versailles since an hour, and perfectly well knew what had happened there: for to the landlord's questions as he supplied him with a bottle of wine which he did not touch, he had answered as follows:

"The Queen is coming along with the King and the Dauphin. They had started at half afternoon, having at last decided to live at the Tuileries; in consequence of which for the future Paris would no longer want for bread, as it would have in her midst, the Baker, the Baker's Wife and the Baker's Boy, as the popular slang dubbed the three 'Royals.'"

As for himself, he was going to hang round to see the procession go by.

This last assertion might be true, although it was easy to tell that his glance was more often bent on the side towards Paris than Versailles, which led one to surmise that he did not feel obliged to tell Boniface exactly what his intentions were.

In a few seconds his attraction seemed gratified, for he spied a man, garbed much like himself, and appearing of the same trade, outlined on the ridge of the road. He walked heavily like one who had journeyed from afar.

His age appeared to be like his awaiter's, that is, what is called the wrong side of forty. His features were those of a common fellow with low inclinations and vulgar instincts.

The stranger's eye was fastened on him with an odd expression as if he wished with a single scrutiny to measure the gold, if any, and the alloy in his composition.

When the wayfarer from the town was within twenty steps of this man lounging in the doorway, the latter stepped inside, poured the wine from the bottle into two glasses and returning to the doorstep with one tumbler held up, he hailed him:

"Hello, mate! it is pretty cold weather, and the road is a long one. What do you say to our having a drop of the red to cheer us up and warm us?"

The workman from town looked round to make sure that he was alone and that the greeting was addressed to him.

"Speaking to me, are you?"

"Who else, as you are alone?"

"And offering me a go of wine?"

"Why not, as we are brothers of the file and bossing-hammer alike? or some at nigh."

"Anybody can belong to a trade," said the other looking hard at the speaker; "but the point is, are you a greenhand or a master of the craft?"

"I reckon we shall tell how far we have learnt the trade while drinking and chatting together."

"All right then!" said the other, walking up to the door, while the inviter showed the table set out with the wine. The man took the tumbler, eyed the contents as if he had doubts, but they disappeared when the stranger poured himself out a second brimmer.

"Why, hang it all, are you getting so proud that you will not drink with a shopmate?"

"No, dash me if I am—here is Good Luck to the Nation!"

The workman's grey eyes were fixed on the toast-giver's.

He tossed off the glass at a draft, and wiped his lips on his sleeve.

"Deuse take it, but it is Burgundy wine," he remarked.

"And good liquor, too, eh? the vintage was recommended to me; and happening along I dropped in, and I am not repenting it. But why not sit down and be at home? there is some more in the bottle and more in the cellar when that is gone."

"I say, what are you working at here?"

"I have knocked off for the day. I finished a job at Versailles and I am going on to Paris with the royal procession as soon as it comes along."

"What procession?"

"Why, the King and the Queen and the little Prince, who are returning to the city with the Fishmarket women and two hundred Assemblymen, all under protection of Gen. Lafayette and the National Guard."

"So the fat old gentleman has decided to come to town?"

"They made him do it."

"I suspected so when I started for Paris at three this morning."

"Hello! did you leave Versailles at three without any curiosity about what was going off?"

"No, no, I itched to know what the gent was up to, being an acquaintance, a chum of mine, by the way, though I am not bragging; but you know, old man, one must get on with the work. I have a wife and children to provide for, and it is no joke now. I am not working at the royal forge."

The listener let what he heard pass without putting any questions.

"So, it was on a pressing job that you went back to Paris?" he only inquired.

"Just that, as it appears, and handsomely paid too," said the workman, jingling some coin in his pocket, "though it was paid for by a kind of servant, which was not polite, and by a German, too, which blocked me from having any pleasant chatter during the work. I am not one for gab, but it amuses one if no harm is spoken of others."

"And it is no harm when harm is spoken of the neighbors, eh?"

Both men laughed, the stranger showing sound teeth against the other's snaggy ones.

"So, then, you have knocked off a good job, wanted doing in a hurry, and well paid?" said the former, like one who advances only a step at a time, but still does advance. "Hard work, no doubt?"

"You bet it was hard. Worse than a secret lock—an invisible door. What do you think of one house inside of another? some one who wants to hide away, be sure. What a game he could have—in or out, as he pleased. 'Your master in?' 'No, sir: just stepped out.' 'You are a liar—he came in just now.' 'You had better look, since you are so cocksure.' So they look round, but I defy them to find the gentleman. An iron door, you will understand, which closes on a beading-framed panel, while it runs on balls in a groove as on wheels. On the metal is a veneer of old oak, so that you can rap with your knuckles on it and the sound is identical with that of a solid plank. I tell you when the job was done, it would take me in myself."

"Where the mischief would you do a job like that? but I suppose you would not tell even a pal?"

"I cannot tell because I do not know."

"What hoodwinked you?"

"Guess again and you will be wrong. A hack was waiting for me at the city turnpike bars. A chap came up and asked: 'Are you so and-so?' I said 'I am.' 'Good, we are waiting for you: jump in.' So I got inside the coach, where they bandaged my eyes, and after the wheels had gone round for about half an hour, a big carriage-door was opened. They took me out and up ten steps of a flight of stairs into a vestibule, where I found a German servant who said to the others: 'Goot! make scarce of yourseluffs; no longer want we you.' They slung their hook out of it, while the blinders were taken me off, and I was shown what I had to do. I had pitched into the work like a good hand, and was done in an hour. They paid me in bran-new gold, tied up my eyes, put me back in the carriage, dropped me on the same spot where I was taken up, wished me safe home—and here I am."

"Without your having seen anything, even out of the tail of the eye? Deuse take me if ever I heard of a bandage which would stop a man catching a glimpse on one side or t'other. Better own up that you had a peep at something?" pursued the stranger.

"Well, I did make a misstep at the first stone of the stairs so that, in throwing up my hands to keep from falling, I got a peep from its disarranging the handkerchief. I saw a regular row of trees on my left hand which made me think that I was in some avenue. That is all, on my honor."

"I can't say it is much. For the main avenue is long and more than one house has a carriage-doorway betwixt the St. Honore Coffeehouse and the Bastile."

"The fact is," said the locksmith, scratching his head, "I don't think I am up to telling the house."

The questioner appeared satisfied, although his countenance did not usually betray his feelings.

"But," exclaimed he, as if skipping to another topic, "are there no good locksmiths at Paris that they have to send to Versailles for one?"

CHAPTER II. THE THREE ODDITIES.

THE locksmith lifted his tumbler to his eye's level, admired the liquor with pleasure, and said after sipping it with gratification:

"Bless you, yes, plenty of locksmiths at Paris."

He drank a few drops more.

"Ay, and masters of the craft." He drank again. "Yes, but there is a difference between them."

"Hang me," said the other, "but I believe you are like St. Eloi, our patron saint, master among the master-workmen."

"Are you one of us?"

"Akin, my boy: I am a gunsmith. All smiths are brothers. This is a sample of my work."

The locksmith took the gun from the speaker's hands, examined it with attention, clicked the hammers and approved with a nod of the sharp action of the lock: but spying the name on the plate, he said:

"Leclere? this won't do, friend, for Leclere is scanty thirty, and we are both a good forty, without meaning to hurt your feelings."

"Quite true, I am not Leclere, but it is the same thing, only a little more so. For I am his master."

"Oh, capital!" chuckled the locksmith; "it is the same as my saying 'I am not the King but I am the same thing, only more so, as I am his master.'"

"Oho," said the other rising and burlesquing the military salute, "have I the honor of addressing Master Gamain, the King of Locksmiths?"

"Himself in person, and delighted if he can do anything for you," replied Gamain, enchanted at the effect his name had produced.

"The devil! I had no idea I was talking to one of the high flyers in our line," said the other. "A man so well considered."

"Of such consequence, do you mean?"

"Well, maybe I have not used the right word, but then I am only a poor smith, and you are the master smith for the master of France. I say," he went on in another tone, "it can't be always funny to have a king for a 'prentice, eh?"

"Why not?"

"Plain enough. You cannot eternally be wearing gloves to say to the mate on your bench: 'Chuck us the hammer or pass the retail file along.'"

"Certainly not."

"I suppose you have to say: 'Please your gracious Majesty, don't hold the drill askew.'"

"Why, that is just the charm with him, d'ye see, for he is a plain-dealer at heart. Once in the forge, when he has the anvil to the fore, and the leathern apron tied on, none would ever take him for the Son of St. Louis, as he is called."

"Indeed you are right, it is astonishing how much he is like the next man."

"And yet these perking courtiers are a long time seeing that."

"It would be nothing if those close around him found that out," said the stranger, "but those who are at a distance are beginning to get an idea of it."

His queer laugh made Gamain look at him with marked astonishment. But he saw that he had blundered in his pretended character by making a witticism, and gave the man no time to study his sentence, for he hastened to recur to the topic by saying:

"A good thing, too; for I think it lowers a man to have to slaver him with Your Majesty here and My Noble Sire there."

"But you do not have to call him high names. Once in the workshop we drop all that stuff. I call him Citizen, and he calls me Gamain, but I ain't what you would call chummy with him, while he is familiar with me."

"That is all very well; but when the dinner hour comes round I expect he sends you off to the kitchen to have your bread and cheese with the flunkeys."

"Oh, Lor', No! he has never done that; quite the other way about, for he gets me to bring in a table all set into the workshop and he will often put his legs under the mahogany with me, particularly at breakfast, saying: 'I shall not bother about having breakfast with the Queen, as I should have to wash my hands.'"

"I can't make this out."

"You can't understand that when the King works like us, he has his hands smeared with oil and rust and filings, which does not prevent us being honest folks, and the Queen would say to him, with her hoity-toity prudish air: 'Dirty beggar, your hands are foul.' How can a man have a fop's hands if he works at the forge?"

"Don't talk to me about that—I might have married high if I could have kept my fingers nice," sighed the stranger.

"Let me tell you that the old chap does not have a lively time in his geographical study or his library; but I believe he likes my company the best."

"That is all very amusing for you, except having to endure so poor a pupil."

"Poor," repeated Gamain. "Oh, no, you must not say that. He is to be pitied, to tell the truth, in his coming into the world as a king, for he is but a man—and having to waste himself on a pack of nonsense instead of sticking to our art, in which he makes good way. He will never be but a third-rate king for he is too honest, but he would have made an excellent locksmith. There is one man I execrate for stealing away his time—that Necker fellow, who made him lose such a lot of time!"

"You mean with his accounts and financing."

"Ay, his fine-Nancy-ing, indeed."

"But you must make a fat thing out of such a lad to bring on."

"No, that is just where you are in error: that is why I bear a grudge to him, Louis the Father of the Kingdom, the Restorer of the French Nation! People believe that I am rich as Creases, while I am as poor as Job."

"You, poor? why, what does he do with all his money?"

"He gives half to the poor and the other half is got away by his parasites, so that he never has any brass. The Coigny, Polignac and Vaudreuil families eat him up, poor dear old boy! One day he wanted to cut down Lord Coigny's appointments, and the gentleman waylaid him at our forge door: after going out for five minutes, the King came back, pale as a ghost, muttering: 'Faith, I believe he would have caned me.' 'Did he get the appointments reduced, Sire?' I inquired. 'I let them stand,' he said: 'what else could I do?' Another time he wanted to scold the Queen for giving Duchess Polignac three hundred thousand francs for the linen for her baby, and what do you think?"

"It is a pretty sum for a baby!"

"Right you are: but it was not enough: the Queen made him give her five hundred thousand. You have only to look how these Polignacs have got on, who had not a penny when they started in, but are running away from France with millions. I should not have minded if they had any talent, but just give those neerdowells a hammer or cold chisel; they could not forge a horseshoe: give them file and screw-driver and see how they would get on at a common lock! However, they can wag the tongue to some purpose, since they hounded the King on so that they leave him in a quagmire. He may flounder out as best he can, with the help of General Lafayette and Mayor Bailly, and Lord Mirabeau. I gave him good advice, but he would not listen to me, and he leaves me with fifteen hundred livres a-year, though I am his trainer, who first showed him to hold a file properly."

"But I suppose that when you worked with him, there were some pickings?"

"But am I working with him now? Since the Taking of the Bastile, I have not set foot inside his palace. Once or twice I met him: the first time, as there was a crowd about in the street, he just bobbed his head; the next, on the Satory Road, he stopped the coach for the coast was clear. 'Good morning, my poor Gamain, how goes it?' he sighed. 'How goes it with you, Sire? but I know it is rough—but that will be a lesson to you.' 'Are your wife and children well?' he said to shift the talk. 'All fine but with appetites like ogres.' 'You must make them a little present from me.' He searched his pockets, but he could rake up only nine louis. 'That is all I carry with me, my poor Gamain,' he said with a kind of groan, 'and I am ashamed to do so little.' Of course, it was small cash for a monarch to give, short of ten gold pieces, so paltry a sum to a work-fellow—So——"

"You refused them?"

"Catch me? No, I said: 'I had better grab, for he will meet somebody else not so delicate as me, who would take them.' Still, he need not fret himself, I shall never walk into Versailles unless I am sent for, and I do not know as I shall then."

"What a grateful heart this rogue has," muttered the stranger, but all he said aloud was: "It is very affecting, Master Gamain, to see devotion like yours survive misfortune. A last glass to the health of your 'prentice."

"Faith, he does not deserve it, but never mind! here's to his health, all the same!" He drank. "Only to think that he had thousands of bottles in his cellar which would beat this, and he never said to a footman: Take a basket of this lush to my friend Gamain!' Not he—he would sooner have it swilled by his Lifeguardsmen, the Swiss, or his Flanders Regiment. They did him a lot of good, I do not think!"

"What did you expect?" questioned the other, sipping his wine, "kings are ungrateful like this one. But hush! we are no longer alone."

In fact, three persons were entering the drinking saloon, two men of the common sort and a fishfag, and they took seats at the table matching that at which Gamain and his "treater" were sitting.

The locksmith raised his eyes to them and stared with an attention making the other smile. They were truly worthy of some remark.

One of the two men was all body: the other all legs: it was hard to say anything about the woman.

All-Body resembled a dwarf: he was under five feet in height: he may have lost an inch or so from his knees knocking although when he stood up, his feet kept apart. Instead of his countenance redeeming the deformity, it seemed to highten it;—for his oily and dirty hair was flattened down on his bald forehead; his eyebrows were so badly shaped as to seem traced at random; his eyes were usually dull but when lighted up sheeny and glassy as the toad's. In moments of irritation, they threw out sparks like a viper's, from concentrated pupils. His nose was flat, and deviated from the straight line so that his prominent cheek bones stood out all the more. Lastly, to complete the hideous aspect, his yellow lips only partly covered the few, black and loose teeth in his twisted mouth.

At first glance you would say that gall, not blood, flowed in his veins.

The other was so opposed to the short-legged one that he seemed a heron on its stilts. The likeness to the bird was the closer from his head being lost between his humped shoulders so as to be distinguished solely by the eyes, like blood-spots, and a long, pointed, beak-like nose. Like the heron, too, he seemed to have the ability to stretch his neck, and put out the eyes of one at a distance. His arms also were gifted with this elasticity, and while seated, he might pick up a handkerchief dropped at his feet without moving his body.

The third person was ambiguous; it being difficult to divine the sex. If a man, he was upwards of thirty-four, wearing a stylish costume of the fishmarket stallkeepers, with lace kerchief and tucker, and gold earrings and chain. His features, as well as could be made out through layers of rouge and flake white, together with beauty-patches of sticking plaster of all fancy shapes, were slightly softened as in degenerate races. As soon as one caught sight of him one wanted to hear him speak in the hope that the voice's sound would give his dubious appearance a stamp by which he could be classed. But it was nothing to the purpose: his soprano voice left the curious observer still deeper plunged into doubt.

The shoes and stockings of the trio were daubed in mud to show that they had been tramping in the road for some time.

"Lord save us, I seem to know that woman, from having met her before," said Gamain.

"Very likely at court," sneered the pretended workman "their manners have been there quite a while and they have been visitors, the fishmarket dames, of late. But," he went on, pulling his cap down on his brow and taking up his gun, "they are here on business: consequently, we had better leave them alone."

"Do you know them?"

"By sight. Do you?"

"I say that I have met the woman before: tell me who the men are and I may put my finger on her name."

"Of the two men, the knock-kneed one is the surgeon, Jean Paul Marat; while the humpback is Prosper Verrieres."

"Aha!"

"Does not that put you on the right track?"

"My tongue to the dogs if it does!"

"The fishwoman is——"

"Wait, it is—but, no—impossible——"

"I see that you will not name him—the fishwoman is the Duke of Aiguillon."

At this utterance of the title, the disguised nobleman started and turned, as well as his companions. They made a movement to rise as men do when in presence of a leader: but the pretended gunsmith laid a finger on his lips and passed them by.

Gamain followed him, believing he was in a dream.

At the doorway he was jostled by a running man, who seemed to be pursued by a mob, shouting:

"Stop him—that is the Queen's hairdresser! stop the hairdresser!"

Among the howling and racing men were two who carried each a human head on a pikestaff. They were those of two Lifeguards, killed at Versailles in defending the Queen from the mob.

"Halloa, it is Leonard," said the strange workman, to the fugitive.

"Silence, do not name me," yelled the barber, dashing into the saloon.

"What do they chase him for?" inquired Gamain.

"The Lord knows," was the response: "maybe they want him to curl the hair of the poor soldiers. In Revolutionary times, fellows have such quaint fancies!"

He mixed in with the throng, leaving Gamain, from whom he had probably extracted all he wanted, to make his way alone to his workshop at Versailles.

CHAPTER III. THE UNDYING MAN.

IT was the more easy for the pretended gunsmith to blend with the crowd as it was numerous.

It was the advance guard of the procession around the King, Queen and the Prince Royal, leaving the court suburb at half past one.

In the royal coach were the Queen, her son, her daughter, called Madam Royale though a child, Count Provence, the King's brother. Lady Elizabeth his sister, and the Queen's favorite lady of the household, Andrea Taverney Countess of Charny.

In a hundred carriages came the National Assemblymen who had declared they would henceforth be inseparable from the monarch.

This mob was about a quarter of an hour ahead of the royal party, and rallied round the two royal guardsmen's heads as their colors. All stopped at the Sevres wine saloon. The collection was of tattered and half-drunken wretches, the scum that comes to the surface whether the inundation is water or lava.

Suddenly, great stir in the concourse, for they had seen the National Guards' bayonets and General Lafayette's white horse, immediately preceding the royal coach.

Lafayette was fond of popular gatherings: he really reigned among the Paris people whose idol he was. But he did not like the lowest orders. Paris, like Rome, had a grade under the mere mob.

In particular, he did not approve of Lynch Law, and he had done his utmost to try to save those aristocrats whom the crowd had executed. It was to hide their trophies and preserve the bloody tokens of victory that the multitude kept on ahead. But on being encouraged by the trio of captains waiting at the Sevres saloon, they decided to keep the heads up and wait for the King, so that he should not be parted from his faithful guards.

The mob was increased by the country folks flocking to the road from all quarters to see the cortege go by. A few cheered, adding their uproar to the howls, hoots and groans of the marching column, but the majority, stood dull and quiet on both sides of the road.

Did this mean that they were for the Royal Family? No: or at least unless they belonged to the court party, everybody, even the upper middle class, suffered more or less from the dreadful famine spreading over the kingdom. If they did not insult the King and Queen, they remained hushed, and the silence of an assemblage is often worse than an insult.

On the other hand the myriads roared with all their lung power: "Hurrah for Lafayette!" who took off his hat now and then or waved the sword in his right hand: and "Long live Mirabeau!" who thrust his head out of the carriage window, where he was one of six, to get a whiff of the air necessary for his broad chest.

Hence, amid the silence for himself, the unfortunate Louis XVI. heard applauded that Popularity which he had lost and that Genius which he had never possessed.

By the King's right side carriage-window walked a man in a black suit whose dress pointed him out as one of the Philosophers, as they were termed, or Revolutionists who worked intellectually for the amelioration of the monarchy. This was the royal honorary physician, Dr. Honore Gilbert. The crowd cheered him at times, for he was a hero of their own. Born a Frenchman, of humble degree, a boy on the estate of the ultra-royalist Baron Taverney, he had educated himself in democratic learning. Falling in love with his master's lovely daughter, Andrea, since Countess of Charny, he had followed her to court. At Paris he became favorite pupil of Rousseau, the revolutionist, and this farther confirmed him in his subversive principles.

But having taken advantage of Andrea while she was powerless under the influence of a mesmeric sleep, he fled the country. He had deposited in sure hands the living evidence of his crime, a boy named Emile (In honor of Rousseau, who wrote a book so called) Sebastian Gilbert, and fled the country. But at the Azores Islands he came in contact with the young lady's brother Philip, who shot him down and believed he left him dead.

But, restored to life by his friend, the Baron Balsamo, otherwise Cagliostro the Magician he accompanied him to America.

The two formed part of the legion of Frenchmen who helped the revolted Thirteen Colonies to throw off the British yoke.

Returning to his country he was arrested at Havre and thown into the Bastile. When that hated prison was stormed by the Parisians led by the Farmer Billet, he was rescued. He had gone to court to learn who had caused this arrest, and to his amazement discovered that its author was the woman whom he had unutterably wronged. Yes, the baron's daughter had married the Queen's favorite, thought by some to be her paramour, Count George Charny, very rich, very brave and altogether fit to create her a power in the realm.

Gilbert had a sincere pity for royalty under a cloud. He was known to the King as the author of certain articles on the way to steer the Ship of State, and his offer to serve him was gladly accepted.

The mob cheered at the remarkable shaking up of the sands in Time's box by which the revolutionary advocate, fresh from the Bastile dungeons, should walk at the side of the King's coach to shield his life from the assassin. No mere touch of rhetoric, for on the royal visit to Paris lately a bullet had cut a button off the doctor's coat and slain a woman in the throng: this graceful gentlemen in black was then a better safeguard than the soldiers whose heads were now garnishing the pikes there in advance.

Queen Marie Antoinette looked with wonder at this doctor, whose stoicism she could not understand, while to it the American manner of forced quiet added more sternness. Without love or devotion for his sovereigns, he carried out what he considered duty towards them, as ready to die for them as those who had the qualities of the loyalist he lacked.

On both sides of the royal coach tramped men and women, in mud six inches deep, while amid the ribbons and rags, the Fishmarket women and porters of the Paris Markets swarmed round waves more compact than the rest of the human sea. These clumps were cannon or ammunition wagons, on which sat women singing at the top of their voices. An old song which had been applied to King Louis XV.'s mistress Jeanne Dubarry, and was now altered to suit Marie Antoinette and the situation of affairs, was their choice. They roared:

"The Baker's wife has got the cash, which costs her very little."

They also kept reiterating: "We shall not want for bread any more, as we have got the Baker, the Baker's Wife and the Baker's Little Boy along."

The Queen seemed to listen to it all without understanding. Between her knees she held her son, who looked at the multitude as frightened princes stare when appalled.

The King watched with a dull and heavy eye. He had little sleep in the night; he had not made a good breakfast though usually a hearty eater; he had no time to have his hair dressed and his beard had grown long. His linen was limp and roughened, too—all things to his disadvantage. Alas, Louis was not the man for emergencies, and this was a period of emergencies. He bent his head when they came: save once when he held his chin up—it was when he walked upon the scaffold.

Lady Elizabeth was the angel of sweetness and resignation placed by heaven beside those doomed creatures to console the King during the Queen's absence; and the Queen after the King's death.

Count Provence, here as everywhere, had the squinting glance of a false man; he knew that he ran no present danger; he was the popular member of the family—no one knew why—perhaps because he remained in France when his brother Artois fled.

Could the King have read his heart, he might not have felt any gratitude to him for what he pledged in the way of devotion.

Countess Andrea seemed of marble. She had recognized the man she most hated in the King's new confidential adviser, and one whom the Queen seemed bound to win to her side. Like a statue, the stir round her seemed not to affect her, and she looked in attire as trim as if fresh from a band-box. One thought was alive within her, fierce and luminous—love for some unknown—perchance her husband, or hate for Gilbert—at whom she darted lightnings involuntarily whenever their glances crossed. But she felt that she might not defy his with impunity, for he was a pupil of Balsamo Cagliostro, the arch-mesmerist, and might sway her with the same art.

A hundred paces on the other side of the little drinking saloon, the royal train stopped. All along the line the clamor doubled.

The Queen bent out of the window and as the movement looked like a bow to the crowd, there was a long murmur. She called Dr. Gilbert.

He went up to the window: as he had kept his hat off all the way, he had no need to bare his head in respect. His attitude showed he was entirely under her orders.

"What are your people shouting and singing?" she requested to know.

The Queen's form of putting the question showed that she had been ruminating it for some time. He sighed as much as to say, it is the same old story.

"Alas, my lady," he proceeded with profound melancholy, "those you call my people, were yours in former times, and it is less than twenty years ago when Lord Brissac, a delightful courtier whom I look in vain for here, showed you the same people shouting for the Dauphin under the City Hall windows and said: 'You behold twenty thousand admirers there.'"

The Queen bit her lips from the impossibility of catching this man in want of a repartee or of respect.

"That is true—it only proves that the many-headed change," she said.

Gilbert bowed this time, without retort.

"I asked you a question, doctor," persisted the lady, with the obstinacy she had for even disagreeable matters.

"Yes, and I answer since your Majesty insists. They are singing that the

Baker's Wife has plenty of money which it gave her no trouble to get. You are aware that they style your Majesty the Baker's Wife?"

"Just as they called me Lady Deficit before. Is there any connection between the nicknames?"

"So much also as the finances are concerned. They mean by your money being easily come by that you had complaisant treasurers such as Calonne in particular, who gave you whatever you asked; the people therefore assume that you got your money readily for the asking."

The Queen's hand was clenched on the red velvet carriage-window ledge.

"So much for what they are singing. Now, for what they bellow out?"

"They say that they shall no longer want for bread since they have the Baker, the Baker's Wife and the Baker's Son among them."

"I expect you to make this second piece of insolence clear."

"You would see that they are not so much to blame as you fancy if you were to look to the intention and not weigh the words of the people. Wrongly or rightfully, the masses believe that a great Grain Trust is carried on at Versailles. This prevents flour from coming freely into the capital. Who feeds the Paris poor? the Baker. Towards whom does the working man and his wife hold out their supplicating hands when their children cry for food? the baker and the baker's wife. Who do they pray to after the Sender of the harvest? the lady of the estate—that is, the loaf-giver, as the name is derived. Are not you three the loaf-givers for the country, the King, yourself and this august child? Do not be astonished at the mighty, blessed name the people give you, but thank them for cherishing the hope that as soon as the King, the Queen and their son are in the midst of the famished thousands, they will no longer be in want."

For an instant the royal lady closed her eyes, and she made the movement of swallowing as though to keep down her hatred as well as bitter saliva which scorched her throat.

"So we ought to thank these howlers for their songs and nick-names upon us?"

"Yes, and most sincerely: the song is but an expression of their good humor as the shouts are of their expectations. The whole explains their desire."

"So they want Lafayette and Mirabeau to live long?"

"Yes," returned Gilbert, seeing that the Queen had clearly heard the cries, "for those two leaders, separated by the gulf over which you hang, may, united, save the monarchy."

"Do you mean that the monarchy has sunk so low that it can be picked up by those two?" queried the lady.

He was going to make some kind of reply when a burst of voices, in dread, with atrocious peals of laughter and a great swaying of the gathering, driving Gilbert closer to the vehicle, announced that he would be needed in defense of the Queen by speech or action. It was the two head-carriers, who, after having made Leonard barb and curl the hair, wanted to have the fun of presenting them to Marie Antoinette—as other roughs, or perhaps the same—had presented the dead heads of sons to their fathers.

The crowd yelled with horror and fell away as these ghastly things came up.

"In heaven's name, do not look to the right," cried Gilbert.

The Queen was no woman to obey such an injunction without a peep to see the reason. So her first movement was to turn her gaze in the forbidden direction and she uttered a scream of fright. But, all of a sudden, as she tore her sight from this horrible spectacle as if they were Gorgon heads, they became fixed as though they met another view even more awful, from which she could not detach it.

This Medusa's head was the stranger's who had been drinking and chatting with Locksmith Gamain in the wine-store: with folded arms, he was leaning against a tree.

The Queen's hand left the window cushion, and resting on Gilbert's shoulder, he felt her clench her nails into its flesh. He turned to see her pale, with fixed eyes and quivering, blanched lips.

He would have ascribed the emotion to the two death's heads but for her not looking at either. The gaze was in another direction, traveling visually in which he descried the object and he emitted a cry of amaze.

"Cagliostro!" both uttered at the same time.

The man at the tree clearly saw the Queen, but all he did was beckon for Gilbert to come to him.

At this point of time the carriages started on once more. By a natural and mechanical impulse the Queen gave Gilbert an outward push to prevent his being run over by the wheel. It looked as though she urged him towards the summoner. Anyhow, he was not sufficiently master of himself not to obey the mandate. Motionless, he let the party proceed; then, following the mock gunsmith who merely looked back to be sure he was followed, he entered behind him a little lane going uphill to Bellevue, where they disappeared behind a wall at the same time as the procession went out of sight in a declivity of the hills, as though plunging into an abyss.

CHAPTER IV. FATALITY.

GILBERT followed his guide half-way up the slope where stood a handsome house. The foregoer pulled out a key and opened a side door intended for the master to go in or come out without the servants knowing when he did so. He left the door ajar to signify that the companion of the journey was to use it. Gilbert entered and shut the door gently but it silently closed itself tightly with a pneumatic arrangement at the hinges which seemed the work of magic. Such an appliance would have been the delight of Master Gamain.

Through luxuriously fitted passages Gilbert finally came into a drawing room, hung with Indian satin tapestry; a fantastic Oriental bird held the lustre in its beak and it emitted a light which Gilbert knew was electricity, though its application thus would have been a puzzle to others than this specialist in advanced science. The lights represented lily-blooms, which again was an anticipation of modern illuminators.

One picture alone adorned this room but it was Raphael's Madonna.

Gilbert was admiring this masterpiece when the host entered by a secret door behind him from a dressing room.

An instant had sufficed for him to wash off the stain and the pencillings and to give his black hair, without any grey, a stylish turn. He had also changed his clothes. Instead of the workman was an elegant nobleman. His embroidered coat and his hands glittering with rings in the Italian style, strongly contrasted with Gilbert's American black coat and his plain gold ring, a keepsake from General Washington.

Count Cagliostro advanced with a smiling open face and held out his hand to Gilbert.

"Dear Master," cried the latter rushing to him.

"Stop a bit," interrupted the other, laughing: "since we have parted, my dear Gilbert, you have made such progress in revolutionary methods at all events, that you are the master at present and I not fit to undo your shoestrings."

"I thank you for the compliment," responded the doctor, "but how do you know I have made such progress, granting I have progressed?"

"Do you believe you are one of those men whose movement is not marked although not seen? Since eight years I have not set eyes on you but I have had a daily report of what you did. Do you doubt I have double-sight?"

"You know I am a mathematician."

"You mean, incredulous? Let me show you, then. In the first place you returned to France on family matters; they do not concern me, and consequently——"

"Nay, dear master, go on," interposed the other.

"Well, you came to have your son Sebastian educated in a boarding school not far from Paris in quiet, and to settle business affairs with your farmer, an honest fellow whom you are now retaining in town against his wishes. For a thousand reasons he wants to be home beside his wife."

"Really, master, you are prodigious!"

"Wait for something stronger. The second time you returned to France because political questions drew you, like many others; besides you had published several political treatises which you sent to King Louis XVI., and as there is much of the Old Man in you—you are prouder for the approval of the King than perhaps you would be of that of my predecessor in your training, Rousseau—who would be higher than a king this day, had he lived—you yearn to learn what is thought of Dr. Gilbert by the descendant of St. Louis, Henry Fourth and Louis XIV. Unfortunately a little matter has kept alive which you did not bear in mind, as a sequel to which I picked you up in a cave in the Azores, where my yacht put in. I restored you from the effects of a bullet in your breast. This little affair concerned Mdlle. Andrea Taverney, become Countess Charny, which she deserves, to save the Queen's reputation, compromised by the King coming upon her and Count Charny by surprise.

"As the Queen could refuse nothing to this saver, she got a blank warrant and committal to prison for you, so that you were arrested on the road out of Havre and taken to the Bastile. There you would be to this day, dear doctor, if the people, prepared for a rising by a person whom you may divine, had not in a day knocked the old building lower than the gutter. I was not sorry, for I had a taste of the fare myself before I was banished the Kingdom. This morning early, you contributed to the rescue of the Royal Family, by running to arouse Lafayette, who was sleeping the sleep of the virtuous; and just now, when you saw me, you were about to make a breastwork of your body for the Queen who seemed threatened—though, between ourselves, she detests you. Is this right? Have I forgotten anything of note, such as a hypnotic seance before the King when Countess Charny was made to disclose how she had led to your imprisonment and how she obtained a certain casket of your papers by one Wolfstep, a police agent? Tell me and if I have omitted any point, I am ready to do penance for it."

Gilbert stood stupefied before this extraordinary man, who knew so well to prepare his march that his hearer was inclined to attribute to him the faculty of comprising heavenly as well as mundane things, and to read in the heart of man.

"Yes, it is thus and you are still the magician, the fortune-teller, the thaumaturgist, Cagliostro!"

The wonder-worker smiled with satisfaction, for it was evident that he was proud of having worked on Gilbert such an impression as the latter's visage revealed.

"And now," continued Gilbert, "as I love you as much as you do me, dear master, and my desire to learn what you have been doing is equal to yours and how I have fared, will you kindly tell me, if I am not intruding too far, in what part of the globe you have exhibited your genius and practiced your power?"

"Oh, I?" said Cagliostro, smiling, "like yourself I have been rubbing shoulders with kings, but with another aim. You go up to them to uphold them; I to knock them over. You try to manufacture a constitutional monarch and will not succeed; I, to make emperors, kings and princes democratic, and I am coming on."

"Are you really?" queried Gilbert with an air of doubt.

"Decidedly. It must be allowed that they were prepared for me by Voltaire, Alembert and Diderot, admirable Mecaenases, sublime contemners of the gods, and also by the example of Frederick the Great, whom we have the misfortune to lose. But you know we are all mortal, except the Count of St. Germain and myself.

"So long as the Queen is fair, my dear Gilbert, and she can recruit soldiers to fight among themselves, kings who fret to push over thrones have never thought of hurling over the altar. But we have her brother, Kaiser Joseph II. who suppresses three-fourths of the monasteries, seizes ecclesiastical property, drives even the Camelite nuns out of their cells, and sends his sister prince of nuns trying on the latest fashions in hats and monks having their hair curled. We have the King of Denmark, who began by killing his doctor Struensee, and who, at seventeen, the precocious philosopher, said: 'Voltaire made a man of me for he taught me to think.' We have the Empress Catherine, who made such giant strides in philosophy that—while she dismembered Poland, Voltaire wrote to her: 'Diderot, Alembert and myself are raising altars to you. We have the Queen of Sweden and many princes in the Empire and throughout Germany.'"

"You have nothing left you but to convert the Pope, my dear master, and I hope you will, as nothing is beyond you."

"That will be a hard task. I have just slipped out of his claws. I was locked up in Castle Sanangelo as you were in the Bastile."

"You don't say so? did the Romans upset the castle as the people of St. Antoine Ward overthrew the Bastile?"

"No, my dear doctor, the Romans are a century behind that point. But, be easy: it will come in its day: the Papacy will have its revolutionary days, and Versailles and the Vatican can shake hands in equality at that era."

"I thought that nobody came alive out of Castle Sanangelo?"

"Pooh! what about Benvenuto Cellini, the sculptor?"

"You had not wings such as he made, had you, and did you flit over the Tiber like a new Icarus?"

"It would be the more difficult as I was lodged for the farther security in the blackest dungeon of the keep. But I did get out, as you see."

"Bribed the jailor with gold?"

"I was out of luck, for my turnkey was incorruptible. But, fortunately, he was not immortal. Chance—the believers say, Providence—well, the Architect of the Universe granted that he should die on the morrow of his refusing to open the prison doors. He died very suddenly! and he had to be replaced."

"The new hand was not unbribable?"

"The day of his taking up his office, as he brought me the soup, he said: 'Eat heartily and get your strength, for we have to do some stiff traveling this night.' By George, the good fellow told no lie. That same night we rode three horses out dead, and covered a hundred miles."

"What did the government say when your disappearance was known?"

"Nothing. The dead and still-warm other jailer was clad in the clothes I left behind; and a pistol was fired in his face; it was laid by his side and the statement was given out that in despair at having no escape and with the useless weapon which I had procured none could tell how, I had blown out my brains. It follows that I am officially pronounced dead and buried; the jailer being interred in my name. It will be useless, my dear Gilbert, my saying that I am alive, for the certificate of my death and burial will be produced to prove that I am no more. But they will not have to do anything of the sort as it suits me to be thought passed away at this date. I have made a dive into the sombre river, as the poets say, but I have come up under another name. I am now Baron Zanone, a Genoese banker. I discount the paper of princes—good paper in the sort of Cardinal Prince Rohan's, you know. But I am not lending money merely for the interest. By the way, if you need cash, my dear Gilbert, say so? You know that my purse, like my heart, is always at your call."

"I thank you."

"Ah, you think to incommode me, because you met me in my dress as a workman? do not trouble about that; it is merely one of my disguises; you know my ideas about life being one long masquerade where all are more or less masked. In any case, my dear boy, if ever you want money, out of my private cash box here—for the grand cash box of the Invisibles is in St. Claude Street—come to me at any hour, whether I am at home or not—I showed you the little, side door; push this spring so—" he showed him the trick—"and you will find about a million ready."

The round top of the desk opened of itself on the spring being pressed, and displayed a heap of gold coin and bundles of banknotes.

"You are in truth a wonderful man!" exclaimed Gilbert; "but you ought to know that with twenty thousand a-year, I am richer than the King. But do you not fear being disquieted in Paris?"

"On account of the matter of the Queen's Necklace for which I was forbid the realm? Go to! they dare not. In the present ferment of minds I have only to speak one word to evoke a riot: you forget that I am friendly with all the popular leaders—Lafayette, Necker, Mirabeau and yourself."

"What have you come to do at Paris?"

"Who knows? perhaps what you went over to the United States to do—found a republic."

"France has not a republican turn of mind," said the other, shaking his head.

"We shall teach her that way, that is all. It has taken fifteen hundred years to rule with a monarchy; in one hundred the Republic will be founded to endure—why not as long?"

"The King will resist; the nobility fly to arms; and then what will you do?"

"We will make a revolution before we have the Republic."

"It will be awful to do that, Joseph," said Gilbert, hanging his head.

"Awful indeed, if we meet many such as you on the road."

"I am not strong, but honest," said the doctor.

"That is worse: so I want to bring you over."

"I am convinced—not that I shall prevent you in your work, but will stay you."

"You are mad, Gilbert; you do not understand the mission of France in Europe. It is the brain of the Old World, and must think freely so that the world will be the happier for its thought. Do you know what overthrew the Bastile?"

"The people."

"No: public opinion. You are taking the effect for the cause."

"For five hundred years they have been imprisoning nobles in the Bastile and it stood. But the mad idea struck an insane monarch one day to lock up thought—the spirit which must be free, and requires space unto immensity, and crack! it burst the walls and the mob surged in at the breach."

"True enough," mused the younger man.

"Twenty-six years ago, Voltaire wrote to Chauvelin: 'All that I see is sowing Revolution round us, and it will inevitably come though I shall not have the bliss to see the harvest. The French are sometimes slow to come into the battle but they get there before the fight is over. Light is so spread from one to another, that it will burst forth in a mass soon, and then there will be a fine explosion. The young men are happy for they will behold splendors. What do you say about the flare-ups of yesterday and what is going on to-day?'"

"Terrible!"

"And what you have beheld in the way of events?"

"Dreadful!"

"We are only at the beginning."

"Prophet of evil!"

"For instance, I was at the house of a man of merit, a doctor of medicine and a philanthropist: what do you think he was busy over?"

"Seeking the remedy for some great disease."

"You have it. He is trying to cure, not death, but life."

"What do you mean?"

"Leaving epigrams aside, I mean that there not being means enough for quitting life, he is inventing a very ingenious machine which he reckons to present to his fellow countrymen, to put fifty or eighty persons to death in an hour. Well, my dear Gilbert, do you believe that so human a philanthropist, so distinguished a physician as Dr. Louis Guillotin, would busy himself about such an instrument unless he felt the want of it?

"I know that this is not so much a novelty as a machine forgotten, as a proof of which I showed it as an image in a glass of water to Marie Antoinette. She was then espoused to the Dauphin of France, now its sovereign, and it was down at Taverney where you were a dependent. The old baron was alive then, and the lady of the manor was Mdlle. Andrea."

"Ah," sighed Gilbert at this reminder of his boyhood.

"But at the first you had eyes only for the servant-maid, Nicole, afterwards Olive Legay, as the Dauphiness, to whom she bore an amazing resemblance by the bye, is the Queen of France. Well I repeat that the future Queen was shown by me this instrument to which I shall suggest no name, though the olden ones are the Maiden, the Widow and the Mannaya in my country. The thing so alarmed her that she swooned dead away. It was in limbo at the era, but you shall see it at work presently if it be successful; and then you must be blind if you do not spy the hand of heaven in it all, it being foreseen that the time would come when the headsman would have his hands too full and that a new method must be devised."

"Count, your remarks were more consoling when we were in America."

"I should rather think they were! I was in the midst of a people who rose and here in society which falls. In our Old World, all march towards the grave, nobility and royalty, and this grave is a bottomless pit."

"Oh, I abandon the nobility to you, count, or rather it threw itself away in the night of the fourth of August; but the royalty must be saved as the national palladium."

"Big words, my dear Gilbert: but did the palladium save Troy? Do you believe it will be easy to save the realm with such a king?"

"But in short he is the descendant of a grand race."

"Eagles that have degenerated into parrots. They have been marrying in and out till they are rundown."

"My dear sorcerer," said Gilbert, rising and taking up his hat, "you frighten me so that I must haste and take my place by the King."

Cagliostro stopped him in making some steps towards the door.

"Mark me, Gilbert," he said, "you know whether I love you or not and if I am not the man to expose myself to a hundred sorrows to aid you to avoid one—well, take this piece of advice: let the King depart, quit France, while it is yet time. In a year, in six months, in three, it will be too late."

"Count, do you counsel a soldier to leave his post because there is danger in his staying?"

"If the soldier were so surrounded, engirt, and disarmed that he could not defend himself: if, above all, his life exposed meant that of half a million of men—yes, I should bid him flee. And you yourself, Gilbert, you shall tell him so. The King will listen to you unless it is all too late. Do not wait till the morrow but tell him to-day. Do not wait till the afternoon but tell him in an hour."

"Count, you know that I am of the fatalist school. Come what come may! so long as I shall have any hold on the King it will be to retain him in France, and I shall stay by him. Farewell, count: we shall meet in the action: perhaps we shall sleep side by side on the battlefield."

"Come, come, it is written that man shall not elude his doom however keen-witted he may be," muttered the magician: "I sought you out to tell you what I said, and you have heard it. Like Cassandra's prediction it is useless, but remember that Cassandra was correct. Fare thee well!"

"Speak frankly, count," said Gilbert, stopping on the threshold to gaze fixedly at the speaker, "do you here, as in America, pretend to make folk believe that you can read the future?"

"As surely, Gilbert," returned the self-asserted undying one, "as you can read the pathway of the stars, though the mass of mankind believe they are fixed or wandering at hazard."

"Well, then—someone knocks at your door."

"Yes."

"Tell me his fate: when he shall die and how?"

"Be it so," rejoined the sorcerer, "let us go and open the door to him."

Gilbert proceed towards the corridor end, with a beating of the heart which he could not repress, albeit he whispered to himself that it was absurd to take this quackering as serious.

The door opened. A man of lofty carriage, tall in stature, and with strong-will impressed on his lineaments, appeared on the sill and cast a swift glance on Dr. Gilbert not exempt from uneasiness.

"Good day, marquis," said Cagliostro.

"How do you do, baron?" responded the other.

"Marquis," went on the host as he saw the caller's gaze still settled on the doctor, "this is one of my friends, Dr. Gilbert. Gilbert, you see Marquis Favras, one of my clients. Marquis, will you kindly step into my sitting-room," continued he as the two saluted each other, "and wait for a few seconds when I shall be with you."

"Well?" queried Gilbert as the marquis bowed again and went into the parlor.

"You wished to know in what way this gentleman would die?" said Cagliostro with an odd smile; "have you ever seen a nobleman hanged?"

"Noblemen are privileged not to die by hanging."

"Then it will be the more curious sight; be on the Strand when the Marquis of Favras is executed." He conducted his visitor to the street door, and said: "When you wish to call on me without being seen and to see none but me, push this knob up and to the left, so—now, farewell—excuse me—I must not make those wait who have not long to live."

He left Gilbert astounded by his assurance, which staggered him but could not vanquish his incredulity.

CHAPTER V. THE CANDLE OMEN.

IN the meantime the Royal Family had continued their road to Paris. The pace was so slow and delayed that it was six o'clock before the carriage containing so much sorrow, hatred, passions and innocence, arrived at the city bars.

During the journey the Dauphin had complained of being hungry. There was no want of bread as many of the pikes and bayonets were holding up loaves and the Queen would have asked Gilbert to get one, if he had been by. She could not ask the mob, whom she held in horror.

"Wait till we are in the Tuileries Palace this evening," she said, hugging the boy to her.

"But these men have plenty," he protested.

"But that is theirs, not ours. And they went all the way to Versailles for it as there was none in Paris, these three days."

"Have they not eaten for three days?" said the Prince. "Then they must be awful hungry, mamma."

Etiquet ordered him to address his mother as Madam, but he was hungry as a poor boy and he called her mamma as a poor boy would his mother.

Ceasing to grieve, he tried to sleep. Poor royal babe, who would cry many times yet for bread before he died.

At the bars a halt was made, not to repose but to rejoice over the arrival. It was hailed with song and dance. A strange scene almost as terrifying in this joy as the others had been for ghastliness.

The fishmarket-women got off their horses, captured from the slain Lifeguardsmen, hanging their swords and carbines to the horns. Other women and the market-girls jumped off their cannon, which appeared in their alarming smoothness.

They all joined hands and danced around the royal carriage. Separating it from the deputies and the National Guard, an omen of what was to follow. This round dance had the good intention to set the enforced guests at ease: the men and women capered, kissed, hugged and sang together. The men lifted up their partners as in Teniers' pictures.

This went on as night was falling, on a dark and rainy day, so that the dancing by the light of torches and the gun-stocks and fireworks, took fantastic effects of light and shade almost infernal.

After half an hour all shouted a general hurrah; all the firearms were shot off at risk of shooting somebody; and the bullets came down in the puddles with a sinister plash.

The prince and his sister wept; they were too frightened to feel hungered.

At the City Hall a line of troops prevented the crowd from entering the place. Here the Queen perceived her foster-brother, and confidential servant, Weber, an Austrian who had followed her fortunes from home, and was trying to pass the cordon and go in with her. To be more useful to the Queen he had put on a National Guard uniform and added the insignia of a staff-officer. The Royal Groom had lent him a horse. Not to excite suspicion he kept at a distance during the journey. Now he ran up at her call.

"What have you come for?" she demanded; "you will be useless here while at the Tuileries you will be needed. If you do not go on before, nothing will be ready for our accommodation."

"Capital idea that," said the King.

The Queen had spoken in German and the King had replied in English as he did not speak the other tongue though understanding it.

The bystanders held foreign tongues in horror, and they murmured and this swelled to a roar when the square opened and let the coach roll through.

The welcoming speech was made by Billy, Mayor of Paris, who played the King a scurvy trick by repeating his answer: "I always come with pleasure and confidence among my good people of Paris," without the word "confidence" which spoilt matters, and he was taken to task by the Queen for it.

It was not till ten o'clock that the royal carriage got back to the Tuileries where Weber had done the best he could for them.

Count Provence had gone to Luxembourg Palace.

Weber had located the Royal Family in Countess Lamarck's rooms, but the comforts were limited. For instance there was no room for Countess Charny at supper and she talked of spending the night in a chair for want of a bed. But knowing the great favor in which the Queen held the countess, they placed a couch for her in the next room to the Queen's.

The latter shuddered at this for she thought of the count being with his wife, and Andrea saw the emotion.

"There must be some corner for me elsewhere," said she; "I will go find it."

"You are right, countess," said the King while Marie Antoinette mumbled something unintelligible. "We will do something better to-morrow."

The King watched the stately countess go out, while he held the plate to his mouth.

"That lady is a delightful creature," he said, "and Charny ought to be happy to find such a phoenix at court."

The Queen leant back in her chair to hide her sensation, not from the speaker, but from his sister Elizabeth, who was frightened lest she had fallen ill.

The Queen did not breathe at ease till alone in her room.

She had heard her daughter say her prayers, speaking a little longer than usual as she was pleading for her brother who had gone to rest forgetting to say his.

Sitting alone at a table, somehow she had the panorama of her life pass before her.

44

She recalled that she was born on the second of November, 1755, the day of the Lisbon earthquake, which swallowed up fifty thousand souls and extended five thousand miles.

She recalled that the room she slept in, in France, at Strasburg, represented the Massacre of the Innocents and so frightened her in the flickering lamplight that she had always retained a terrible memory of her first night on French soil.

She recalled how, stopping at Taverney House, she had been shown in the gardens by Baron Balsamo the image of an unknown instrument for decapitation: this was the man who, under the name of Cagliostro, had exercised a fatal influence on her destiny, as witness his hand in the Queen's Necklace trial; though she was advised that he had perished in the papal dungeons as a magician and atheist, had she not seen him this day in the mob during the halt at Sevres?

She recalled that in Madam Lebrun's portrait she had unwittingly made her pose as the unfortunate Henrietta Maria of England, in her portrait, as Wife of Charles I. the Beheaded.

She recalled how, when she got out of her coach for the first time at Versailles, in that Marble Court where so much blood lately flowed on her behalf, a lightning stroke had flashed so extraordinarily that Marshal Richelieu had said: "An evil omen!" albeit he was a cynic not easily startled by superstition.

She was recalling all this when a reddish cloud, from her eyes being strained, thickened around her, and one of the four candles in the candelabrum went out without evident cause.

While she was looking at it, still smoking, it seemed to her that the next taper to it paled sensibly, and turning red and then blue in the flame, faded away and lengthened upward, as if to quit the wick, from which it leaped altogether. It was extinguished, as though by an unseen breath from below.

She had watched the death of this with haggard eyes and panting bosom, and her hands went out towards the candlestick proportionable to the eclipse.

When gone out, she closed her eyes, drew back in her armchair, and ran her hand over her forehead, streaming with perspiration.

When she opened them anew, after ten minutes, she perceived that the flame of the third candle was affected like the rest.

She believed it was a dream or that she was under some hallucination. She tried to rise but seemed nailed to her chair. She wanted to call her daughter, whom she would not have aroused a few minutes before for a second crown, but her voice died away in her throat. She tried to turn her head but it was rigid as if the third light expiring attracted her eyes and breath. Like the other pair, it changed hue and swaying to one side and the other, finally shot itself out.

Then fear had such mastery that speech returned to her and that made her feel restored in courage.

"I am not going to distress myself because three candles happened to go out," she said; "but if the fourth suffers the same fate, then woe is me!"

Suddenly, without going through the transitions of the others, without lengthening or fluttering to left or right as if the death-angel wing had wafted it, the fourth flame went out.

She screamed with terror, rose, reeled and fell to the floor.

At this appeal the door opened and Andrea, white and silent in her night-wrapper appeared like a ghost on the sill. When she had revived her mistress with the mechanical action of one impelled by sheer duty, the Queen remembered all the presage, and aware that it was a woman beside her, flung her arms round her neck, and cried:

"Save me, defend me!"

"Your Majesty needs no defense among her friends," said Andrea, "and you appear free of the swoon in which you fell."

"Countess Charny," gasped the other, letting go of her whom she had embraced, and almost repelling her in the first impulse.

Neither the feeling nor the expression had escaped the lady. But she remained motionless to impassibility.

"I shall undress alone," faltered the Queen. "Return to your room, as you must require sleep."

"I shall go back, not to sleep but to watch over your Majesty's slumber," returned Andrea, respectfully curtseying to the other and stalking away with the solemn step of a vitalized statue.

CHAPTER VI. THE REVOLUTION IN THE COUNTRY.

OUR intention being to temporarily abandon the fortunes of our high and mighty characters to follow those of more humble but perhaps no less engaging heroes, we take up with Sebastian Gilbert whom his father, immediately after his release from the Bastile, confided to a young peasant named Ange Pitou, foster-brother of the youth, and despatched them to the latter's birthplace, Villers Cotterets.

It was eighteen leagues from the city, and Gilbert might have sent them down by stage-coach or his own carriage; but he feared isolation for the son of the mesmerists' victim, and nothing so isolates a traveler as a closed carriage.

Ange Pitou had accepted the trust with pride at the choice of the King's honorary physician. He travelled tranquilly, passing through villages trembling with the thrill from the shock of the events at Paris as it was the commencement of August when the pair left town.

Besides Pitou had kept a helmet and a sabre picked up on the battlefield where he had shown himself more brave than he had expected. One does not help in the taking of a Bastile without preserving some heroic touch in his bearing subsequently.

Moreover he had become something of an orator; he had studied the Classics and he had heard the many speeches of the period, scattered out of the City Hall, in the mobs, during lulls in the street fights.

Furnished with these powerful forces, added to by a pair of ponderous fists, plenty of broad grins, and a most interesting appetite for loiters-on who did not have to pay the bill, Pitou journeyed most pleasantly. For those inquisitive in political matters, he told the news, inventing what he had not heard, Paris having a knack that way which he had picked up.

As Sebastian ate little and spoke hardly at all, everybody admired Pitou's vigorous paternal care.

They went through Haramont, the little village where the mother of one and the nurse of the other had died and was laid in earth.

Her living home, sold by Pitou's Aunt Angelique, her sister-in-law, had been razed by the new owner, and a black cat snarled at the young men from the wall built round the garden.

But nothing was changed at the burying-ground; the grass had so grown that the chances were that the young peasant could not find his mother's grave. Luckily he knew it by a slip of weeping willow, which he had planted; while the grass was growing it had grown also and had become in a few years a tolerable tree.

Ange walked directly to it, and the pair said their prayers under the lithe branches which Pitou took in his arms as they were his mother's tresses.

Nobody noticed them as all the country folk were in the field and none seeing Pitou would have recognized him in his dragoon's helmet and with the sword and belt.

At five in the afternoon they reached their destination.

While Pitou had been away from Haramont three years, it was only as many weeks since he quitted Villers Cotterets, so that it was simple enough that he should be recognized at the latter place.

The two visitors were reported to have gone to the back door of Father Fortier's academy for young gentlemen where Pitou had been educated with Sebastian, and where the latter was to resume his studies.

A crowd collected at the front door where they thought Pitou would come forth, as they wanted to see him in the soldier's appurtenances.

After giving the doctor's letter and money for the schooling to Abbé Fortier's sister, the priest being out for a walk with the pupils, Pitou left the house, cocking his helmet quite dashingly on the side of his head.

Sebastian's chagrin at parting was softened by Ange Pitou's promise to see him often. Pitou was like those big, lubberly Newfoundland dogs who sometimes weary you with their fawning, but usually disarm you by their jolly good humor.

The score of people outside the door thought that as Pitou was in battle array he had seen the fights in Paris and they wanted to have news.

He gave it with majesty; telling how he and Farmer Billet, their neighbor, had taken the Bastile and set Dr. Gilbert free. They had learnt something in the Gazettes but no newspaper can equal an eye-witness who can be questioned and will reply. And the obliging fellow did reply and explain and at such length that in an hour, one of the listeners suddenly remarked that he was flagging and said:

"But our dear Pitou is tired, and here we are keeping him on his legs, when he ought to go home, to his Aunt Angelique's. The poor old girl will be delighted to see him again."

"I am not tired but hungry," returned the other. "I am never tired but I am always sharpset."

Before this plain way of putting it, the throng broke up to let Pitou go through. Followed by some more curious than the rest, he proceeded to his father's sister's house.

It was a cottage where he would have been starved to death by the pious old humbug of an old maid, but for his poaching in the woods for something that they could eat while the superfluity was sold by her to have the cash in augmentation of a very pretty hoard the miser kept in a chair cushion.

As the door was fastened, from the old lady being out gossiping, and Pitou declared that an aunt should never shut out a loving nephew, he drew his great sabre and opened the lock with it as it were an oyster, to the admiration of the boys.

Pitou entered the familiar cottage with a bland smile, and went straight up to the cupboard where the food was kept. He used in his boyish days to ogle the crust and the hunk of cheese with the wish to have magical powers to conjure them out into his mouth.

Now he was a man: he went up to the safe, opened it, opened also his pocket-knife, and taking out a loaf, cut off a slice which might weigh a fair two pounds.

He seemed to hear Aunt Angelique snarl at him, but it was only the creak of the door hinges.

In former times, the old fraud used to whine about poverty and palm him off with cheap cheese and few flavors. But since he had left she got up little delicacies of value which lasted her a week, such as stewed beef smothered in carrots and onions; baked mutton with potatoes as large as melons; or calvesfoot, decked with pickled shallots; or a giant omelet sprinkled with parsley or dotted with slices of fat pork of which one sufficed for a meal even when she had an appetite.

Pitou was in luck. He lighted on a day when Aunt Angelique had cooked an old rooster in rice, so long that the bones had quitted the flesh and the latter was almost tender. It was basking in a deep dish, black outside but glossy and attractive within. The coxcomb stuck up in the midst like Ceuta in Gibraltar Straits.

Pitou had been so spoilt by the good living at Paris that he never even reflected that he had never seen such magnificence in his relative's house.

He had his hunk of bread in his right hand: he seized the baking dish in his left and held it by the grip of his thumb in the grease. But at this moment it seemed to him that a shadow clouded the doorway.

He turned round, grinning, for he had one of those characters which let their happiness be painted on their faces.

The shadow was cast by Angelique Pitou, drier, sourer, bonier, not bonnier, and more mean than ever.

Formerly, at this sight, Pitou would have dropped the bread and dish and fled.

But he was altered. His helmet and sword had not more changed his aspect than his mind was changed by frequenting the society of the revolutionary lights of the capital.

Far from fleeing, he went up to her and opening his arms he embraced her so that his hands, holding the knife, the bread and the dish, crossed behind her skeleton back.

"It is poor Pitou," he said in accomplishing this act of nepotism.

She feared that he was trying to stifle her because she had caught him red-handed in plundering her store. Literally, she did not breathe freely until she was released from this perilous clasp.

She was horrified that he did not express any emotion over his prize and at his sitting in the best chair: previously he would have perched himself on the edge of a stool or the broken chair. Thus easily lodged he set to demolishing the baked fowl. In a few minutes the pattern of the dish began to appear clean at the bottom as the rocks and sand on the seashore when the tide goes out.

In her frightful perplexity she endeavored to scream but the ogre smiled so bewitchingly that the scream died away on her prim lips.

She smiled, without any effect on him, and then turned to weeping. This annoyed the devourer a little but did not hinder his eating.

"How good you are to weep with joy at my return," he said. "I thank you, my kind aunt."

Evidently the Revolution had transmogrified this lad.

Having tucked away three fourths of the bird he left a little of the Indian grain at the end of the dish, saying:

"You are fond of rice, my dear auntie: and, besides, it is good for your poor teeth."

At this attention, taken for a bitter jest, Angelique nearly suffocated. She sprang upon Pitou and snatched the lightened platter from his hand, with an oath which would not have been out of place in the mouth of an old soldier.

"Bewailing the rooster, aunt?" he sighed.

"The rogue—I believe he is chaffing me," cried the old prude.

"Aunt," returned the other, rising majestically, "my intention was to pay you. I have money. I will come and board with you, if you please, only I reserve the right to make up the bill of fare. As for this snack, suppose we put the lot at six cents, four of the fowl and two of bread."

"Six? when the meat is worth eight alone and the bread four," cried the woman.

"But you did not buy the bird—I know the old acquaintance by his nine years comb. I stole him for you from under his mother and by the same token, you flogged me because I did not steal enough corn to feed him. But I begged the grain from Miss Catherine Billet; as I procured the bird and the food, I had a lien on him, as the lawyers say. I have only been eating my own property."

"Out of this house," she gasped, almost losing her voice while she tried to pulverize him with her gaze.

Pitou remarked with satisfaction that he could not have swallowed one grain more of rice.

"Aunt, you are a bad relative," he said loftily. "I wanted you to show yourself as of old, spiteful and avaricious. But I am not going to have it said that I eat my way without paying."

He stood on the threshold and called out with a voice which was not only heard by the starers without but by anybody within five hundred paces:

"I call these honest folk for witnesses, that I have come from Paris afoot, after having taken the Bastile. I was hungered and tired, and I have sat down under my only relation's roof, and eaten, but my keep is thrown up at me, and I am driven away pitilessly!"

He infused so much pathos in this exordium that the hearers began to murmur against the old maid.

"I want you to bear witness that she is turning from her door a poor wayfarer who has tramped nineteen leagues afoot; an honest lad, honored with the trust of Farmer Billet and Dr. Gilbert; who has brought Master Sebastian Gilbert here to Father Fortier's; a conqueror of the Bastile, a friend of Mayor Bailly and General Lafayette."

The murmuring increased.

"And I am not a beggar," he pursued, "for when I am accused of having a bite of bread, I am ready to meet the score, as proof of which I plank down this silver bit—in payment of what I have eaten at my own folk's."

He drew a silver crown from his pocket with a flourish, and tossed it on the table under the eyes of all, whence it bounced into the dish and buried itself in the rice. This last act finished the mercenary aunt; she hung her head under the universal reprobation displayed in a prolonged groan. Twenty arms were opened towards Pitou, who went forth, shaking the dust off his brogans, and disappeared, escorted by a mob eager to offer hospitality to a captor of the Bastile, and boon-companion of General Lafayette.

CHAPTER VII. THE ABDICATION IN A FARMHOUSE.

AFTER having appeased the duties of obedience, Pitou wished to satisfy the cravings of his heart. It is sweet to obey when the order chimes in with one's secret sympathies.

Ange Pitou was in love with Catherine, daughter of farmer Billet who had succored him when he fled from his aunt's and with whom he had taken the trip to Paris which returned him a full-fledged hero to his fellow-villagers.

When he perceived the long ridge of the farmhouse roofs, measured the aged elms which twisted to stand the higher over the smoking chimneys, when he heard the distant lowing of the cattle, the barking of the watchdogs, and the rumbling of the farm carts, he shook his casque on his head to tighten its hold, hung the calvary sabre more firmly by his side, and tried to give himself the bold swagger of a lover and a soldier. As nobody recognized him at the first it was a proof that he had fairly succeeded.

The farmhands responded to his hail by taking off their caps or pulling their forelocks.

Through the dininghall window pane Mother Billet saw the military visitor. She was a comely, kind old soul who fed her employes like fighting cocks. She was, like other housewives, on the alert, as there was talk of armed robbers being about the country. They cut the woods down and reaped the green corn. What did this warrior's appearance signify? attack or assistance?

She was perplexed by the clodhopper shoes beneath a helmet so shining and her supposition fluctuated between suspicion and hope.

She took a couple of steps towards the new-comer as he strode into the kitchen, and he took off his headpiece not to be outdone in politeness.

"Ange Pitou?" she ejaculated. "Whoever would have guessed that you would enlist."

"Enlist indeed?" sneered Pitou, smiling loftily.

As he looked round him, seeking someone, Mistress Billet smiled, divining who he was after.

"Looking for Catherine?" she asked unaffectedly.

"To present her with my duty," said Pitou.

"She is ironing," responded Mrs. Billet; "but sit ye down and talk to me."

"Quite willing, mother." And he took a chair.

In all the doorways and windows the servants and laboring men flocked to see their old fellow. He had a kindly glance for them all, a caress in his smile for the most part.

"So you come from town, Ange?" began Mother Billet. "How did you leave the master?"

"He is all right, but Paris is all wrong."

The circle of listeners drew in closer.

"What about the King?" inquired the mistress.

Pitou shook his head and clacked his tongue in a way humiliating to the head of the monarchy.

"And the Queen?"

Pitou said never a word.

"Oh," groaned the crowd.

Pitou was aching for Catherine's coming.

"Why are you wearing a helmet?"

"It is a trophy of war," rejoined the young peasant. "A trophy is a tangible testimonial that you have vanquished an enemy."

"Have you vanquished an enemy, Pitou?"

"An enemy—pooh!" said the valiant one, disdainfully. "Ah, good Mother

Billet, you do not know that Farmer Billet and yours truly took the Bastile between us."

This speech electrified the auditory. Pitou felt the breath on his hair and the helmet mane, while their hands grasped the back of his chair.

"Do tell us what our master has done," pleaded Mrs. Billet, proud and tremulous at the same time.

Pitou was hurt that Catherine did not leave her linen to come and hear such a messenger as he was. He shook his head for he was growing discontented.

"It will take a time," he observed.

"Are you hungry, or thirsty?"

"I am not saying no."

Instantly all the men and maids bustled about so that Pitou found under his hand goblets, mugs, bread, meat, cheese, without realizing the extent of his hint. He had a hot liver, as the rustics say: that is, he digested quickly. But he had not shaken down the Angelican fowl in rice; he tried to eat again but had to give up at the second mouthful.

"If I begin now," he said, "I should have to do it all over again when Miss Catherine comes."

While they were all hunting after the young girl, Pitou happened to look up and saw the girl in question leaning out of a window on the upper landing. She was gazing towards Boursonne Woods.

"Oh," he sighed, "she is looking towards the manor of the Charnys. She is in love with Master Isidor Charny, that is what it is."

He sighed again, much more lamentably than before.

Taking the farmer's wife by the hand as the searchers returned fruitless in their search, he took her up a couple of the stairs and showed her the girl, mooning on the window sill among the morning glories and vines.

"Catherine!" she called: "Come, Catherine, here is Ange Pitou, with news from town."

"Ah," said Catherine coldly.

So coldly that Pitou's heart failed him as he anxiously waited for her reply.

She came down the stairs with the phlegm of the Flemish girls in the old Dutch paintings.

"Yes, it is he," she said, when on the floor.

Pitou bowed, red and trembling.

"He's wearing a soldier's helmet," said a servant-woman in her young mistress's ear.

Pitou overheard and watched for the effect. But her somewhat pallid though evercharming face showed no admiration for the brazen cap.

"What is he wearing that thing for?" she inquired.

This time indignation got the upperhand in the peasant.

"I am wearing helmet and sabre," he retorted proudly, "because I have been fighting and have killed Swiss and dragoons: and if you doubt me, Miss Catherine, you can ask your father, and that is all."

She was so absent-minded that she appeared to catch the latter part of the speech alone.

"How is my father?" asked she; "and why does he not return home with you? Is the news from Paris bad?"

"Very," replied the young man.

"I thought that all was settled," the girl objected.

"Quite true, but all is unsettled again."

"Have not the King and the people agreed and is not the recall of

Minister Necker arranged?"

"Necker is not of much consequence now," said Pitou jeeringly.

"But that ought to satisfy the people."

"It falls so short of that, that the people are doing justice on their own account and killing their enemies."

"Their enemies? who are their enemies?" cried the girl astonished.

"The aristocrats, of course," answered the other.

"Whom do you call aristocrat?" she asked, turning paler.

"Why, naturally, they that have grand houses, and big properties, and starve the nation—those that have everything while we have nothing; that travel on fine horses or in bright coaches while we jog on foot."

"Heavens," exclaimed the girl, so white as to be corpselike.

"I can name some aristo's of our acquaintance," continued he, noticing the emotion. "Lord Berthier Sauvigny, for instance, who gave you those gold earrings you wore on the day you danced with Master Isidore. Well, I have seen men eat the heart of him!"

A terrible cry burst from all breasts and Catherine fell back in the chair she had taken.

"Did you see that?" faltered Mother Billet, quivering with horror.

"And so did Farmer Billet. By this time they have killed or burnt all the aristocrats of Paris and Versailles. What do you call it dreadful for? you are not of the higher classes, Mother Billet."

"Pitou, I did not think you were so bloodthirsty when you started for Paris," said Catherine with sombre energy.

"I do not know as I am so, now; but——"

"But then do not boast of the crimes which the Parisians commit, since you are not a Parisian and did not do them."

"I had so little hand in them that Farmer Billet and me were nigh slaughtered in taking the part of Lord Berthier—though he had famished the people."

"Oh, my good, brave father! that is just like him," said Catherine, excitedly.

"My worthy man," said Mrs. Billet with tearful eyes. "What has he been about?"

Pitou related that the mob had seized Foulon and Berthier for being the active agents for higher personages in the great Grain Ring which held the corn from the poor, and torn them to pieces, though Billet and he had tried to defend them.

"The farmer was sickened and wanted to come home, but Dr. Gilbert would not let him."

"Does he want my man to get killed there?" sobbed poor Mother Billet.

"Oh, no," replied Pitou. "It is all fixed between master and the doctor. He is going to stay a little longer in town to finish up the revolution. Not alone, you understand, but with Mayor Bailly and General Lafayette."

"Oh, I am not so much alarmed about him as long as in the gentlemen's company," said the good old soul with admiration.

"When does he think of returning?" inquired the daughter.

"I don't know in the least."

"Then, what have you come back for?"

"To bring Sebastian Gilbert to Father Fortier's school, and you, Farmer Billet's instructions."

Pitou spoke like a herald, with so much dignity that the farmer's wife dismissed all the gapers.

"Mrs. Billet," began the messenger, "the master wants you to be worried as little as possible, so he thinks that while he is away, the management of the farm should be in other hands, younger and livelier."

"Oh!"

"Yes, and he has selected Miss Catherine."

"My daughter to rule in my house," cried the woman, with distrust and inexpressible jealousy.

"Under your orders," the girl hastened to say, while reddening.

"No, no," persisted Pitou, who went on well since he was in full swing: "I bear the commission entire: Master Billet delegates and authorizes Miss Catherine to see to all the work and govern the house and household in his stead."

As Billet was infallible in his wife's eyes, all her resistance ceased instantly.

"Billet is right," she declared after a glance at her daughter; "she is young but she has a good head, and she can even be headstrong. She can get along outdoors better than me; she knows how to make folks obey. But to be running about over field and hills will make a tomboy of her——"

"Fear nothing for her," interposed Pitou with a consequential air; "I am here and I will go around with her."

This gracious offer, by which Ange probably intended to make an effect, drew such a strange glance from Catherine that he was dumbfounded.

Pitou was not experienced in feminine ways but he guessed by her blush that she was not giving complete acquiescence, for he said with an agreeable smile which showed his strong teeth between the large lips:

"Even the Queen has a Lifeguard. Besides, I may be useful in the woods."

"Is this also in my husband's instructions?" queried Madam Billet who showed some tendency towards cutting sayings.

"Nay," said Catherine, "that would be an idle errand and father would not have set it for Master Pitou while he would not have accepted it."

Pitou rolled his frightened eyes from one to the other: all his castle in the air came tumbling down. A true woman, the younger one understood his painful disappointment.

"Did you see the girls in Paris with the young men tagging at their gown-tails?"

"But you are not a girl, after you become mistress of the house," remonstrated Pitou.

"Enough chatter," interrupted Mother Billet; "the mistress of the house has too much work to do. Come, Catherine, and let me turn over things to you, as your father bids us."

As soon as the house was placed under the new ruler the servants and workmen were presented to her as the one from whom in the future orders would flow. Each departed with the alacrity shown by the new officials at the beginning of a fresh term.

"What about me?" inquired Pitou, left alone and going up to the girl.

"I have no orders for you. What do you think of doing?"

"What I did before I went away."

"Then you worked for my father and mother. I have nothing in your line, for you are a scholar and a fine Paris gentleman now."

"But look at the muscle in my arms," protested the poor fellow in desperation. "Why do you force me to die of hunger under the pretence that I am a learned man? Are you ignorant that Epictetus the philosopher was a tavern waiter to earn his bread, and that Æsop the fabulist had to work for a living? and yet they were more learned than ever I shall be. But Master Billet sent me down here to help on the farm."

"Be it so; but my father can force you to do things that I should shrink from imposing upon you."

"Don't shrink, and impose on me. You will see that I can stand anything. Besides you have books to keep and accounts to make out; and my strong point is figuring and ciphering."

62

"I do not think it enough for a man," rejoined Catherine.

"Am I good for nothing, then?" groaned Pitou.

"Well, live here a bit," she said; "I will think it over and we shall see what turns up."

"You want to think it over, about my staying. What have I done to you, Miss Catherine? you do not seem to be the same as before."

Catherine shrugged her shoulders very slightly. She had no good reasons to fear Pitou and yet his persistency worried her.

"Enough of this," she said, "I am going over to Fertemilon."

"I will saddle a horse and go with you."

"No; stay where you are."

She spoke so imperiously that the peasant remained riveted to the spot, hanging his head.

"She thinks I am changed, but," said he, "it is she who is another sort altogether."

When he was roused by hearing the horse's hoofs going away, he looked out and saw Catherine riding by a side path towards the highway.

It occurred to him that though she had forbid him to accompany her, she had not said he must not follow her.

He dashed out and took a short cut through the woods, where he was at home, till he reached the main road. But though he waited a half-hour, he saw nobody.

He thought she might have forgotten something at the farm and started back for it; and he returned by the highway. But on looking up a lane he spied her white cap at a distance.

Instead of going to Fertemilon, as she distinctly stated, she proceeding to Boursonne.

He darted on in the same direction but by a parallel line.

It was no longer to follow her but to spy her.

She had spoken a falsehood. In what end?

He was answered by seeing her thrash her horse into the trot in order to rejoin a horseman who rode to meet her with as much eagerness as she showed on her part.

On coming nearer, as the pair halted at meeting, Pitou recognized by his elegant form and stylish dress the neighboring lord, Isidore Charny. He was brother of the Count of Charny, lieutenant of the Royal Lifeguards, and accredited as favorite of the Queen.

Pitou knew him well and lately from having seen him at the village dances where Catherine chose him for partner.

Dropping to the ground in the brush and creeping up like a viper, he heard the couple.

"You are late to-day, Master Isidore," began Catherine.

"To-day?" thought the eavesdropper; "it appears that he has been punctual on other meetings."

"It is not my fault, my darling Kate," replied the young noble. "A letter from my brother delayed me, to which I had to reply by the bearer. But fear nothing, I shall be more exact another time."

Catherine smiled and Isidore pressed her hand so tenderly that Pitou felt upon thorns.

"Fresh news from Paris?" she asked. "So have I. Did you not say that when something alike happens to two persons, it is called sympathy?"

"Just so. Who brings you news?"

"Pitou."

"And pray who is Pitou?" asked the young noble with a free and easy air

Alexandre Dumas

which changed the red of the listener's cheek to crimson.

"You know well enough," was her reply: "Pitou is the farmboy that my father took on out of charity: the one who played propriety for me when I went to the dance."

"Lord, yes—the chap with knees that look like knots tied in a rope."

Catherine set to laughing. Pitou felt lowered; he looked at his knees, so useful lately while he was keeping pace with a horse, and he sighed.

"Come, come, do not tear my poor Pitou to pieces," said Catherine; "Let me tell you that he wanted to come with me just now—to Fertemilon, where I pretended I was going."

"Why did you not accept the squire—he would have amused you."

"Not always," laughed the girl.

"You are right, my pet," said Isidore, fixing his eyes, brilliant with love, on the pretty girl.

She hid her blushing face in his arms closing round it.

Pitou closed his eyes not to see, but he did not close his ears, and the sound of a kiss reached them. He tore his hair in despair.

When he came to his senses the loving couple were slowly riding away.

The last words he caught were:

"You are right, Master Isidore; let us ride about for an hour which I will gain by making my nag go faster—he is a good beast who will tell no tales," she added, merrily.

This was all: the vision vanished. Darkness fell on Pitou's spirit and he said:

"No more of the farm for me, where I am trodden on and made fun of. I am not going to eat the bread of a woman who is in love with another man, handsomer, richer and more graceful than me, I allow. No, my place is not in the town but in my village of Haramont, where I may find those who will think well of me whether my knees are like knots in a rope or not."

He marched towards his native place, where his reputation and that of his sword and helmet had preceded him, and where glory awaited him, if not happiness. But we know that perfect bliss is not a human attribute.

CHAPTER VIII. ANOTHER BLOW.

AS everybody in his village would be abed by ten o'clock, Pitou was glad to find accommodation at the inn, where he slept till seven in the morning. At that hour everybody had risen.

On leaving the Dolphin Tavern, he noticed that his sword and casque won universal attention. A crowd was round him in a few steps.

Undoubtedly he had attained popularity.

Few prophets have this good fortune in their own country. But few prophets have mean and acrimonious aunts who bake fowls in rice for them to eat up the whole at a sitting. Besides, the brazen helmet and the heavy dragoon's sabre recommended Pitou to his fellow-villager's attention.

Hence, some of the Villers Cotterets folk, who had escorted him about their town, were constrained to accompany him to his village of Haramont. This caused the inhabitants of the latter to appreciate their fellow-villager at his true worth.

The fact is, the ground was prepared for the seed. He had flitted through their midst before so rapidly that it was a wonder he left any trace of memory: but they were impressed and they were glad of his second appearance. They overwhelmed him with tokens of consideration, begged him to lay aside his armor, and pitch his tent under the four lime trees shading the village green.

Pitou yielded all the more readily as it was his intention to take up residence here and he accepted the offer of a room which a bellicose villager let him have furnished. Settling the terms, the rent per annum being but six livres, the price of two fowls baked in rice, Ange took possession, treated those who had accompanied him to mugs of cider all round, and made a speech on the doorsill.

His speech was a great event, with all Haramont encircling the doorstep. Pitou had studied a little; he had heard Paris speechifying inexhaustibly; there was a space between him and General Lafayette as there is between Paris and Haramont, mentally speaking.

He began by saying that he came back to the hamlet as into the bosom of his only family. This was a touching allusion to his orphanage for the women to hear.

Then he related that he and Farmer Billet had gone to Paris on hearing that Dr. Gilbert had been arrested and because a casket Gilbert had entrusted to his farmer had been stolen from him by the myrmidons of the King under false pretences. Billet and he had rescued the doctor from the Bastile by attacking it, with a few Parisians at their back. At the end of his story his helmet was as grand as the cupola of an observatory.

He ascribed the outbreak to the privileges of the nobility and clergy and called on his brothers to unite against the common enemy.

At this point he drew his sabre and brandished it.

This gave him the cue to call the Haramontese to arms after the example of revolted Paris.

The Revolution was proclaimed in the village.

All echoed the cry of "To arms!" but the only arms in the place were those old Spanish muskets kept at Father Fortier's.

A bold youth, who had not, like Pitou, been educated under his knout, proposed going thither to demand them. Ange wavered, but had to yield to the impulse of the mob.

"Heavens," he muttered: "if they thus lead me before I am their leader, what will it be when I am at their head?"

He was compelled to promise to summon his old master to deliver the firearms. Next day, therefore, he armed himself and departed for Father Fortier's academy.

He knocked at the garden door loud enough to be heard there, and yet modestly enough not to be heard in the house.

He did it to tranquilize his conscience, and was surprised to see the door open; but it was Sebastian who stood on the sill.

He was musing in the grounds, with an open book in his hand.

He uttered a cry of gladness on seeing Pitou, for whom he had a line in his father's letter to impart.

"Billet wishes you to remind him to Pitou and tell him not to upset the men, and things on the farm."

"Me? a lot I have to do with the farm," muttered the young man: "the advice had better be sent on to Master Isidore."

But all he said aloud was: "Where is the father?"

Sebastian pointed and walked away. Priest Fortier was coming down into the garden. Pitou composed his face for the encounter with his former master.

Fortier had been almoner of the old hunting-box in the woods and as such was keeper of the lumber-room. Among the effects of the hunting establishment of the Duke of Orleans were old weapons and particularly some fifty musketoons, brought home from the Ouessant battle by Prince Joseph Philip, which he had given to the township. Not knowing what to do with them, the section selectmen left them under charge of the schoolmaster.

The old gentleman was clad in clerical black, with his cat-o'-nine tails thrust into his girdle like a sword. On seeing Pitou, who saluted him, he folded up the newspaper he was reading and tucked it into his band on the opposite side to the scourge.

"Pitou?" he exclaimed.

"At your service as far as he is capable," said the other.

"But the trouble is that you are not capable, you Revolutionist."

This was a declaration of war, for it was clear that Pitou had put the abbe out of temper.

"Hello! why do you call me a Revolutionist? do you think I have turned the state over all by myself?"

"You are hand and glove with those who did it."

"Father, every man is free in his mind," returned Pitou. "I do not say it in Latin for I have improved in that tongue since I quitted your school. Those whom I frequent and at whom you sneer, talk it like their own and they would think the way you taught it to be faulty."

"My Latin faulty?" repeated the pedagogue, visibly wounded by the ex-pupil's manner. "How comes it that you never spoke up in this style when you were under my—whip—that is, roof?"

"Because you brutalized me then," responded Pitou: "your despotism trampled on my wits, and liberty could not lay hold of my speech. You treated me like a fool, whereas all men are equal."

"I will never suffer anybody to utter such rank blasphemy before me," cried the irritated schoolmaster. "You the equal of one whom nature and heaven have taken sixty years to form? never!"

"Ask General Lafayette, who has proclaimed the Rights of Man."

"What, do you quote as an authority that traitor, that firebrand of all discord, that bad subject of the King?"

"It is you who blaspheme," retaliated the peasant: "you must have been buried for the last three months. This bad subject is the very one who most serves the King. This torch of discord is the pledge of public peace. This traitor is the best of Frenchmen."

"Oh," thundered the priest, "that ever I should believe that the royal authority should sink so low that a goodfornothing of this sort invokes Lafayette as once they called on Aristides."

"Lucky for you the people do not hear you," said Pitou.

"Oho, you reveal yourself now in your true colors," said the priest triumphantly: "you bully me. The people, those who cut the throats of the

70

royal bodyguard; who trample on the fallen, the people of your Baillys, Lafayettes and Pitous. Why do you not denounce me to the people of Villers Cotterets? Why do you not tuck up your sleeves to drag me out to hang me up to the lamppost? where is your rope—you can be the hangman."

"You are saying odious things—you insult me," said Pitou. "Have a care that I do not show you up to the National Assembly!"

"Show me up? I will show you up, sirrah! as a failure as a scholar, as a Latinist full of barbarisms, and as a beggar who comes preaching subversive doctrines in order to prey upon your clients."

"I do not prey upon anybody—it is not by preying I live but by work: and as for lowering me in the eyes of my fellow-citizens, know that I have been elected by them commander of the National Guards of Haramont."

"National Guards at Haramont? and you, Pitou, the captain? Abomination of desolation! Such gangs as you would be chief of must be robbers, footpads, bandits, and highwaymen."

"On the contrary, they are organized to defend the home and the fields as well as the life and liberties of all good citizens. That is why we have [illegible] oc me to—for the arms."

"Arms? oh, my museum?" shrieked the schoolmaster. "You come to pillage my arsenal. The armor of the paladins on your ignoble backs. You are mad to want to arm the ragamuffins of Pitou with the swords of the Spaniards and the pikes of the Swiss."

The priest laughed with such disdainful menace that Pitou shuddered in every vein.

"No, father, we do not want the old curiosities, but the thirty marines' guns which you have."

"Avaunt!" said the abbe, taking a step towards the envoy.

"And you shall have the glory of contributing to deliver the country of the oppressors," said Pitou, who took a backward step.

"Furnish weapons against myself and friends," said the other, "give you guns to be fired against myself?" He plucked his scourge from his belt. "Never, never!"

He waved the whip over his head.

"But your refusal will have a bad effect," pleaded Pitou, retreating, "you will be accused of national treason, and of being no citizen. Do not expose yourself to this, good Father Fortier!"

"Mark me a martyr, eh, Nero? is that what you intend?" roared the priest, with flaring eye and much more resembling the executioner than the victim.

"No, father, I come as a peaceful envoy to——"

"Pillage my house for arms as your friends gutted the Soldiers' Home at Paris."

"We received plenty of praise for that up there," said Ange.

"And you would get plenty of strokes of the whip down here."

"Look out," said Pitou, who had backed to the door, and who recognized the scourge as an old acquaintance, "you must not violate the rights of man!"

"You shall see about that, rascal."

"I am protected by my sacred character as an ambassador——"

"Are you?"

And just as Pitou had to turn after getting the street door open, for he had backed through the hall, the infuriated schoolmaster let him have a terrible lash where his backplate would have to be unusually long to defend him. Whatever the courage of the conqueror of the Bastile, he could not help emitting a shriek of pain as he bounded out among the crowd expecting him.

At the yell, neighbors ran forth from their dwellings and to the profound general astonishment all beheld the young man flying with all swiftness under his helmet and with his sabre, while Father Fortier stood on the doorstep, brandishing his whip like the Exterminating Angel waves his sword.

CHAPTER IX. PITOU BECOMES A TACTICIAN.

OUR hero's fall was deep. How could he go back to his friends without the arms? How, after having had so much confidence shown in him, tell them that their leader was a braggart who, in spite of his sword and helmet, had let a priest whack him in the rear?

To vaunt of carrying all before him with Father Fortier and fail so shamefully—what a fault!

To obtain the muskets, force or cunning was the means. He might steal into the school and steal out the arms. But the word "steal," sounded badly in the rustic's ears. There were still left some people in France who would call this the high-handed outrage of brigands.

So he recoiled before force and treachery.

His vanity was committed to the task, and prompted a fresh direction for his searches.

General Lafayette was Commander-in-chief of the National Guards of France; Haramont was in France and had a National Guards company. Consequently, General Lafayette commanded the latter force. He could not tolerate that his soldiers at Haramont should go unarmed when all his others were armed. To appeal to Lafayette, he could apply to Billet who would address Gilbert, and he the general.

Pitou wrote to Billet but as he could not read, it must be Gilbert who would have the letter placed before him.

This settled, he waited for nightfall, returned to his lodgings mysteriously and let his friends there see that he was writing at night. This was the large square note which they also saw him post next day:

"DEAR AND HONORED FRIEND BILLET:

"The Revolutionary cause gains daily hereabouts and while the aristocrats lose, the patriots advance. The Village of Haramont enrolls itself in the active service of the National Guard; but it has no arms. The means to procure them lies in those who harbor arms in quantity should be made to surrender the overplus, so that the country would be saved expense. If it pleases General Lafayette to authorize that such illegal magazines of arms should be placed at the call of the townships, proportionately to the number of men to be armed, I undertake for my part to supply the Haramont Arsenal with at least thirty guns. This is the only means to oppose a dam to the contra-Revolutionary movements of the aristocrats and enemies of the Nation.

"Your fellow-Citizen and most humble Servant,

"Ange Pitou."

When this was written the author perceived that he had omitted to speak to his correspondent of his wife and daughter. He treated him too much in the Brutus style; on the other hand, to give Billet particulars about Catherine's love affair was to rend the father's heart; it was also to re-open Pitou's bleeding wounds. He stifled a sigh and appended this P. S.

"Mistress Billet and Miss Catherine and all the household are well, and beg to be remembered to Master Billet."

Thus he entangled neither himself nor others.

The reply to this was not slow in coming. Two days subsequently, a mounted express messenger dashed into Haramont and asked for Captain Ange Pitou. His horse was white with foam. He wore the uniform of a staff-officer of the Parisian National Guards.

Judge of the effect he produced and the trouble and throbs of Pitou! He went up to the officer who smiled, and pale and trembling he took the paper he bore for him. It was a response from Billet, by the hand of Gilbert.

Billet advised Pitou to move moderately in his patriotism.

He enclosed General Lafayette's order, countersigned by the War Minister, to arm the Haramont National Guards.

The bearer was an officer charged to see to the arming of cities on the road.

Thus ran the Order:

"All who possess more than one gun or sword are hereby bound to place the excess at the disposal of the chief officials in their cantons. The Present Measure is to be executed throughout the entire country."

Red with joy, Pitou thanked the officer, who smiled again, and started off for the next post for changing horses.

Thus was our friend at the high tide of honor: he had received a communication from General Lafayette, and the War Minister.

This message served his schemes and plans most timely.

To see the animated faces of his fellows, their brightened eyes and eager manner; the profound respect all at once entertained for Ange Pitou, the most credulous observer must have owned that he had become an important character.

One after another the electors begged to touch the seal of the War Department.

When the crowd had tapered down to the chosen friends, Pitou said:

"Citizens, my plans have succeeded as I anticipated. I wrote to the Commander-in-chief your desire to be constituted National Guards, and your choice of me as leader. Read the address on the order brought me."

The envelope was superscribed: "Captain Ange Pitou, Commander of the National Guards. Haramont."

"Therefore," continued the martial peasant, "I am known and accepted as commander by the Chief of the Army. You are recognized and approved as Soldiers of the Nation by General Lafayette and the Minister of War."

A long cheer shook the walls of the little house which sheltered Pitou.

"I know where to get the arms," he went on. "Select two of your number to accompany me. Let them be lusty lads, for we may have a difficulty."

The embryo regiment chose one Claude Tellier sergeant and one Desire Maniquet lieutenant. Pitou approved.

Accompanied by the two, Captain Pitou proceeded once more to Villers Cotterets where he went straight to the mayor to be still farther supported in his demand.

On the way he was puzzled why the letter from Billet, written by Gilbert, asked no news of Sebastian.

On the way he fretted over a paragraph in the letter from Billet, written as it was by Dr. Gilbert, which read:

"Why has Pitou forgot to send news about Sebastian and why does not the boy himself write news?"

Meanwhile, Father Fortier was little aware of the storm he had aroused; and nobody was more astounded when a thunderclap came to his door. When it was opened he saw on the sill the mayor, his vice, and his secretary. Behind them appeared the cocked hats of two gendarmes, and half-a-dozen curious people behind them.

"Father Fortier," said the mayor, "are you aware of the new decree of the Minister of War?"

"No, mayor," said he.

"Read it, then."

The secretary read the warrant to take extra arms from the domiciles. The schoolmaster turned pale.

"The Haramont National Guard have come for the guns."

Fortier jumped as if he meant to fly at the guardsmen.

Judging that this was the nick for his appearance, Pitou approached, backed by his lieutenant and sergeant.

"These rogues," cried the abbe, passing from white to red, "these scums!"

The mayor was a neutral who wanted things to go on quietly; he had no wish to quarrel with the altar or the guard-house; the invectives only called forth his hearty laugh.

"You hear how the reverend gentleman treats the Haramont National Guards," he said to Pitou and his officers.

"Because he knew us when boys and does not think we have grown up," said Ange, with melancholy mildness.

"But we have become men," roughly said Maniquet, holding out towards the priest his hand, maimed by a gun going off prematurely while he was poaching on a nobleman's warren. Needless to say he was determined the nobility should pay for this accident.

"Serpents," said the schoolmaster in irritation.

"Who will sting if trodden on," retorted Sergeant Claude, joining in.

In these threats the mayor saw the extent of the Revolution and the priest martyrdom.

"We want some of the arms here," said the former, to conciliate everybody.

"They are not mine but belong to the Duke of Orleans," was the reply.

"Granted," said Pitou, "but that does not prevent us asking for them all the same."

"I will write to the prince," said the pedagogue loftily.

"You forget that the delay will avail nothing," interposed the mayor; "the duke is for the people and would reply that they ought to be given not only the muskets but the old cannon."

This probability painfully struck the priest who groaned in Latin: "I am surrounded by foes."

"Quite true, but these are merely political enemies," observed Pitou; "we hate in you only the bad patriot."

"Absurd and dangerous fool," returned the priest, in excitement which

The Hero of the People

gave him eloquence of a kind, "which is of us the better lover of his country, I who wish to keep cruel weapons in the shade, or you demanding them for civil strife and discord? which is the true son, I who seek palms to decorate our common mother, or you who hunt for the steel to rend her bosom?"

The mayor turned aside his head to hide his emotion, making a slight nod as much as to say: "That is very neatly put." The deputy mayor, like another Tarquin, was cropping the flowers with his cane. Ange was set back, which caused his two companions to frown.

Sebastian, a Spartan child, was impassible. Going up to Pitou he asked him what was the to-do.

"An order signed by General Lafayette, and written by my father?" he repeated when briefly informed. "Why is there any hesitation in obeying it?"

He revealed the indomitable spirit of the two races creating him in his dilated pupils, and the rigidity of his brow.

The priest shuddered to hear the words and lowered his crest.

"This is rebellion," continued Sebastian; "beware, sir!"

"Thou, also?" cried the schoolmaster, draping himself in his gown after the manner of Caesar.

"And I," said Pitou, comprehending that his post was at stake. "Do you style me a traitor, because I came to you with the olive branch in my hand to ask the arms, and am forced this day to wrench them from you under support of the authorities? Well, I would rather appear as a traitor to my duties than give a favoring hand to the Anti-Revolution. The Country forever and above all! hand over the arms, or we will use ours!"

The mayor nodded on the sly to Pitou as he had to the priest to signify: "You have said that finely."

The speech had thunderstricken the priest and electrified the hearers. The mayor slipped away, and the deputy would have liked to follow his example, but the absence of the two principal functionaries would look bad.

78

He therefore followed the secretary, who led the gendarmes along to the museum, guided by Pitou who, instructed in the place was also instructed on the place of deposit.

Like a lion cub, Sebastian bounded with the patriots. The schoolmaster fell half dead on a chair.

The invaders wanted to pillage everything, but Pitou only selected thirty-three muskets, with an extra one, a rifle, for himself, together with a straight sword, which he girded on.

The others, made up into two bundles, were carried by the joyous pair of officers in spite of the weight, past the disconsolate priest.

They were distributed to the Haramontese that evening, and in presenting a gun to each, Pitou said, like the Spartan mother giving out the buckler: "Come home with it, or go to sleep on it!"

Thus was the little place set in a ferment by Pitou's act. The delight was great to own a gun where firearms had been forbidden lest the lords' game should be injured and where the long oppression of the gamekeepers had infused a mania for hunting.

But Pitou did not participate in the glee. The soldiers had weapons but not only was their captain ignorant how to drill them but to handle them in file or squad.

During the night his taxed brain suggested the remedy.

He remembered an old friend, also an old soldier, who had lost a leg at the Battle of Fontenoy; the Duke of Orleans gave him the privilege to live in the woods, and kill either a hare or a rabbit a-day. He was a dead shot and on the proceeds of his shooting under this license he fared very well.

His manual of arms might be musty but then Pitou could procure from Paris the new Drill-book of the National Guards, and correct what was obsolete by the newest tactics.

He called on old Clovis at a lucky moment as the old hunter was saddened by his gun having burst. He welcomed the present of the rifle which Ange brought him and eagerly embraced the opportunity of paying him in kindness by teaching him the drill.

Each day Pitou repeated to his soldiery what he had learnt overnight from the hunter, and he became more popular, the admired of men, children and the aged. Even women were quieted when his lusty voice thundered: "Heads up—eyes right! bear yourselves nobly! look at me!" for Pitou looked noble.

As soon as the manoeuvres became complicated, Pitou went over to a large town where he studied the troops on the parade grounds, and picked up more in a day from practice than from the books in three months.

Thus two months passed by, in fatigue, toil and feverish excitement.

Pitou was still unhappy in love, but he was satiated with glory. He had run about so much, so moved his limbs, and whetted his mind, that you may be astonished that he should long to appease or comfort his heart. But he was thinking of that.

CHAPTER X. THE LOVER'S PARTING.

MANY times after drill, and that followed nights spent in learning the tactics, Pitou would wander in the skirts of Boursonne Wood to see how faithful Catherine was to her love-trysts.

Stealing an hour or two from her farm and house duties, the girl would go to a little hunting-box, in a rabbit warren belonging to Boursonne Manor, to meet the happy Isidore, the mortal more than ever proud and handsome, when all the country was in suffering around him.

What anguish devoured poor Pitou, what sad reflections he was driven to make on the inequality of men as regards happiness.

He whom the pretty maids were ogling, preferred to come and mope like a dog whipped for following the master too far from home, at the door of the summerhouse where the amorous pair were billing and cooing.

All because he adored Catherine and the more as he deemed her vastly superior to him. He did not regard her as loving another, for Isidore Charny had ceased to be an object of jealousy. He was a lord, handsome and worthy of being loved: but Catherine as a daughter of the lower orders ought not for that reason disgrace her family or drive Pitou to despair.

Meditation on this cut him with sharp edges and keen points.

"She showed no proper feeling in letting me go from the farm," he mused, "and since I went off, she has not inquired whether I starved to death or not. What would Father Billet say if he knew how his friends are thus cast off, and his business neglected? What would he say if he heard that, instead of looking after the working people, his daughter goes to keep appointments with the aristocrat, Lord Charny? He would not say much, but he would kill her. It is something to have the means of revenge in one's hand," thought Pitou.

But it is grander not to use them.

Still, Pitou had learnt that there is no benefit in doing good unless the actions are known to the person befriended.

Would it be possible to let Catherine know that he was helping her?

He knew that she came through the woods to go to the hunting-box, and it was very easy for him to plant himself under the trees, a book in hand as if he were studying, where she would be sure to come along.

Indeed, as he was pretending to pore over the "Perfect National Guardsman," after having watched her to her rendezvous, he heard the soft shutting of a door. The rustle of a dress in the brush came next. Catherine's head appeared above the bushes, looking with an apprehensive air all round for fear somebody would see her.

She was ten paces from her rustic worshipper, who kept still with the book on his knee. But he no longer looked on it but at the girl so that she should mark that he saw her.

She uttered a slight faint, stifled scream, recognized him, became pale as though death had flitted by and grazed her, and, after a short indecision betrayed in her trembling and the shrug of her shoulders, she flew wildly into the underwood and found her hitched-up horse in the forest. She mounted and fled.

Pitou's plot was well laid and she had fallen into it.

He went home, half-frightened, half-delighted.

He perceived a number of details most alarming in the accomplished trick.

The following Sunday was appointed for a grand military parade at Haramont. Sufficiently drilled, the Haramontese meant to give warlike exercises. Several rival villages also making military studies, were to contest with them in the career of arms.

The announcement drew a great crowd, and the people in holiday attire gathered on the green, where they feasted frugally on homemade cake and fruit, washed down with spring water.

Some of the spectators were the gentry and squires, come to laugh at the clowns playing at soldiers.

Haramont had become a centre, for four corps of other Guards came hither, headed by fife and drum.

Among the farmers, came Catherine and Mother Billet on horseback.

This was at the same time as the Haramont National Guard marched up, with fife and drum, with Commander Pitou on a borrowed white horse, in order that the likeness should be complete to General Lafayette reviewing the National Guards at Paris.

Without joking, if he did not look stylish and aristocratic, he was noble and valiant and pleasant to behold.

This company of Guards had shining muskets, the national cockades, and marched with most satisfactory time in two files. It had won the tribute before reaching the parade ground.

Out of the corner of his eye, Pitou saw that Catherine changed color. From that moment the review had more interest to him than anything in the world.

He passed his men through the simple manual of arms, and they did it so smartly and neatly that it elicited applause.

Not so with the competitors, who were irregularly armed and had not been trained steadily. Others exaggerated from their conceit what they could have done properly.

On the whole imperfect results.

For the grand array, Pitou was outranked in seniority by an army sergeant who took the general command; but unhappily he had grasped more than he could hold: he bunched his men, lost grip of some files, let a company meander under the surrounding trees, and finally lost his head so that his own soldiers began to grumble.

From the Haramont side rose a shout:

"Let Pitou try!"

"Yes, yes Pitou!" caught up the other villagers, furious at their inferiority being manifested through their own instructors.

Pitou jumped on his white charger, and replacing himself at the head of his troop, become the rallying point of the little army, uttered a word of command so superbly that the oaks shivered. On the instant, and as by miracle, order was re-established: the movements fitted in with one another with such uniformity that the enthusiasm did not disturb the regularity. Pitou so well applied the theory of the instruction books and the practice of old Clovis that he obtained immense success.

Formed into a hollow square, the whole army raised but one voice and proclaimed him Colonel on the spot.

Bathed in perspiration and drunk with glory, Pitou got down off his horse and received the people's felicitations when he alighted.

But at the same time he glanced round for Catherine. He heard her voice by his side; he had no need to hunt for her, as she had come to him. Great was this triumph.

"Have you not a word for us, Captain Pitou?" she demanded, with a laughing air belied by her pale face; "I suppose you have grown proud since you are a great general?"

"Oh, no," responded he, saluting, "I am not that, but just a poor fellow who loves his country and desires to serve her."

This reply was carried away on the waves of the multitude and was proclaimed sublime by the acclamation in unison.

"Ange, I want to speak with you," whispered Catherine. "Do come back to the farm with mother and me."

"All right."

Catherine had already arranged that they should be alone together on the road. She had switched her mother into the train of several neighbors and gossips who held her in talk so that the girl could walk through the woods with the National Guardsman.

"Why have you kept aloof from the farm so long?" began Catherine when they were beneath the hoary oaks. "It is bad behavior on your part."

Pitou was silent, for it hurt him to hear Catherine tell lies.

"But, I have something else to speak about," she continued, seeing that he was avoiding her with his usually straight and loyal glance. "The other day I saw you in the copse. Did you know me?"

"Not at first, but I did know you."

"What were you doing there in hiding?"

"Why should I be in hiding? I was studying a military book."

"I only thought that curiosity——"

"I am not a Peeping Tom."

She stamped testily with her small foot.

"You are always stuck there and it is not a regular place for students."

"It is very secluded—nothing disturbs one there."

"Nothing? do you stay there any length of time?"

"Sometimes whole days."

"And have you been in the habit of making that your resort?" she inquired quickly.

"Since a good while back."

"It is astonishing that I should not have seen you before," she said, lying so boldly that Pitou was almost convinced.

But he was ashamed for her sake; he was timid from being in love and this led him to be guarded.

"I may have dozed off," he replied; "it has happened when I have taxed my brain too much."

"Then in your sleep you would not have noticed where I strayed for shade—I would go as far as the walls of the old shooting-lodge."

"What lodge?" questioned Pitou.

"The Charny Hunting-lodge," replied she, blushing from his innocence being too thickly laid on not to be suspicious. "It is there grow the finest houseleeks in the section. I burnt myself while ironing and wanted to make a poultice of them."

As if willing to believe her, he looked at her hands.

"No, not my hand, my foot," she said quickly. "I—I dropped the iron: but it has done me good; you see, that I do not limp."

"She did not limp either when she scampered through the wood like a fawn," thought Ange.

She imagined she had succeeded and that Pitou had seen and heard nothing. Giving way to delight, mean in so fine a spirit, she said:

"So Captain Pitou is riding his high horse; proud of his new rank, he scorns us rustics from being a military officer."

Pitou felt wounded. Even a dissimulated sacrifice almost requires some reward, and as Catherine only mystified Pitou or jested at him, no doubt contrasting him with the intelligent Charny, all his good intentions vanished. Self-esteem is a charmed serpent, on which it is perilous to step unless you crush it once for all.

"It seems to me that you are the haughty one," he returned, "for you drove me off the farm on the grounds that there was no work for me. I haven't told Master Billet so far I have arms for earning my bread, thank God! However, you are the mistress under your own roof. In short, you sent me away. Hence, as you saw me at the Charny Lodge, and we were not enemies, it was your place to speak to me instead of running away like a boy stealing apples."

The viper had bitten; Catherine dropped out of her calm.

"I, run away?" she exclaimed.

"As though fire had broken out on the farm. I had not time to shut up my book before you were on the back of Younker, where he was concealed in the foliage, after barking an ashtree, and ruining it."

"What do you mean by ruining?"

"That is right enough," continued Pitou: "while you were gathering houseleeks, Younker was browsing, and in an hour a horse eats a heap of stuff. It must have taken quite an hour for him to strip that sized tree of bark. You must have collected enough plants to cure all the wounds inflicted in taking the Bastile—it is a great thing for poultices!"

Pale and in despair, Catherine could not find a word to speak. Pitou was silent also, as he had said quite enough.

Mother Billet, stopping at the road forks, was bidding adieu to her cronies.

"What does the officer say?" queried the woman.

"He says goodnight to you, Mother Billet."

"Not yet," cried Catherine with a desperate tone. "Tell me the truth—are we no longer friends?"

Pitou felt his secret well up to his lips: but it was all over with him if he spoke; so he bowed mutely with respect which touched her heart; gave Mother Billet a pleasant smile, and disappeared in the dense wood.

"Is that what is called love?" Pitou monologued to himself; "it is sweet at times and then again bitter."

He returned to Haramont, singing the most doleful of rural ballads to the mournfullest tunes.

Luckily he did not find his warriors in any such mood. On the contrary, they were preparing for a feast and they had set aside the chair of honor for their Caesar who had overcome the other villages' Pompeys.

Dragged by his officers into the banquet room, he saluted in silence in return for the greetings, and with the calmness we know as his, attacked the roast veal and potatoes. His action lasted so long that his "digester" was filled while his heart was freed of gall. At the end of a couple of hours he perceived that his grief was no worse.

He stood up when his brother revellers could not stand, while the ladies had fled before the dessert. He made a speech on the sobriety of the Spartans—when all were dead drunk. He said that it was healthier to take a stroll than sleep under the table.

Alone he set the example; he asked of the shadows beneath the glades, why he should be so stern towards a young woman, made for love, grace and sweetness; one who might also cherish a fancy at the outset of life? Alas, why had she not fancied him?

Why should an ugly, uncouth bear like him inspire amorous sentiments in a pretty girl, when a handsome young nobleman—a very peacock beside him—was there to glitter and enchant?

He reasoned that, dazzled by Charny's brilliancy, she would not see Pitou's real value if he acted harshly towards her. Consequently, he ought to behave nicely to her.

The good soul, heated white hot by wine and love, vowed to make Catherine ashamed of having scorned the affection of such a sterling lover as he was.

He could not admit that the fair, chaste and proud Catherine was anything like a plaything to the dashing gallant, or a bright flirt, smiling on the lace ruffles and spurred boots.

Some day Master Isidore would go to the city to marry a countess, and the romance would end by his never looking at Catherine again.

To prove to the maid that he was not ugly, he resolved to take back any harsh words he had used; to do which it was necessary for him to see her.

He started through the woods for the Billet Farm, slashing the bushes with his stick—which blows the shrubs returned with usury.

During this time Catherine was pensively following her mother.

A few steps from the farm was a swamp. The road narrows there so that two horses can hardly go abreast. Mother Billet had gone through and the girl was about to follow when she heard a whistle.

In the shadow she spied the laced cap of Isidore's groom. She let her mother ride on and waited for the messenger.

"Master wants to see you very particular this evening at eleven, wherever you like," said the man.

"Good gracious, has anything bad happened to him?" she said.

"I do not know; but he had a letter from town sealed with black wax. I have been waiting an hour for you."

Ten o'clock struck on the village church bell. Catherine looked round her.

"This place is dark and out of the way," she said; "I will await your Master here."

At the fixed time she ran out to the spot, warned by the sound of a galloping horse. It was Isidore, attended by the groom, who stood at a space while the noble advanced, without getting off his horse.

He held out his arms to her, lifted her on the stirrup, kissed her and said:

"My brother Valence was killed yesterday at Versailles and my brother the count calls me. I am off, Catherine!"

"Oh," she moaned painfully, as she furiously embraced him, "if they have killed him, they will kill you as well."

"Catherine, whatever betides, my eldest brother awaits me; Catherine, you know that I love you."

"Oh, stay, stay," she cried, only knowing one thing—that her beloved talked of leaving her.

"But, honor, Catherine—my murdered brother! vengeance!"

"Oh, what an unhappy girl I am," moaned she, collapsing, palpitating but rigid in the horseman's arms.

Resigned, for she at last comprehended that the brother's summons was an order, she glided to the ground after a farewell kiss.

He turned his eyes, sighed and wavered for a time; but, attracted by the imperative order received, he set his horse to the gallop, and flung Catherine a final farewell.

The lackey followed him across the country.

Catherine remained on the ground, where she had dropped, barring the way with her body.

Almost immediately a man appeared on the hill, striding towards the farm. In his rapid course he could not fail to stumble on the body. He staggered and rolled in the fall, and his groping hands touched the inert form.

"Catherine—dead!" he yelled so that the farm dogs' took up the howling. "Who has killed Catherine?"

He knelt down, pale and ice-cold, beside the inanimate body with its head across his knee.

CHAPTER XI. THE ROAD TO PARIS.

ON this same evening, a no less grave event set the college of Father Fortier in an uproar. Sebastian Gilbert had disappeared about six o'clock and had not been found up to midnight by the most active search.

Nobody had seen him save Aunt Angelique, who, coming from the church, where she let out the chairs, had thought to see him going up a lane. This report added to the schoolmaster's disquiet. He knew that the youth had strange delusions, during which he believed he was following a beautiful lady; more than once when on a walk he had seen him stare at vacancy and if he plunged too deeply into the copse, he would start the best pedestrians of the class after him.

But he had never gone off in the night.

This time, he had taken the road to Haramont, and Angelique had really seen him. He was going to find Pitou. But the latter left the village by one end, to go and see Catherine, at the same time as the doctor's son quitted it by the other.

Pitou's door was open, for the captain was still simple in his habits. He lit the candle and waited: but he was too fretful. He found a sheet of paper, half of that on which Pitou had inscribed the name of his company of soldiers, and wrote as follows:

"My dear Pitou: I have come to tell you of a conversation I overheard between Father Fortier and the Villers Cotterets Vicar. Fortier is in connivance with the aristocratic party of Paris and says that a counter-revolutionary movement is hatching at Versailles. The cue was given when the Queen wore the black cockade and trampled the tricolor under-foot. This threat already made me uneasy about my father, who is the aristocrats' enemy, as you know: but this time it is worse.

"The vicar has returned the priest's visit, and as I feared for my father, I listened to their talk to hear the sequel to what I overheard by accident last time. It appears, my dear Pitou, that the people stormed Versailles and killed a great many royalists, among them Lord Valence Charny.

"Father Fortier said: 'Speak low, not to startle little Gilbert, whose father has gone to Versailles and may be killed in the lot!'

"You understand, Pitou, that I did not wait for more, but I have stolen away and I come to have you take me back to Paris. I will not wait any longer, as you may have gone to lay snares in the woods and would not be home till to-morrow. So I proceed on my road to Paris. Have no anxiety as I know the way and besides I have two gold pieces left out of the money my father gave me, so that I can take a seat in the first conveyance I catch up with.

"P. S.—I make this rather long in order to explain my departure, and to delay me that you may return before I finish. But no, I have finished, and you have not come, so that I am off. Farewell, until we meet again! if nothing has happened to my father and he runs no danger, I will return. If not, I shall ask his leave to stay beside him. Calm Father Fortier about my absence; but do not do so until it is too late for him to overtake me. Good-bye, again!"

Knowing his friend's economy, he put out the candle, and set off.

He went by the starlight at first till he struck through byways the main road at Vauciennes. At the branch of the Paris and Crespy roads, he had to stop as he did not know which to take. They were both alike. He sat down discouraged, partly to rest, partly to reflect, when he heard the galloping of horses from Villers Cotterets way.

He waited to ask the riders the information he wanted. Soon he saw two shadows in the gloom, one riding at a space behind the other so that he judged the foremost to be the master and the other his groom.

He walked out three steps from the roadside to accost him when the horseman clapped his hand to his holster for a pistol.

"I am not a thief, sir," cried Sebastian, interpreting the action correctly, "but a boy whom recent events at Versailles calls thither to seek his father. I do not know which of these roads I ought to take to get to Paris—point it out, please, and you will do me a great service."

The speaker's stylish language and his juvenile tone did not seem unknown to the rider, who reined in his steed, albeit he seemed in haste.

"Who are you, my boy, and how comes it you are out on the highway at such an hour?" he inquired.

"I am not asking you who you are—only my road—the way for a poor boy to reach his father in distress."

In the almost childish voice was firmness which struck the cavalier.

"My friend, we are on the road to Paris," he replied: "I have only been there twice and do not know it very well, but I am sure this is the right one."

Sebastian drew back a step offering his thanks. The horses had need of getting their wind and started off again not very rapidly.

"My Lord Viscount," said the lackey to his master, "do you not recognize that youth?"

"No: though I fancied——"

"It is young Sebastian Gilbert, who is at boarding school, at Abbé Fortier's; and who comes over to Billet's Farm with Ange Pitou."

"You are right, by Jove!" Turning his horse and stopping, he called out: "Is this you, Sebastian?"

"Yes, my lord," returned the boy, who had known the horseman all the time.

"Then, come, and tell me how I find you here?"

"I did tell you—I want to learn that my father in Paris is not killed or hurt."

"Alas, my poor boy," said Isidore with profound sadness, "I am going to town on the like errand: only I have no doubt; one of my brothers, Valence, was slain at Versailles yesterday."

"Oh, I am so sorry," said the youth, holding out his hand to the speaker, which the latter took and squeezed.

"Well, my dear boy, since our fate is akin," said the cavalier, "we must not separate; you must like me be eager to get to Paris."

"Oh, dear, yes!"

"You can never reach it on foot."

"I could do it but it would take too long; so I reckon on taking a place in a stage going my way, and get what lift I can do the journey."

"Better than that, my boy; get up behind my man."

Sebastian plucked his hands out of the other's grasp.

"I thank you, my lord," said he in such a tone that the noble understood that he had hurt the youth's feelings by offering to mount him behind his inferior.

"Or, better still, now I think of it," he went on, "take his place. He can come on afterwards. He can learn where I am by asking at the Tuileries Palace."

"I thank you again, my lord," replied the adolescent, in a milder voice, for he had comprehended the delicacy of the offer: "I do not wish to deprive you of his services."

It was hard to come to an arrangement now that the terms of peace were laid down.

"Better again, my dear Sebastian. Get up behind me. Dawn is peeping: at ten we shall be at Dammartin, half way; there we will leave the two horses, which would not carry us much farther, under charge of Baptistin, and we will take the post-chaise to Paris. I intended to do this so that you do not lead to any change in my arrangements."

"If this be true, then, I accept," said the young man, hesitating but dying to go.

"Down with you, Baptistin, and help Master Sebastian to mount."

"Thanks, but it is useless," said the youth leaping up behind the gentleman as light as a schoolboy.

The three on the two horses started off at the gallop, and disappeared over the ridge.

CHAPTER XII. THE SPIRIT MATERIALIZED.

AT five next afternoon, Viscount Charny and Sebastian reached the Tuileries Palace gates. The name of his brother passed Isidore and his companion into the middle courtyard.

Young Gilbert had wanted to go to the house in Honore Street where his father dwelt, but the other had pointed out that as he was honorary physician to the Royal Household, he might be at the palace, where the latest news of him could be had.

While an usher made inquiries, Sebastian sat on a sofa and Isidore walked up and down the sitting-room.

In ten minutes the man returned: Count Charny was with the Queen; Dr. Gilbert had had nothing happen to him; he was supposed to be with the King, as a doctor was with his Majesty. If it were so, he would be informed on coming out that a person was waiting to see him.

Isidore was much affected in parting with him as his joy at recovering his father made the loss of his brother more painful.

At this the door opened for a servant to call: "The Viscount of Charny is asked for in the Queen's apartments."

"You will wait for me," said Isidore; "unless your father comes, promise me, Gilbert, for I am answerable for you to the doctor."

"Yes, and receive my thanks in the meantime," rejoined Sebastian, resuming his place on the sofa as the Viscount left the room with the domestic.

Easy about his father's fate, and himself, certain that the good intent would earn his forgiveness for the journey, he went back in memory to Father Fortier, and on Pitou, and reflected on the trouble which his flight and his note would cause them severally.

And naturally, by the mechanism of ideas, he thought of the woods around Pitou's home, where he had so often pursued the ghost in his reverie. The White Lady seen so oft in visions, and once only in reality, he believed in Satory Wood, appearing and flitting away in a magnificent carriage drawn by a galloping pair.

He recalled the profound emotion this sight had given him and half plunged in dreams anew, he murmured:

"My mother?"

At this juncture, a door in the wall over against him opened. A woman appeared. This appearance was so much in harmony with what happened in his fancy, that he started to see his ghost take substance. In this woman was the vision and the reality—the lady seen at Satory.

He sprang up as though a spring had acted under his feet.

His lips tightened on one another, his eyes expanded, and the pupils dilated. His heaving breast in vain endeavored to form a sound.

Majestic, haughty and disdainful, the lady passed him without any heed. Calm as she was externally, yet her pale countenance, frowning brow and whistling respiration, betrayed that she was in great nervous irritation.

She crossed the room diagonally, opened another door, and walked into a corridor.

Sebastian comprehended that she was escaping him, if he did not hasten. He still looked as if apprehensive that it was a ghost, but then darted after her, before the skirt of her silken robe had disappeared round the turning of the lobby.

Hearing steps behind her, she walked more briskly as if fearing pursuit.

He quickened his gait as much as he could, fearing as the corridor was dark that he might miss her. This caused her to accelerate her pace also, but she looked round.

He uttered a cry of joy for it was clearly the vision.

Seeing but a boy with extended arms and understanding nothing why she should be chased, the lady hurried down a flight of stairs. But she had barely descended to one landing than Sebastian arrived at the end of the passage where he called out:

"Lady, oh, lady!"

This voice produced a strange sensation throughout the hearer; she seemed struck in the heart by a pain which was half delight, and from the heart a shudder sent by the blood through all her veins.

Nevertheless, as all was a puzzle to her; she doubled her speed, and the course resembled a flight.

They reached the foot of the stairs at the same time.

It was the courtyard into which the lady sped. A carriage was waiting for her, for a servant was holding the door open. She stepped in swiftly and took her seat.

Before the door could be closed, Sebastian glided in between it and the footman, and seizing the hem of her dress, kissed with frenzy and cried:

"Oh, lady!"

Looking at the pretty boy who had frightened her at first, she said in a sweeter voice than she usually spoke, though it was yet shaken with fear and emotion:

"Well, my little friend, why are you running after me? why do you call me? what do you want?"

"I want to see you, and kiss you," replied the child. "I want to call you 'Mother,'" he added in so low a voice that only she could hear him.

She uttered a scream, embraced him, and approaching him as by a sudden revelation, fastened her ardent lips on his brow. Then, as though she dreaded someone coming to snatch away this child whom she had found, she drew him entirely into the vehicle, pushed him to its other side, shut the door with her own hand, and lowering the glass to order: "Drive to No. 9 Coq-Heron Street, the first carriage-doorway from Plastriere Street," she shut the window instantly.

Turning to the boy she asked his name.

"Sebastian? come, Sebastian, come here, on my heart."

She threw herself back as if going to swoon, muttering: "What new sensation is this? can it be what is called happiness?"

The journey was one long kiss of mother and son.

She had found this son by a miracle, whom the father had torn from her in a terrible night of anguish and dishonor; he had disappeared with no trace but the abductor's tracks in the snow; this child had been detested until she heard its first wail, whereupon she had loved him; this child had been prayed for, called for, begged for. Her brother had uselessly hunted for him over land and ocean. For fifteen years she had yearned for him, and despaired to behold him again; she had begun to think no more of him but as a cherished spirit. Here he was, running and crying after her, seeking her, in his turn, calling her "Mother!"

He was pillowed on her heart, pressing on her bosom, loving her filially although he had never seen her, as she loved him with maternal affection. Her pure lips recovered all the joys of a lost life in this first kiss given her son.

Above the head of mankind is Something else than the void in which the spheres revolve: in life there is Another Thing than chance and fatality.

After fourteen years she was taken back to the house where he was born, this offspring of the union of the mesmerist Gilbert and the daughter of the House of Taverney, his victim. There he had drawn the first breath of life and thence his father had stolen him.

This little residence, bought by the late Baron Taverney, served as lodging for his son when he came to town, which was rarely, and for Andrea, when she slept in town.

After her conflict with the Queen, unable to bear meeting the woman who loved her husband, Andrea had made up her mind to go away from the rival, who visited on her retaliation for all her griefs, and whom the woes of the Queen, great though they were, always remained beneath the sufferings of the loving woman.

All concurred then in making this evening a happy one for the ex-Queen's maid of honor. Nothing should trouble her. Instead of a room in a palace where the walls are all ears and eyes, she was harboring her child in her own little, secluded house.

As soon as she was closeted with Sebastian in her boudoir, she drew him to a lounge, on which were concentrated the lights from both candles and fire.

"Oh, my boy, is it really you?" she exclaimed with a joy which still quivered with lingering doubt.

"Mother!" ejaculated Sebastian with an outburst of the heart, flowing like refreshing dews on Andrea's burning heart and enfevered veins.

"And the meeting to be here," said she, looking round with terror towards the room whence he had been stolen.

"What do you mean by 'Here?'"

"Fifteen years ago, my boy, you were born in this room, and I bless the mercy of the Almighty that you are miraculously restored to me."

"Yes, miraculously indeed," said the youth, "for if I had not feared for my father——"

Andrea closed her eyes and leaned back, so sharp was the pang shooting through her.

"If I had not set out alone in the night, I should not have been perplexed about the road: and then I should not have been recognized by Lord Isidore Charny, who offered his help and conducted me to the Tuileries——"

Her eyes re-opened, her heart expanded and her glance thanked heaven: for it increased the miracle that Sebastian should be led to her by her husband's brother.

"I should not have seen you passing through the palace and not following you might never have called you 'Mother!' the word so sweet and tender to utter."

Recalled to her bliss, she hugged him again and said:

"Yes, you are right, my boy; it is most sweet: but there is perchance another one more sweet and tender; 'My son!' which I say to you as I press you to my heart. But in short," she suddenly said, "it is impossible that all should remain mysterious around us. You have explained how you come here, but not how you recognized me and ran after me, calling me your mother."

"How can I tell? I do not myself know," replied Sebastian, looking at her with love unspeakable. "You speak of mysteries? all is mysterious about you and me. List to me, and I will tell you what seems a prodigy."

Andrea bent nearer.

"It is ten years since I knew you. You do not understand. I have dreams which my father calls hallucinations."

At the reminder of Gilbert, passing like a steel point from the boyish lips, Andrea started.

"I have seen you twenty times, mother. In the village, while playing with the other schoolboys, I have followed you as you flitted through the woods and pursued you with useless calls till you faded away. Crushed by fatigue I would drop on the spot, as if your presence alone had sustained me."

This kind of second existence, this living dream, too much resembled what the medium herself experienced for her not to understand him.

"Poor darling," she said as she pressed him more closely, "it was vainly that hate strove to part us. Heaven was bringing us together without my suspecting it. Less happy than you, I saw my dear child neither in dream nor reality. Still, when I passed through that Green Saloon I felt a shiver; when I heard your footsteps behind mine, giddiness thrilled my heart and brain; when you called me 'Lady' I all but stopped; when you called me 'Mother!' I nearly swooned; when I embraced you, I believed."

"My mother," repeated Sebastian, as if to console her for not having heard the welcome title for so long.

"Yes, your mother," said the countess, with a transport of love impossible to describe.

"Now that we have found each other," said the youth, "and as you are contented and happy at our union, we are not going to part any more, tell me?"

She shuddered: she was enjoying the present to the exclusion of the past and totally closing her eyes on the future.

"How I should bless you, my poor boy, if you could accomplish this miracle!" she sighingly murmured.

"Let me manage it; I will do it. I do not know the causes separating you from my father,"—Andrea turned pale—"but they will be effaced by my tears and entreaties, however serious they may be."

"Never," returned the countess, shaking her head.

"I tell you that my father adores you," said Sebastian, who believed that the woman was in the wrong from the way his father had forbidden him ever to mention her name.

Her hands holding the speaker's relaxed but he did not notice this, as he continued:

"I will prepare him to greet you; I will tell him all the happiness you give me; one of these days, I will take you by the hand and lead you to him, saying: 'Here she is, father—look, how handsome she is!'"

Repulsing Sebastian, she sprang up.

"Never," repeated she, while he stared with astounded eyes for she was so white as to alarm him. This time her accent expressed a threat rather than fright.

She recoiled on the lounge; in that face he had seen the hard lines which

Raphael gives to irritated angels.

"Why do you refuse to receive my father?" he demanded, in a sullen voice.

At these words, the lightning burst as at the contact of two clouds.

"Why? do you ask me why? well, never shall you know."

"Still, I ask why," said Sebastian, with firmness.

"Because, then," said Andrea, incapable of self-restraint under the sting of the serpent gnawing at her heart, "because your father is an infamous villain!"

He bounded up from the divan and stood before her.

"Do you say that of my father," he cried, "of Dr. Gilbert, who brought me up and educated me, the only friend I ever knew? I am making a mistake—you are no mother of mine!"

She stopped him darting towards the door.

"Stay," she said, "you cannot know, ought not understand, may not judge."

"No; but I can feel, and I feel that I love you no more."

She screamed with pain.

Simultaneously, a diversion was given to the emotion overwhelming her by the sound of a carriage coming up to the street doorway. Such a shudder ran over her that he thrilled in sympathy.

"Wait, and be silent," she said so that he was subjugated.

"Who am I to announce?" she heard the old footman demand in the ante-room.

"The Count of Charny; and inquire if my lady will do me the honor to receive me?"

"Into this room, child," said Andrea, "he must not see you—he must not know that you exist!"

She pushed the frightened youth into the adjoining apartment.

"Remain here till he shall have gone, when I will relate to—No, nothing of that can be said? I will so love you that you will not doubt that I am your own loving mother."

His only reply was a moan.

At this moment the door opened and the servant, cap in hand, acquitted himself of the errand entrusted to him.

"Show in the Count of Charny," she said in the firmest voice she could find.

As the old man retired, the nobleman appeared on the sill.

CHAPTER XIII. HUSBAND AND WIFE.

COUNT CHARNY was clad in black, mourning for his brother slain two days before.

This mourning was not solely in his habit, but in the recesses of his heart, and his pallid cheeks attested what grief he had undergone. Never are handsome faces finer than after sorrow, and the rapid glance of his wife perceived that he had never looked more superb.

She closed her eyes an instant, slightly held back her head to draw a full breath and laid her hand on her heart which seemed about to break.

When she opened them, after a second, Charny was in the same place.

"Is the carriage to wait?" inquired the servant, urged by the footman at the door.

An unspeakable look shot from the yearning eyes of the visitor upon his wife, who was dazed into closing her own again, while she stood breathless as though she had not noticed the glance or heard the question. Both had penetrated to her heart.

Charny sought in this lovely living statue for some token to indicate what answer he should make. As her shiver might be read both ways, he said: "Bid the coachman wait."

The door closed and perhaps for the first time since their wedding the lord and his lady were alone together.

"Pardon me," said the count, breaking the silence, "but is my unexpected call intrusion? I have not seated myself and the carriage waits so that I can depart as I came."

"No, my lord, quite the contrary," quickly said Andrea. "I knew you were well and safe, but I am not the less happy to see you after recent events."

"You have been good enough then to ask after me?"

"Of course; yesterday, and this morning, when I was answered that you were at Versailles; and this evening, when I learnt that you were in attendance on the Queen."

Were those last words spoken simply or did they contain a reproach? Not knowing what to make of them, the count was evidently set thinking by them. But probably leaving to the outcome of the dialogue the lifting of the veil lowered on his mind for the time, he replied almost instantly:

"My lady, a pious duty retained me at Versailles yesterday and this day; one as sacred in my eyes brought me instantly on my arrival in town beside her Majesty."

Andrea tried in her turn to discover the true intent of the words. Thinking that she ought to respond, she said:

"Yes, I know of the terrible loss which—you have experienced." She had been on the point of saying "we," but she dared not, and continued: "You have had the misfortune to lose your brother Valence de Charny."

The count seemed to be waiting for the clue, for he had started on hearing the pronoun "Your."

"Yes, my lady. As you say, a terrible loss for me, but you cannot appreciate the young man, as you little knew poor Valence, happily."

In the last word was a mild and melancholy reproach, which his auditor comprehended, though no outward sign was manifested that she gave it heed.

"Still, one thing consoles me, if anything can console me; poor Valence died doing his duty, as probably his brother Isidore will die, and I myself."

This deeply affected Andrea.

"Alas, my lord," she asked, "do you believe matters so desperate that fresh sacrifices of blood are necessary to appease the wrath of heaven?"

"I believe that the hour comes when the knell of kings is to peal; that an evil genius pushes monarchy unto the abysm. In short I think, if it is to fall, it will be accompanied, and should be so, by all those who took part in its splendor."

"True, but when comes that day, believe that it will find me ready like yourself for the utmost devotion," said Andrea.

"Your ladyship has given too many proofs of that devotion in the past, for any one to doubt it for the future—I least of all—the less as I have for the first time flinched about an order from the Queen. On arriving from Versailles, I found the order to present myself to her Majesty instantly."

"Oh," said Andrea, sadly smiling; "it is plain," she added, after a pause, "like you, the Queen sees the future is sombre and mysterious and wishes to gather round her all those she can depend on."

"You are wrong, my lady," returned Charny, "for the Queen summoned me, not to bid me stand by her, but to send me afar."

"Send you away?" quickly exclaimed the countess, taking a step towards the speaker. "But I am keeping you standing," she said, pointing to a chair.

So saying, she herself sank, as though unable to remain on foot any longer, on the sofa where she had been sitting with Sebastian shortly before.

"Send you away? in what end?" she said with emotion not devoid of joy at the thought that the suspected lovers were parting.

"To have me go to Turin to confer with Count Artois and the Duke of Bourbon, who have quitted the country."

"And you accepted?"

"No, my lady," responded Charny, watching her fixedly.

She lost color so badly that he moved as if to assist her, but this revived her strength and she recovered.

"No? you have answered No to an order of the Queen's, my lord?" she faltered, with an indescribable accent of doubt and astonishment.

"I answered that I believed my presence here at present more necessary than in Italy. Anybody could bear the message with which I was to be honored;

I had a second brother, just arrived from the country, to place at the orders of the King, and he was ready to start in my stead."

"Of course the Queen was happy to see the substitute," exclaimed Andrea, with bitterness she could not contain, and not appearing to escape Charny.

"It was just the other way, for she seemed to be deeply wounded by the refusal. I should have been forced to go had not the King chanced in and I made him the arbiter."

"The King held you to be right?" sneered the lady with an ironical smile: "he like you advised your staying in the Tuileries? Oh, how good his Majesty is!"

"So he is," went on the count, without wincing: "he said that my brother Isidore would be well fitted for the mission and the more so as it was his first visit to court, so that his absence would not be remarked. He added that it would be cruel for the Queen to require my being sent away from you at present."

"The King said, from me?" exclaimed Andrea.

"I repeat his own words, my lady. Looking round and addressing me, he wanted to know where the Countess of Charny was. 'I have not seen her this evening,' said he. As this was specially directed to me, I made bold to reply. 'Sire,' I said, 'I have so seldom the pleasure of seeing the countess that I am in the state of impossibility to tell where she is; but if your Majesty wishes to know, he might inquire of the Queen who, knowing, will reply!' I insisted as I judged from the Queen looking black, that some difference had arisen between you."

Andrea was so enwrapt in the listening that she did not think of saying anything.

"The Queen made answer that the Countess of Charny had gone away from the palace with no intention to return. 'Why, what motive can your best friend have in quitting the palace at this juncture?' inquired the King.

'Because she is uncomfortable here,' replied the Queen who had started at the title you were given. 'Well, that may be so; but we will find accommodation for her and the count beside our own rooms,' went on the King. 'You will not be very particular, eh, my lord?' I told him that I should be satisfied with any post as long as I could serve him in it. 'I know it well: so that we only want the lady called back from—' the Queen did not know whither you had departed. 'Not know where your friend has gone?' exclaimed the King. 'When my friends leave me I do not inquire after them.' 'Good, some woman's quarrel,' said Louis; 'my Lord Charny, I have to speak a while with the Queen. Kindly wait for me and present your brother who shall start for Turin this evening. I am of your opinion that I shall require you and I mean to keep you by me.' So I sent for my brother who was awaiting me in the Green Saloon, I was told."

At the mention, Andrea, who had nearly forgotten Sebastian in her interest in her husband's story, was made to think of all that had passed between mother and son, and she threw her eyes with anguish on the bedroom door where she had placed him.

"But you must excuse me for talking of matters but slightly interesting you while you are no doubt wishful to know why I have come here."

"No, my lord, what you say does engage me," replied the countess; "your presence can only be agreeable on account of the fears I have felt on your account. I pray you to continue. The King asked you to wait for him and to bring your brother."

"We went to the royal apartments, where he joined us in ten minutes. As the mission for the princes was urgent he began by that. Their Highnesses were to be instructed about what had happened. A quarter of an hour after the King came, my brother was on the road, and the King and I were left alone. He stopped suddenly in pacing the room and said: 'My lord, do you know what has passed between the Queen and the countess?' I was ignorant. 'Something must have happened,' he went on, 'for the Queen is in a temper fit to massacre everybody, and it appears to me unjust to the countess—which is odd, as the Queen usually defends her friends through thick and thin, even when they are wrong.' 'I repeat I know nothing, but I venture to assert that the countess has done no wrong—even if we cannot admit that a queen ever does so.'"

"I thank your lordship for having so good an opinion of me," said Andrea.

"'I suppose as the countess has a house in town that she has retired there,' I suggested. 'Of course! I will give you leave of absence till to-morrow on condition that you bring back the countess,' said the King."

Charny looked at his wife so fixedly that she was unable to bear the glance and had to close her eyes.

"Then, seeing that I was in mourning, he stayed me to say that my loss was one of those which monarchs could not repair; but that if my brother left a widow or a child he would help them, and would like them presented to him, at any rate; the Queen should take care of the widow and he would of the children."

Charny spoke with tears in his voice.

"I daresay the King was only repeating what the Queen had said," remarked the lady.

"The Queen did not honor me with a word on the subject," returned Charny, "and that is why the King's speech affected me most deeply. He ended by bidding me 'Go to our dear Andrea; for though those we love cannot console us they can mourn with us, and that is a relief.' Thus it is that I come by the King's order, which may be my excuse, my lady," concluded the count.

"Did you doubt your welcome?" cried the lady, quickly rising and holding out both hands to him.

He grasped them and kissed them; she uttered a scream as though they were redhot iron, and sank back on the divan. But her hands were clinging to his and he was drawn down so as to be placed sitting beside her.

But it was then that she thought she heard a noise in the next room, and she started from him so abruptly that he rose and stood off a little, not knowing to what to attribute the outcry and the repulsion so suddenly made.

Leaning on the sofa back, he sighed. The sigh touched her deeply.

At the very time when the bereaved mother found her child, something like the dawn of love beamed on her previously dismal and sorrowful horizon. But by a strange coincidence, proven that she was not born to happiness, the two events were so combined that one annulled the other: the return of the husband thrust aside the son's love as the latter's presence destroyed the budding passion.

Charny could not divine this in the exclamation and the starting aloof, the silence full of sadness following, although the cry was of love and the retreat from fear, not repulsion.

He gazed upon her with an expression which she could not have mistaken if she had been looking up.

"What answer am I to carry to the King?" he inquired emitting a sigh.

"My lord," she replied, starting at the sound and raising her clear and limpid eyes to him, "I suffered so much while in the court that I accepted the leave to go when accorded by the Queen, with thankfulness. I am not fitted to live in society, and in solitude I have found repose if not happiness. My happiest days were those spent as a girl at Taverney and in the convent of St. Denis with the noble princess of the House of France, the Lady Louise. But, with your lordship's permission, I will dwell in this summerhouse, full of recollections which are not without some sweetness in spite of their sadness."

Charny bowed at this suggestion of his permission being sought, like a man who was obeying an order, far more than granting a request.

"As this is a fixed resolve," he said, marking how steady she was with all her meekness, "am I to be allowed to call on you here?"

She fastened her eyes on him, usually clear but now full of astonishment and blandness.

"Of course, my lord," was her response, "and as I shall have no company, you can come any time that your duties at the palace allow you to set aside a little while to me."

Never had Charny seen so much charm in her gaze, or such tenderness in her voice. Something ran through his veins, like the shudder from a lover's first kiss. He glanced at the place whence he had risen when Andrea got up; he would have given a year of life to take his seat there again if she would not once more repel him. But the soldier was timid, and he dared not allow himself the liberty.

On her part, Andrea would have given ten years, sooner than only one, to have him in that place, but, unfortunately, each was ignorant of the other's mood, and they stood still, in almost painful expectation.

"You were saying that you had to endure a great deal at court. Was not the Queen pleasant towards you?"

"I have nothing to blame her Majesty for," replied the ex-lady of honor, "and I should be unjust if I did not acknowledge her Majesty's kind treatment."

"I hinted at this, because I have lately noticed that the friendship seemed to show a falling off," continued the count.

"That is possible, and that is why I am leaving the court."

"But you will live so lonely?"

"Have I not always lived so, my lord?" sighed Andrea, "as maid—wife— " she stopped, seeing that she was going too far.

"Do you make me a reproach?"

"What right have I in heaven's name to make reproaches to your lordship?" retorted the countess: "do you believe I have forgot the circumstances under which we were plighted? Just the opposite of those who vow before the altar reciprocal love and mutual protection, we swore eternal indifference and complete separation. The blame would be to the one who forgot that oath."

Charny caught the sigh which these words had not entirely suppressed, from the speaker's heart.

"But this is such a small dwelling," he said: "a countess in one sitting room with only another to eat in, and this for repose——"

She sprang in between him and the bedroom, seeing Sebastian behind the door, in her mind's eye.

"Oh, my lord, do not go that way, I entreat you," she exclaimed, barring the passage with her extended arms.

"Oh, my lady," said he, looking at her so pale and trembling, with fright never more plain on a human face, "I knew that you did not like me: but I had no idea you hated me to this degree."

Incapable of remaining any longer beside his wife without an outburst, he reeled for a space like an intoxicated man; recovering himself, he rushed out of the room with an exclamation of pain which echoed in the depths of the hearer's heart.

She watched him till he was out of sight; she listened till she could no longer hear his departing carriage, and then with a breaking heart, dreading that she had not enough motherly love to combat with this other passion, she darted into the bedroom, calling out:

"Sebastian," but no voice replied.

By the trembling of the night-lamp in a draft she perceived that the window was open. It was the same by which the child was kidnapped fifteen years before.

"This is justice," she muttered; "did he not say that I was no more his mother?"

Comprehending that she had lost both husband and child at the period when she had recovered them, Andrea threw herself on the couch, at the end of her resignation and her prayers exhausted.

Suddenly it seemed to her that something more dreadful than her sorrowful plight glided in between grief and her tears.

She looked up and beheld a man, after climbing in at the open window, standing on the floor.

She wished to shriek and ring for help; but he bent on her the fascinating gaze which caused her the invincible lethargy she remembered Cagliostro could impose upon her: but in this mesmerist and his spell-binding look and bearing, she recognized Gilbert.

How was it the execrated father stood in the stead of his beloved son?

CHAPTER XIV. IN SEARCH OF THEIR SON.

IT was Dr. Gilbert who was closeted with the King when the usher inquired after him on the order of Isidore and the entreaty of Sebastian.

The upright heart of Louis XVI. had appreciated the loyalty in the doctor's. After half an hour, the latter came forth and went into the Queen's ante-chamber, where he saw Isidore.

"I asked for you, doctor, but I have another with me who wants still more to see you. It will be cruel to detain you from him: so let us hasten to the Green Saloon."

But the room was empty and such was the confusion in the palace that no servant was at hand to inform them what had become of the young man.

"It was a person I met on the road, eager to get to Paris and coming here on foot only for my giving him a ride."

"Are you speaking of the peasant Pitou?"

"No, doctor—of your son, Sebastian."

At this, the usher who had taken Isidore away returned.

He was ignorant of what had happened but, luckily, a second footman had seen the singular disappearance of the boy in the carriage of a court lady.

They hastened to the gates where the janitor well recalled that the direction to the coachman was "No. 9 Coq-Heron Street, first carriage entrance from Plastriere Street."

"My sister-in-law's," exclaimed Isidore, "the countess of Charny!"

"Fatality," muttered Gilbert. "He must have recognized her," he said in a lower tone.

"Let us go there," suggested the young noble.

Gilbert saw all the dangers of Andrea's son being discovered by her husband.

"My lord," he said, "my son is in safety in the hands of the Countess of Charny, and as I have the honor to know her, I think I can call by myself. Besides it is more proper that you should be on your road; for I presume you are going to Turin, from what I heard in the King's presence."

"Yes, doctor."

"Receive my thanks for your kindness to Sebastian, and be off! When a father says he is not uneasy, you need feel no anxiety."

Isidore held out his hand which the revolutionist shook with more heartiness than he had for most of his class; while the nobleman returned within the palace, he went along to the junction of the streets Coq-Heron and Plastriere.

Both were painful memories.

In the latter he had lived, a poor boy, earning his bread by copying music, by receiving instruction from the author Rousseau. From his window he had contemplated Andrea at her own casement, under the hands of her maid, Nicole, his first sweetheart, and to that window he had made his way by a rope and by scaling the wall, to view more closely and satisfy his passion for the high-born lady who had bewitched him.

Rousseau was dead, but Andrea was rich and nobler still; he had also attained wealth and consideration.

But was he any happier than when he walked out of doors to dip his crust in the waters of this public fountain?

He could not help walking up to the door where Rousseau had lived. It was open on the alley which ran under the building to the yard at the back as well as up to the attic where he was lodged.

He went up to the first floor back, where the window on the landing gave a view of the rear house where Baron Taverney had dwelt.

No one disturbed him in his contemplation; the house had come down in the world; no janitor; the inhabitants were poor folk who did not fear thieves.

The garden at Taverney's house was the same as a dozen years before. The vine still hung on the trellis which had served him as ladder in his night clamberings within the enclosure.

He was unaware whether Count Charny was with his wife, but he was so bent on learning about Sebastian that he meant to risk all.

He climbed the wall and descended on the other side. In the garden nothing obstructed him, and thus he reached the window of Andrea's Bedroom.

In another instant, as related, the two enemies stood face to face.

The lady's first feeling was invincible repugnance rather than profound terror.

For her the Americanized Gilbert, the friend of Washington and Lafayette, aristocratic through study, science and genius, was still the hangdog Gilbert of her father's manor house, and the gardener's boy of Trianon Palace.

Gilbert no longer bore her the ardent love which had driven him to crime in his youth, but the deep and tender affection, spite of her insults and persecutions, of a man ready to do a service at risk of his life.

With the insight nature had given him and the justice education implanted, Gilbert had weighed himself: he understood that Andrea's misfortunes arose from him, and he would never be quits with her until he had made her as happy as he had the reverse.

But how could he blissfully affect her future.

It was impossible for him yet to comprehend.

On seeing this but to so much despair, again the prey to woe, all his fibres of mercy were moved for so much misery.

Instead of using his hypnotic power to subdue her, he spoke softly to her, ready to master her if she became rebellious.

The result was that the medium felt the ethereal fluid fade away like a dissolving fog, by Gilbert's permission, and she was able to speak of her own free will.

"What do you want, sir? how came you here?"

"By the way I used before," replied the doctor. "Hence you can be easy—no one will know of it. Why? because I come to claim a treasure, of no consequence to you, but precious to me, my son. I want you to tell what has become of my son, taken away in your carriage and brought here."

"How do I know? taught by you to hate his mother, he has fled."

"His mother? are you really a mother to him?"

"Oh, you see my grief, you have heard my cries, and looking on my despair, you ask me if I am his mother?"

"How then are you ignorant what has become of him?"

"But I tell you he has fled; that I came into this room for him and found the window open and the room vacant."

"Where could he have gone—good God!" exclaimed Gilbert. "It is past midnight and he does not know the town."

"Do you believe anything evil has befallen him?" asked she, approaching.

"We shall hear, for it is you who shall tell me."

And with a wave of the hand he began anew to plunge her into the mesmeric sleep.

She uttered a sigh and fell off into repose.

"Am I to put forth all my will power or will you answer voluntarily?" asked Gilbert when she was under control.

"Will you tell the boy again that I am not his mother?"

"That depends. Do you love him?"

"Ardently, with all my soul."

"Then you are his mother as I am his father, for it is thus I love him. Loving him, you shall see him again. When did you part from the boy?"

"About half an hour ago, when Count Charny called. I had pushed him into this room."

"What were his last words?"

"That I was no more his mother: because I had told him that you were a villain."

"Look into the poor boy's heart and see what harm you wrought."

"Oh, God forgive me," said Andrea: "forgive me, my son."

"Did Count Charny suspect the boy was here?"

"No, I am sure."

"Why did he not stay?"

"Because he never stays long with me. Oh, wretch that I am," she interrupted herself, "he was returning to me after refusing that mission—because he loves me—he loves me!"

Gilbert began to see more clearly into this drama which his eye was first to penetrate.

"But do you love him?" he demanded.

"I see your intention is good: you wish to make up to me for the grief you have caused: but I refuse the boon coming from you. I hate you and wish to continue in my hatred."

"Poor mortality," muttered the philosopher, "have you had so much happiness that you can dally with a certain amount offered you? so you love him?"

"Yes. Since first I saw him, as the Queen and I sat with him in a hackney-carriage in which we returned from Paris to Versailles one night."

119

"You know what love is, Andrea," queried Gilbert, mournfully.

"I know that love has been given as a standard by which we can measure how much sadness we can endure," replied she.

"It is well: you are a true woman and a true mother: a rough diamond, you were shaped by the stern lapidary known as Grief. Return to Sebastian."

"Yes, I see him leaving the house with clenched hands and knit brow. He wanders up the street—he goes up to a woman and asks her for St. Honore Street——"

"My street: he was seeking for my house. Poor child! he will be there awaiting me."

"Hold! he has gone astray—he is in New St. Roch Street. Oh, he does not see that vehicle coming down Sourdiere Street, but I see the horses—Ah!"

She drew herself up with an awful scream, maternal anguish depicted on her visage, down which rolled tears and perspiration.

"Oh, if harm befalls him, remember that it will recoil on your head," hissed Gilbert.

"Ah," sighed Andrea in relief, without hearing or heeding him, "God in heaven be praised! it is the horse's breast which struck him, and he is thrown out of the rut of the wheel. There he lies, stunned, but he is not killed. Only swooned. Hasten to help him. It is my son! They form a crowd round him: is there not a doctor or surgeon among them all?"

"Oh, I shall run," said Gilbert.

"Wait," said Andrea, stopping him by the arm, "they are dividing to let help come. It is the doct—oh, do not let that man approach him—I loathe him—he is a vampire, he is hideous!"

"Oh, for heaven's sake, do not lose sight of Sebastian," said Gilbert, shuddering.

"This ghoul carries him away—up the street—into the blind alley, called

St. Hyacinthe: where he goes down some steps. He places him on a table where books and printed papers are heaped. He takes off his coat and rolls up his sleeve. He ties the arm with bandages from a woman as dirty and hideous as himself. He finds a lance in a case—he is going to bleed him. Oh, I cannot bear to see my son's blood flow. Run, run, and you will find him as I say."

"Shall I awaken you at once with recollection: or would you sleep till the morning and know nothing of what has happened?"

"Awaken me at once with full memory."

Gilbert described a double curve with his hands so that his thumbs came upon the medium's eyelids; he breathed on her forehead and said merely:

"Awake!"

Instantly her eyes became animated; her limbs were supple; she looked at Gilbert almost without terror, and continuing, though aroused, the impulse in her vision, she cried:

"Oh, run, run, and snatch the boy from the hands of that man who causes me so much fright!"

CHAPTER XV. THE MAN WITH THE MODEL.

WITH no need to be spurred in his quest, Gilbert darted through the rooms and as it would have taken too long to climb the walls, he made for the front door, which he opened himself and bounded out on the street.

Knowing Paris intimately, he reached the spot indicated by Andrea in her vision without delay and his first question to a storekeeper, who had witnessed the accident to the boy, confirmed the statement.

He proceeded straightway to the door in the alley, and knocked.

"Who knocks?" challenged a woman's voice.

"I, the father of the wounded child whom you succored," replied the knocker.

"Open, Albertine," said a man's voice: "it is Dr. Gilbert."

He was let into a cellar, or rather cavern, down some moldering steps, lighted by a lamp set on the table cumbered with printed papers, books and manuscripts as Andrea had described.

In the shadow, and on a mattress, young Gilbert lay, but held out his arms to his father, calling him. However powerful the philosophical command in Gilbert, paternal love overruled decorum, and he sprang to the boy whom he pressed to his breast, with care not to hurt his bruised chest or his cut arm. After a long, fond kiss, he turned to thank the good Samaritan. He was standing with his feet far apart, one hand on the table, the other on his hip, lit by the lamp of which he had removed the shade the better to illumine the scene.

"Look, Albertine," said he, "and with me thank the chance enabling me to do a good turn for one of my brothers."

The speaker was a green and sallow man, like one of those country clowns whom Latona's wrath pursued and who was turning to a frog. Gilbert shuddered, thinking that he had seen this abortion before as through a sheet of blood.

He drew nearer to Sebastian and hugged him once more. But triumphing over his first impulse, he went back to the strange man who had so appalled Andrea in the second-sight vision, and said:

"Receive all the thanks of a father, sir, for having preserved his son: they are sincere and come right from his heart."

"I have merely done my duty as prescribed by nature and recommended by science," replied the other. "I am a man, and as Terence says, nothing human is foreign to me; besides, I have a tender heart, and cannot see even an insect suffer; consequently still less my fellow man."

"May I learn to what fervent philanthropist I have the honor to speak?"

"Do you not know your brother-physician?" said the surgeon, laughing in what he wanted to seem benevolence though it was ghastly. "I know you, Dr. Gilbert, the friend of the American patriots, and of Lafayette!" He laid peculiar stress on this name. "The republican of America and France, the honorable Utopist who has written magnificent articles on constitutional government, which you sent to Louis XVI. from the States, and for which he lodged you in the Bastile, the moment you touched French soil. You wanted to save him by clearing the road to the future, and he opened that into jail— regular royal gratitude!"

He laughed again, this time terribly and threateningly.

"If you know me it is a farther reason for me to insist on learning to whom I am indebted."

"Oh, it is a long while since we made acquaintance," said the surgeon. "Twenty years, sir, on the dreadful night of the thirtieth of May, 1770; the night when the fireworks exploded by accident among the people in the Paris square, and injured and killed many who came to rejoice over the wedding of the Archduchess and our Prince Royal, but who had to curse their names. You were but a boy whom Rousseau brought to me, wounded and crushed almost to death, and I bled you on a board amid the dead and the cut-off limbs. Yet that awful night is a pleasant memory to me for I was able to save many existences by my steel knowing where to dissever to preserve life and where to cut to spare pain."

"You are Jean Paul Marat, then," cried Gilbert, falling back a step despite himself.

"Mark, Albertine, that my name makes some effect," said Marat with a sinister laugh.

"But I thought you were physician to Count Artois; why are you in this cave, why lighted by this smoky lamp?"

"I was the Prince's veterinary surgeon, you mean. But he emigrated? no prince, no stables; no stables, no vet. Besides, I gave in my resignation, for I would no longer serve the tyrants."

The dwarf drew himself up to the full extent of his form.

"But, in short, why are you in this hole?"

"Because, Master Philosopher, I am a sound patriot writing to decry the ambitious; Bailly fears me, Necker detests me, and Lafayette sets the National Guard on to hunt me down and has put a price on my head— the aspiring dictator! but I brave him! out of my hole, I pursue him, and denounce the Caesar. Do you know what he has done? He has had fifteen thousand snuffboxes made with his portrait on them, which hides some trick. So I entreat all good citizens to smash them when found. It is the rallying sign for the great Royalist Plot, for you cannot be ignorant that Lafayette is conspiring with the Queen while poor Louis is blubbering scalding tears over the blunders the Austrian is leading him into.

"The Queen," said Gilbert pensively.

"Yes; don't tell me that she is not plotting: lately she gave away so many white cockades that white ribbon went away up in the market. It is a fact, for I had it from one of the workgirls of Bertin the dressmaker, her Prime Minister in Fashions, who used to say: 'I have been discussing matters this morning with her Majesty.'"

"And how do you denounce such things?" inquired the doctor.

"In my newspaper, the one I have just started, twenty numbers having appeared. It is 'The Friend of the people or the Parisian Publicist,' an impartial political organ. To pay for the paper and the printing—look behind you—I have sold the sheets and blankets off my bed."

Turning, Gilbert indeed saw that Sebastian lay on the mattress absolutely bare, but he had fallen asleep, overcome with pain and fatigue. He went up to him to see that it was not a swoon, but reassured by the regular breathing he, returned to this journalist, who irresistibly inspired him with the interest we feel for a hyena, tiger or other wild beast.

"Who help you in this gigantic work?" he inquired.

"My staff?" sneered Marat. "Ha, ha, ha! the geese fly in files: the eagle soars alone. My helpers are these," and he showed his head and hands. "I write the whole paper single handed—I can show you the copy, though it runs into sixteen pages octavo sometimes, and often I use small type though I commenced with large. So, it is not merely a newspaper—but a personality—it is Marat!"

"Enormous labor—how do you manage it?" asked the other doctor.

"It is the secret of nature—a compact I have made with death. I have given ten years of my life, so that I need no rest by day and no sleep by night. My existence is summed up in writing: I do it day and night. Lafayette's police coop me up in this cell, where they chain me body and soul to my work: they have doubled my activity. It was heavy on me at first but I am inured to it. It delights me now to see poor humanity through this airhole, by the narrow and slanting beam. From my gloomy den I judge mankind living, and science and politics without appeal. With one hand I demolish the savants, with the other the politicians. I shall upset the whole state of things, like Samson destroying the Temple, and under the ruins perhaps crushing me, I shall bury the throne!"

In spite of himself the hearer shuddered: in his rags and the poverty-stricken vault this man repeated very nearly what Cagliostro had said in his palace under his embroidered clothes.

"But when you are so popular, why do you not try for a nomination in the National Assembly?" he asked.

"Because the day has not come for that," replied the demagogue; expressing his regret, he continued, "Oh, were I a tribune of the masses, sustained by only a few thousand of determined men, I answer for the Constitution being perfectly safe in six weeks: the political machine should move better: no villain would dare play ticks with it: the Nation should be free and happy: in less than a year, it should be flourishing and redoubtable: and thus would it remain while I was erect."

The vain creature was transformed under Gilbert's eyes: his eyes became bloodshot; his yellow skin shone with sweat; the monster became great in his hideousness as another is grand in his beauty.

"Yes, but I am not a representative," he proceeded, resuming his train of ideas from where he had interrupted himself: "I have not the thousands of followers. No, but I am a journalist, and have my weapons and ammunition, my subscribers and readers, for whom I am an oracle, a prophet and a diviner. I have my following for whom I am a friend, and I lead them on, trembling, from treachery to treachery, discovery to discovery, from one dreadful thing to another. In the first number of The Friend of the People, I denounced the upper classes saying that there were six hundred guilty wretches in France and that number of ropes-ends would do the job: but I made a mistake, ha, ha! The deeds of the fifth and sixth of October opened my eyes and I see that we must hang twenty thousand of the patricians."

Gilbert smiled, for fury elevated to this point, seemed madness to him.

"Why, there is not enough hemp in France to do this work, and rope would go up in price," he said.

"That is why I am looking round for some other means," returned Marat, "more expeditious and novel. Do you know whom I expect this evening? one of our brother medicos, a member of the National Assembly whom you must know by name, Dr. Guillotin——"

"The one who moved that the Assembly, expelled from the Session Hall at Versailles, should meet in the Tennis Court a learned man?"

"Do you know what this able citizen has discovered? a marvellous machine which kills without pain, for death must be punishment not torture; he has invented it and we shall try it one of these mornings."

Gilbert started: this was the second time that this brother Invisible reminded him of the Chief, Cagliostro; no doubt this death-machine was the same he had spoken of.

"But you are lucky—a knock! it is he. Run and open the door, Albertine."

The hag, who was the wife—rather the female mate of Marat—rose from the stool on which she was squatting, and staggered half asleep towards the door.

Giddy with terror, Gilbert went instinctively towards Sebastian, ready to take him in his arms and flee.

"Just think of an automatic executioner," said Marat, enthusiastically, "with no need of a man to set it going; which can, if the knife is changed a couple of times, cut off three hundred heads a-day!"

"And add," said a bland, melodious voice, behind Marat, "which can cut off these heads without other sensation than a slight coolness around the neck."

"Oh, is this you, doctor?" exclaimed Marat, turning towards a dapper little man of forty or so, whose gentle demeanor and spruce dress made a marked contrast with his host: in his hand he carried a small box such as children's toys are kept in. "What are you bringing us?"

"A model of my machine, my dear Marat. But I see Dr. Gilbert here, unless I mistake," said the little dandy, trying to pierce the obscurity.

"The same, sir," said the other visitor bowing.

"Enchanted to meet you, sir; you are only too welcome, and I shall be happy to have the opinion of so distinguished a man on my invention. I must tell you, my dear Marat, that I have found a skillful carpenter, named Guidon, to make my machine on the working scale. He is dear, though, wanting five thousand five hundred francs; but no sacrifice is too great for me to make for humanity. In two months it will be built, and we can try it: I shall propose it to the Assembly. I hope you will approve of it in your excellent new paper, though, in sober earnest, the machine recommends itself, as you will see with your own eyes, Dr. Gilbert. But a few lines in the People's Friend will do no harm."

"Be easy on that score; it is not a few lines but a whole number that I shall dedicate to it."

"You are too good, Marat; but I am not going to let you puff a pig in a poke."

He took out of his pocket a much smaller box, in which a sound indicated that some little live thing or several such were fidgeting in their prison. This noise did not escape Marat's subtle hearing.

"What have you got there?" he asked, putting out his hand towards the box.

"Mind," said the doctor, drawing it back, "do not let them escape as we could not catch them again; they are mice whose heads we are going to nick off with the machine. What, are you going to leave us, Dr. Gilbert?"

"Alas, yes, sir, to my great regret; but my son, wounded by being run over by a horse just now, has been relieved by Friend Marat, to whom I also owe my own life in an almost similar affair. I have to thank him again. The boy needs a fresh bed, cares and repose: so that I cannot witness your interesting experiment."

"But you will come and see the one with the real machine, in two months, you promise, doctor?"

"I pledge my word."

"Doctor," said Marat, "I need not say, keep my abode secret. If your friend Lafayette were to discover it he would have me shot like a dog, or hung like a thief."

"Shooting, hanging," exclaimed Guillotin. "But we shall put an end to these cannibal deaths. We shall have a death, soft, easy, instantaneous, such as old people, disgusted with their life and wishful to pass away like sages and philosophers, will prefer to a natural one. Come and see how it works, Marat!"

And without troubling any farther about Dr. Gilbert, the enthusiast opened his larger box and began to set up on the table a model apparatus which the surgeon regarded with curiosity equal to his enthusiasm.

Gilbert profited by their being so engaged, to carry away Sebastian, guided by Albertine who fastened up the outer door after him.

Once in the street, he felt the night wind chill the perspiration gathered on his brow.

"Heavens," he muttered, "what will happen to a city where the cellars perhaps hide five hundred lovers of mankind who are occupied with such work as we have a sample of there? one day they will perform in broad daylight before the crowd."

It was little distance to his house in St. Honore Street.

The cold revived Sebastian but his father would not let him walk. When he knocked at his door, a heavy step was heard approaching.

"Is that you, Dr. Gilbert?" challenged one within.

"That is Pitou's voice," said the boy.

"Praise heaven, Sebastian is found," shouted Pitou on opening the door. "Master Billet," he shouted still more loudly, "Sebastian is found, and all right, I hope, doctor?"

"Without any serious hurt, anyway," replied the other, "Come, Sebastian."

He carried his son up to his bed.

Pitou followed with the light; by his mud-bespattered shoes and stockings it was plain that he had come a long journey.

Indeed, after taking the broken-hearted Catherine home and learning from her lips that her deep sorrow came from Isidore Charny being called away to Paris, he took leave of her and Mother Billet, weeping by her bedside, and went home to Haramont. He walked so slowly that he did not get there until daybreak.

He fell off to sleep so that it was not till he awoke, that he found the youth's letter. Immediately he started to overtake him.

He girded up with a leather strap, took some bread and with a walking stick in his fist, proceeded to town, where he arrived at eight that night.

He found neither the doctor nor his son at home—only Farmer Billet.

This hearty, robust man, unnerved by the bloody scenes witnessed since the Taking of the Bastile, of which enterprise he was the leader, had no news for Pitou.

Their sad waiting was rewarded by the double arrival.

Though tranquil about Sebastian, Pitou, when sent to bed had his budget to unfold to the farmer. Let no reader think that he revealed Catherine's secrets and spoke of her amour with the young noble. The honest soul of the Commander of the Haramont National Guard would not stoop to that story. But he told Billet that the harvest was bad, the barley a failure, part of the wheat wind-laid, and the barns but a third full—and that he had found Catherine on the road.

Billet was little vexed about the grain, but the illness of his daughter distressed him.

He ran to Dr. Gilbert with a sad face as the latter was finishing this note to Andrea: "Be of good heart; the child is found, with no one hurt."

"Dr. Gilbert, you were right to retain me in town where I might be useful; but everything has been going wrong in the country while the good man is away."

Gilbert agreed with his friend that a hearty buxom girl like Catherine should not faint on the public road. Feeling with a parent, he responded:

"Go home, my dear Billet, since land and family call you. But do not forget that I shall claim you in the name of the country."

Thus Billet returned home after an absence of three months, although he had intended to be away only a week.

Pitou followed him, bearing twenty-five louis destined from Gilbert for the equipment and maintenance of the Haramont National Guard.

Sebastian stayed with his father.

CHAPTER XVI. THE PORTRAIT OF CHARLES FIRST.

A WEEK has passed since the events related. Everybody was saying: The Revolution is finished; the King is delivered from Versailles, and his courtiers and evil counsellors. The King is placed in life and actuality. He had heretofore the license to work wrong; now he has full liberty to do good.

The dread from the riots had brought the conservatives over to the royalty. The Assembly had been frightened, too, and saw that it depended on the King. A hundred and fifty of its members took to flight.

The two most popular men, Lafayette and Mirabeau, became royalists. The latter wanted the other to unite with him to save the crown, but while honorable Lafayette had a limited brain, he did not see the orator's genius.

Mirabeau was all for the Duke of Orleans, whom Lafayette advised, nay, ordered to quit the kingdom.

"But suppose I come back without your permission?" said the prince.

"Then, I hope you will do me the honor to cross swords with me at the first battle," replied the marquis.

He was the veritable ruler and the duke had to depart; he did not return until called to be King of the French.

Lafayette had saved the Queen and protected the King; he was perfectly a royalist.

But still, like Gilbert, he was not so much the friend of the King as of the crown.

The monarch had too just a mind not to see this clearly.

Although he had not seen the doctor lately he remembered that this was his day of duty and he called him.

The King was pacing the bedroom, but stopping now and then to look at the Vandyke picture of Charles First, now in the Louvre.

The sovereign of England is painted as a Cavalier, with his horse, as ready for flight as for battle.

This picture seemed fatally the goal of the King's wanderings.

At the step, Louis turned round.

"Oh, is it you, doctor?" he said. "Come in, I am glad to see you." Leading him up to the painting he said: "Do you know this? where did you see it?"

"In Lady Dubarry's house, when I was a boy, but it deeply struck me."

"Yes, she pretended to be descended from the page who holds the horse. Jeanne Dubarry was the woman chosen by Marshal Richelieu to be the sole feminine ruler over the worn-out monarch Louis XV. and to induce him to shut up the infamous Deerpark, which was the harem ruining the old man. She was an adroit actress and played her part marvellously. She entertained while making sport of him, and he became manly because she persuaded him he was so."

He stopped as if blaming himself for his imprudence in speaking of his grandfather thus openly before a stranger; but one glance at Gilbert's frank face encouraged him, for he saw that he could speak all to a man who understood every thing.

"This melancholy, lofty face," went on the King, referring to the portrait, "was placed in the strange Egeria's boudoir, where it heard her impudent laughs and saw her lascivious gambols. Merrily she would take Louis by the arm and show him Charles, saying: 'Old gossip, this King had his neck cut through because he was too weak towards his Parliament. Take warning about your own!' Hence Louis broke up his Parliament and died peacefully on his throne. Thereupon we exiled the poor woman, for whom we ought to have been most indulgent. The picture was packed away in the lumber room of Versailles and I never thought about it. Now, how comes it here, in my bedroom? why does it haunt me?" He shook his head. "There is some fate in this."

"Fatality, if the portrait reads no lesson, Sire; Providence if it does. What does it say to your Majesty?"

"That Charles lost his throne from having made war on his subjects, and James the Second for having tired his own."

"Like me, then, it speaks the truth."

"Well?" inquired the sovereign, questioning the doctor with his glance.

"Well, I beg to ask for your answer to the portrait."

"Friend Gilbert, I have resolved on nothing: I will take the cue from circumstances."

"The people fear that your Majesty purposes war upon them."

"No, sir," he rejoined, "I cannot make war on them without foreign support and I know the state of Europe too well to rely on that. The King of Prussia offers to enter France at the head of a hundred thousand men; but I too well know his ambitious and intriguing spirit—a petty monarchy which wishes to become a great one, thriving on turmoil and hoping to catch some fish like another Silesia. On her part, Austria places a hundred thousand men at my call; but I do not like my brother-in-law Leopold, a two-faced Janus, whose mother, Marie Theresa, had my father poisoned.

"My brother Artois proposes the support of Sardinia and Spain, but I do not trust those powers, led by Artois. Beside him is Calonne, in other words, the Queen's worst enemy, the one who annotated with his own hand the pamphlet of the Countess Lamotte Valois anent the conspiracy of the Queen's Necklace, for which she was branded. I know all that is going on yonder. In their last council a debate ensued about deposing me and appointing a regent who would be probably my dear, very dear brother Count Provence. Prince Conde suggested marching with an enemy upon Lyons, 'whatever happened me at Paris!'

"It is another thing with the Great Empress Catherine; she confines herself to advice, bless her! you can understand that when you reflect that she is at table digesting Poland and cannot rise until she has finished her feast. She gives me advice which aims to be sublime but is only ridiculous, considering what has lately occurred. She says: 'Monarchs ought to proceed on their course like the moon in her orbit, without being disturbed by the baying of curs!'—that is, the protests of the common people. It appears that the Russian curs merely bark; ours do some biting, as you may learn of my poor Lifeguardsmen, torn to pieces by them."

"The people thought that your Majesty was going to quit the country."

"Doctor," said the King after hesitating, and he laid his hand on the other's shoulder, "I have promised you the truth and you shall have it thoroughly. Such a matter has been broached; it is the opinion of many faithful servitors surrounding me that I ought to flee. But on the sixth of October night, when weeping in my arms, the Queen besought me never to flee without her, and that we should all depart together, to be saved or die in company. I shall keep my word; and as I do not think that we could flee in such a number without being stopped, a dozen times before we got to the frontier, I conclude that we shall never get away."

"Well, Sire, there is indeed no need of the foreigners. What would be the use until you shall exhaust your own resources? My advice is that we are only beginning the fight and that the Taking of the Bastile and the attack on the Palace at Versailles are only the two first acts in the tragedy to be played by France under the eyes of Europe."

"I hope you are mistaken, sir," replied Louis, slightly turning pale: "My police tell me nothing like this."

"I have no police or information to check them; but in my position I am the natural conductor between the heavens and what is still concealed in the bowels of the earth. Sire, what we have experienced is merely the rumble that runs before the earthquake; we have yet to meet the lava, the fire and the smoke. I fear that the Revolutionary torrent will run ahead of us. There are only two methods to save yourself. One is to place yourself on the foremost breaker and be carried on with it."

"I do not wish to go where it would carry me."

"The second is to place a barrier across the tide. It is Genius and Popularity in one dam: and it is named Mirabeau."

"The King looked Gilbert in the face as though he had misunderstood him; then turning to the portrait, he said:

"What would you have replied, Charles Stuart, if when you felt the ground quake beneath your feet, some one had suggested your leaning on Cromwell?"

"He would have refused, and rightly; for there is no likeness between Cromwell and Mirabeau." Such was Gilbert's answer.

"They were both traitors."

"Sire," replied the other with profound respect but invincible firmness; "neither were traitors: Cromwell was a rebellious subject, and Mirabeau is a discontented nobleman."

"What is he discontented with?"

"With his father, who locked him up in prison; the courts which condemned him to death; with the King who miscomprehended and still miscomprehends his genius."

"The spirit of a public man is honesty," said the King quickly.

"The reply is fine, worthy of Titus, Trajan or Marcus Aurelius, unluckily many examples arise to the contrary."

"How can you ask me to confide in a man who has a price?"

"Because he is a man of his price. If he will sell himself for a million, it is a bargain. Do you think he is worth twice a Polignac?"

"You are pleading for a friend."

"I have not that honor: but he has a friend who is of the Queen's party, too."

"Count Lamarck? We cast it up to him every day."

136

"On the contrary, your Majesty ought to dissuade him breaking the friendship with him, under pain of death. Mirabeau is a noble, an aristocrat, a King's-man above all. He was elected by the people because the nobles scorned him and he had sublime disdain of the means to attain an end which genius thirsted for. You may say that he will never quit the party of his constituents to join the court party? Why is there not union of the court and plebeians? Mirabeau could make them one. Take him, my lord! To-morrow, rebuffed by your despisal, he may turn against you, and then you will say, as the portrait of your Martyr King will say: All is lost!"

"I will talk this over with the Queen, sir," said the monarch, having turned pale and hesitatingly glanced at the royal portrait. "She may decide on speaking with Mirabeau: but I will not. I like to be able to shake hands with those I confer with, and I could never take the hand of a Mirabeau, though my life, my liberty, and my throne were at stake—After she shall have seen him, we will see——"

"I pray God that it will not be too late."

"Do you believe the peril so imminent?"

"Sire, do not let the portrait of Charles First be removed from your room," said Gilbert; "it is a good adviser."

Bowing, he went forth as another visitor appeared on the sill. He could not restrain from a cry of surprise. This gentleman was Marquis Favras, whom he had met at Cagliostro's a week or so before and to whom the magician had predicted a near and shameful death.

CHAPTER XVII. THE KING ATTENDS TO PRIVATE MATTERS.

LOUIS the King displayed the usual irresolution in dealing with Favras' proposition, approved by the Queen, to make a rush out of the kingdom. He reflected all the night and at breakfast called for Count Charny.

He was still at table when the officer walked in.

"Won't you take breakfast with me, count?"

Charny was obliged to excuse himself from the honor as he had broken his fast.

"I must ask you to wait a while as I never care to speak of important matters while at meals and I have something to talk over with your lordship. Let us speak of other matters for the moment. Of yourself, for instance. I hear that you are badly lodged here; somewhere in the garret, my lord, while the countess is lodging in Paris."

"Sire, I am in a room of my own choice: the countess is dwelling in her own house in Coq-Heron Street."

"I must confess my ignorance; is it near the palace?"

"Tolerably, Sire."

"What does this mean that after only three years of married life, you have separate establishments?"

"Sire, I have no answer to make than that my lady wishes to live alone. I have not had the pleasure of seeing her since your Majesty sent me for news. That is, better than a week ago."

The King understood grief more readily than melancholy and noticed the difference in the tone.

"Count, there is some of your fault in this estrangement," said the monarch, with the familiarity of the family man, as he called himself.

"The man must be to blame when so charming a woman keeps aloof from him. Do not tell me that this is none of my business: for a king can do a great deal by speaking a word. You must treat the lady ungratefully, for she loves you dearly—or did when Lady Taverney."

"Sire, you know that one must not dispute with a king."

"I do not know that the signs were visible to me alone; but this I know very well that on that dreadful October night, when she came to join us, she did not lose sight of you throughout, and her eyes expressed all her soul's anguish, so much so that I saw her make a movement to fling herself between you and danger when the Bullseye Saloon door was beaten down."

Count Charny was not softened; he believed he had seen something of this sort: but the details of his recent interview with his wife were too distinct for him to have his opinion shaken.

"I was paying all the more attention to her," went on Louis, "from the Queen having said when you were sent to the City Hall while I was on my journey to Paris, that she almost died of distress in your absence and of joy at your return."

"Sire," replied Charny with a sad smile, "God had allowed those who are born above us to receive in birth as a privilege of their rank, the gift of seeing deeper into one's heart than oneself can do; the King and the Queen have perceived secrets unrevealed to me: but my limited vision prevents me seeing the same. Therefore I beg to be employed on any dangerous errand or one that would take me to a distance without considering the great love of the Countess of Charny. Absence or danger will be equally welcome, coming at least for my part."

"Nevertheless, a week ago, you appeared wishful to stay in town when the Queen desired to despatch you to Italy."

"I deemed my brother adequate for the position and reserved myself for a mission more difficult or dangerous."

"Then count, this is the very time when I have a difficult task to entrust to you, that with danger to you in the future, that I spoke of the countess's isolation and wished her to have a lady friend's company while I took away her husband."

"I will write to the countess, yes, write: for from the way she last received me, I ought in that manner acquaint her with my movements."

"Say no more on this head; I will talk it over with the Queen during your absence," said Louis, rising. "Faith, the medical lights are right to say that things look differently as you handle them before or after a hearty meal. Come into my study, count; I feel in a mood to talk straight out to you."

Charny followed, thinking how much Majesty lost by this material side, for which the proud Marie Antoinette was always carping at him.

CHAPTER XVIII. THE KING ATTENDS TO PUBLIC MATTERS.

THOUGH the King had been only a fortnight in the Tuileries he had two places fitted out completely for him. The forge was one, the study the other.

Charny walked up to the desk at which his royal master seated himself without looking round at the papers with which he was familiar.

"Count Charny," began the King at last, yet seeming to halt, "I noticed one thing, on the night of the attack by the rioters, you stood by me while you set your brother on guard over the Queen."

"Sire, it was my right as head of my family, as you are chief of the realm, to die for you."

"That made me think, that if ever I had a secret errand, difficult and dangerous, I could rely on your loyalty as a Frenchman, and on your heart as a friend's."

"Oh, Sire, however the King may raise me, I have no pretension to believe that I shall be more than a faithful and thankful subject."

"My lord, you are a grave man though but thirty-six; you have not passed through recent events without drawing some conclusion from them. What do you think of the situation and what would be your means to relieve me, if you were my Premier?"

"Sire, I am a soldier and a seaman," returned Charny, with more hesitation than embarrassment, "these high social questions fly over my head."

"Nay, you are a man," said the sovereign with a dignity in holding out his hand which sprang from the quandary; "another man, who believes you to be his friend, asks you, purely and simply, what you, with your upright heart and healthy mind, would do in his place."

"Sire, in a no less serious position, the Queen asked my opinion: the day after the Taking of the Bastile, when she wanted to fling the foreign legions upon the mobs. My reply would have embroiled me with her Majesty had I been less known to her and my respect and devotion less plain. I said that your Majesty must not enter these walls as a conqueror if he could not as a father of his people."

"Well, my lord, is not that the counsel I followed? The question is was I right? am I here as a King or a captive?"

"Speaking in full frankness, I disapproved of the banquet at Versailles, supplicating the Queen not to go there; I was in despair when she threw down the tricolor and set up the black cockade of Austria."

"Do you believe that led really to the attack on the palace?"

"No, Sire; but it was the cover for it. You are not unjust for the lower orders; they are kindly and love you—they are royalist. But they are in pain from cold and hunger; beneath and around them are evil advisers, who urge them on, and they know not their own strength. Once started they become flood or fire, for they overwhelm or they consume."

"Well, what am I to do? supposing, as is natural enough, I do not want to be drowned or burned."

"We must not open the sluices to the flood or windows to the flame. But pardon me forgetting that I should not speak thus, even on a royal order——"

"But you will on a royal entreaty. Count Charny, the King entreats you—to continue."

"Well, Sire, there are two strata of the lower orders, the soil and the mud; the one which may be reposed upon and the other which will yield and smother one. Distrust one and rest on the other."

"Count, you are repeating at two hours' interval, what Dr. Gilbert told me."

"Sire, how is it that after taking the advice of a learned man, you ask that of a poor naval officer like me?"

142

"Because there is a wide difference between you, I believe. Dr. Gilbert is devoted to royalty and you to the King. If the principle remains safe, he would let the King go."

"Then there is a difference between us, for the King and the principle are inseparable for me," responded the nobleman; "under this head it is that I beg your Majesty to deal with me."

"First, I should like to hear to whom you would apply in this space of calm between two storms perhaps, to efface the wreck made by one and soothe the coming tempest."

"If I had the honor and the misfortune to be the wearer of the crown, I should remember the cheers I heard round my carriage, and I should hold out my hands to General Lafayette and Member Mirabeau."

"Can you advise this when you detest one and scorn the other?"

"My sympathies are of no moment, the whole question is the safety of the crown and the salvation of the monarchy."

"Just what Dr. Gilbert says," muttered the hearer as though speaking to himself.

"Sire, I am happy to be in tune with such an eminent man."

"But if I were to agree to such a union and there should be failure, what think you I ought to do?"

"Think of your safety and your family's."

"Then you suggest that I should flee?"

"I should propose that your Majesty should retire with such regiments as are reliable and the true nobles to some fortified place."

"Ah," said the King with a radiant face: "but among the commanders who have given proof of devotion, you knowing them all, to which would you confide this dangerous mission, of guarding and removing the King?"

"Sire," replied Charny, after hesitation, "it is not because ties of friendship—almost of family—attach me to a certain nobleman that I name him, but because he is known for his steadfast devotion; as Governor of the Leeward Islands, he not only protected our possessions in the Antilles, but captured some islands from the British: he had been charged with various commands, and at present he is General Governor, I believe, at Metz—this is the Marquis of Bouille. Were I a father, I should trust my son to him; a subject, I would confide the King!"

At the name the hearer could not repress an outcry of joy. He held out a letter, saying:

"Read this address, my lord, and see if Providence itself did not inspire me to apply to you."

The address ran: "To Lord François Claude Amour, Marquis of Bouille, General Commander at Metz."

"After what has happened, I do not feel that I ought to keep anything back from you. I have thought of this flight before, but in all the propositions was the hand of Austria beckoning me into a trap, and I have recoiled. I do not love Austria more than you do yourself."

"Sire, you forget that I am the faithful subject of the King and the Queen of France." He emphasized the second title.

"I have already told you, count," went on the King, "that you are a friend, and I can speak the more frankly as the prejudice I cherished against the Queen is completely effaced from my mind. But it was against my will that I received into my house the double enemy of my line, as an Austrian and a Lorrainer. After ten years' struggle it was despite my will that I had to charge Lord Breteuil with the management of my household and the government of Paris; make the Premier of the Archbishop of Toulouse, an atheist; lastly, pay to Austria the millions she extorted from the Low Countries. At present speaking, who succeeds the dead Maria Theresa, to counsel and direct the Queen? Her brother Joseph II., who is luckily dying. He is advised by old women of councillors who sway the Queen of France through her hairdresser Leonard and her dressmaker Bertin.

"They are pensioned by us while they are leading her to alliance with Austria. Austria has always been fatal to France, either as foe or friend, as when she put the dagger in Jacques Clement's or Ravaillac's or Damien's to slay our kings. Formerly it was Catholic and devout Austria, but she is abjuring now and is partly philosophical under Joseph; rashly, she runs against her own sword, Hungary: without foresight, she lets the Belgian priesthood rob her of the finest jewels in her crown, the Low Countries; become the vassal of Russia, she wears out her troops in fighting for it against the Turks, our allies. No, my lord, I hate Austria and I will not trust to her. But I was saying that her overtures of flight were not the only ones. I have had one proposed by Marquis Favras. Do you know him?"

"He was the captain in the Belgunze Regiment, and lieutenant in the Count of Provence's own Guards."

"You have hit it with the latter shot. What think you of him?"

"He is a brave soldier and a loyal gentleman. Unfortunately he has no means and this makes him restless and fit for mad projects and hazardous attempts. But he is a man of honor who will die without retreating a step, or uttering a complaint in order to keep his word. He may be trusted to make a dash but not to manage an enterprise."

"He is not the leader," said the King, with marked bitterness; "that is Provence, who finds the means and manages all; devoted to the end, he will remain while Favras bears me hence. This is not the plot of Austria but of the fugitive princes and peers."

"But why should not your Majesty's brother go with you? why would he remain?"

"Through devotion, and also to be at hand in case the people should be tired of revolution and seek a regent. I tell you what all know, my dear count, and what your brother wrote me yesterday from Turin. They debate about deposing me and ruling by a regent. You see that unless in an extremity I can no sooner accept the Favras plan than the Austrian. This is what I have said to nobody, my dear count, but yourself, and I do it in order that nobody, not even the Queen," he laid stress on the last three words, "can make you more devoted to them than to me, since they cannot show more confidence."

"Sire, am I to keep the journey a secret from everybody?" inquired Charny, bowing.

"It little matters, count, that it should be known whither you go, as long as the design is unknown. You know the situation, my fears and hopes, better than my Minister Necker and my adviser Gilbert. Act accordingly; I put the scissors and the thread in your hands—disentangle or cut, as you see fit."

He held the letter open for him to read:

Tuileries Palace, Oct. 29th.

"I hope, my lord, that you continue contented with your post as Governor of Metz. Count Charny, Lieutenant of my Lifeguards, passing through your city, will inquire if among your desires are any I can gratify. In that event I will take the opportunity to be agreeable to you as I do this one to renew the assurance of my feelings of esteem for your lordship.

"Louis."

"Now, my Lord Charny," said the King, "you have full power to make promises to Bouille if you think he needs any; only do not commit me farther than I can perform."

For the second time he held out his hand.

Charny kissed it with emotion forefending any fresh pledges, and went forth, leaving his master convinced that he had acquired by his trust, the heart of the servitor, better than by offerings of wealth and favors such as he had lavished in the days of his power.

CHAPTER XIX. A LOVING QUEEN.

CHARNY left the King with his heart full of opposing feelings.

The primary one, mounting to the surface over the tumultuous waves of turbulent thoughts, was deep gratitude for the boundless confidence testified to him.

This imposed duties the more holy from his conscience not being dumb. He remembered his wrongs towards this worthy monarch who laid his hand on his shoulder as on a true friend at the time of danger.

The more Charny felt guilty towards his master, the more ready he was to devote himself to him.

The more this respectful allegiance grew the lesser became the less pure emotion which he had cherished for the Queen during years.

This is the reason why he—having lost the vague hope which led him towards Andrea for the test, as if she was one of those flowering shrubs on the precipice edge by which a falling man can save himself—grasped with eagerness this mission diverging him from the court. Here he felt the double torment of being still loved by the woman whom he was ceasing to love and of not being loved by her whom he was beginning to adore.

Profiting by the coldness lately introduced into his relations with the Queen, he went to her rooms with the intention of leaving a note to tell of his departure when he found Weber awaiting him.

The Queen wished to see him forthwith, and there is no eluding the wishes of crowned heads in their palace.

Marie Antoinette was in the opposite mood to her visitor's, she was recalling her harshness towards him and his devotion at Versailles; at the sight of the count's brother laid dead across her threshold she had felt a kind of remorse; she confessed to herself that had this been the count she would have badly paid him for the sacrifice.

But had she any right to expect aught else than devotion of Charny?

She admitted that she was stern and unfair towards him, when the door opened and the gentleman appeared in the irreproachable costume of the military officer on duty.

But there was in his deeply respectful bearing something chilly which repelled the magnetic flow from the Queen's heart, to go and seek in his the tender, sweet and sad memories collected during four years.

The Queen looked round her as though to try to ascertain why he remained on the sill, and when assured it was a matter of his will, she said:

"Come, my lord: we are alone."

"I see that, but I do not see what in that fact should alter the bearing of a subject to his sovereign."

"When I sent Weber for you I thought that fond friends were going to speak with one another."

Charny smiled bitterly.

"I understand that smile and that you say, inwardly, the Queen was unjust at Versailles and is capricious here."

"Injustice or caprice, a woman is allowed anything," returned Charny: "a queen more than all."

"Whatever the caprice, my friend," said Marie with all the witchingness she could put in a voice or smile, "the Queen cannot do without you as adviser or the woman without you as loved friend."

She held out her hand, a little thinned but still worthy of a lovely statue. He kissed it respectfully and was about to let it fall when he felt her retain his.

"I ought to have wept with you over the loss of your brother, slain for my sake: well, I have been weeping these ten days since I have not seen you: they are falling yet."

Ah, if Charny could have surmised what a quantity of tears would follow those, no doubt the immense grief would have made him fall at her feet, and ask pardon for any grievances she had against him.

But the future is enveloped in mystery which no human hand can unveil before the hour and the black garb which Marie Antoinette was to wear to the scaffold, was too thickly embroidered with gold for one to spy the gloom of it.

"Believe, my lady," he said, "that I am truly grateful for your remembrance of me and sorrow for my brother? unfortunately I must be brief as the King has entrusted me with a mission so that I leave in an hour."

"What, do you abandon us like the others?"

"I repeat it is a mission."

"But you refused the like a week ago!"

"In a week much happens in a man's existence to alter his determination."

"Do you depart alone?" she asked, making an effort.

She breathed again when he answered: "Alone."

"Where do you go?" she asked, recovering from her weakness.

"It is the King's secret, but he has none from you."

"My lord, the secret is ours alike," said Marie Antoinette haughtily. "But is it abroad or in the kingdom?"

"The King alone can give your Majesty the desired information."

"So you go away," said she, with profound sorrow overcoming the irritation from Charny's reserve, "to run into dangers afar, and I am not to know what they are!"

"Wheresoever I go, you will have a devoted heart daring all for you: and the dangers will be light since I expose my life in the service of the two sovereigns whom I most venerate on earth."

The Queen uttered a sob which seemed to tear out her heart; and she said with a hand on her throat as if to keep down her gorge.

"It is well—go! for you love me no longer."

Charny felt a thrill run through him; it was the first time this haughty woman and ruler had bowed unto him.

At any other time and under any other circumstances, he must have fallen at her feet if only to crave pardon; but the remembrance of what had happened between him and the King recalled all his strength.

"My lady," he said, "I should be a scoundrel if, after all the tokens of kindness and confidence the King has showered on me, I were to assure your Majesty of anything but my respect and devotion."

"It is very well," said she; "you are free to go."

But when he departed without looking behind him, she waited till she heard him, not returning, but continuing his departure, in the carriage which rolled out of the courtyard.

She rang for her foster-brother.

"Weber," she ordered, "go to the Countess of Charny's residence and say I must speak with her this evening. I had an appointment with Dr. Gilbert, but I postpone that till the morning."

She dismissed him with a wave of the hand.

"Yes, politics to-morrow," she mused: "besides my conversation with Andrea may influence me on the course I take."

CHAPTER XX. WITHOUT HUSBAND—WITHOUT LOVER.

THE Queen was wrong for Charny did not go to his wife's house. He went to the Royal Post to have horses put to his own carriage. But while waiting, he wrote a farewell to Andrea which the servant who took his horses home, carried to her.

She was still dwelling over it, having kissed it with profound feeling, when Weber arrived. Her answer to him was simply that she would conform to her Majesty's orders. And she proceeded to the palace without dread as without impatience.

But it was not so with the Queen. Feverish, she had welcomed Count Provence coming to see how Favras had been received, and she committed the King more deeply than he had pledged himself.

Provence went away delighted, thinking that the King would be removed, thanks to the money he had borrowed from the Genoese banker Zannone, and to Favras and his Hectors. Then he stood a chance of becoming Regent of the realm, perhaps foreseeing that he would yet be King as Louis XVIII.

If the forced departure of the King failed, he would take to flight with what was left of the loan, and join his brothers in Italy.

On his leaving, the Queen went to Princess Lamballe, on whom she made it a habit to pour her woes or her joys in the absence of her other favorites, Andrea or the Polignacs.

Poor martyr! who dares grope in the darkness of alcoves to learn if this friendship were pure or criminal, when inexorable History was coming with feet red-shod in blood, to tell the price you paid for it?

Then she went to dinner for an hour, where both chief guests were absent in thought, the King thinking of Charny's quest, the Queen of the Favras enterprise.

While the former preferred anything to being helped by the foreigners, the Queen set them first: for of course they were her people. The King was connected with the Germans, but then the Austrians are not German to the Germans.

In the flight she was arranging she saw no such crimes as she was afterwards taxed with: she felt justified in calling in the mailed hand to avenge her for the slights and insults with which she was deluged.

The King, as we have shown him, distrusted kings and princes. He relied on the priests. He approved of all the decrees against nobles and classes but not of the decree against the priests, which he vetoed. For them he risked his greatest dangers. Hence the Pope, unable to make a saint of him, made him a martyr.

Contrary to her habit, the Queen gave little time to her children this day; untrue to her husband in heart, she had no claim on their endearments. Such odd contradictions are known only to woman's heart.

The Queen retired early to her own rooms, where she shut herself up with Weber as door-ward. She alleged that she had letters to write.

The King little noticed her going, as some minor events engrossed him; the Chief of Police was coming to confer with him.

The Assembly had changed the old form in public documents of "King of France and Navarre" to "King of the French": and it was debating on the Rights of Man, when it had better be seeing to the Bread Question, more pressing than ever. The arrival of the "Baker" and his family from Versailles had not fed the famished people and the bakeries had strings of customers at their doors.

But the Assemblymen did not have to dance attendance for a loaf, and they had a special baker, one François in Marchepalu Street, who set aside rolls for them out of every baking.

The head of the police was discussing the bread riots with the ruler when Weber ushered Andrea into his mistress's presence.

Though she expected her, Marie Antoinette started when her visitor was announced.

When they were girls together, at Taverney, they had made a kind of agreement of love and duties exchanged in which the higher personage had always had the advantage.

Nothing annoys rulers so much as senses of obligation, particularly in matters of affection.

While thinking she had reproaches to cast on her friend, the Queen felt under a debt to her.

Andrea was always the same: pure and cool as the diamond but cutting and invulnerable like it, too.

"Be welcome, Andrea, as ever," said the Queen to this cold, walking ghost.

The countess shivered for she recognized some of the tone the Queen used to speak with when the Dauphiness.

"Needs must I tell your Majesty that she should not have had to send for me without the royal residence, if I had always been spoken to, in that tone?" said the countess.

Nothing could better help the Queen than this opening: she greeted it as facilitating her course.

"Alas, you ought to know that all womankind have not your immutable serenity," she said; "I, above all, who had to ask your aid so generously accorded——"

"The Queen speaks of a time forgotten by me and I believed gone from her memory."

"The reply is stern," said the other: "you might naturally hold me as ungrateful: but what you took for ingratitude was but impotence."

"I should have the right to accuse you, if ever I had asked you for anything and my wish were opposed," said the countess, "but how can your Majesty expect me to complain when I have sought nothing?"

"Shall I tell you that it is just this indifference which shocks me; yes, you seem a supernatural being brought from another sphere in some whirlwind, and thrown among us like the crystal aerolites. One is daunted by her weakness beside the never-weakening; but in the end assurance returns, for supreme indulgence must be in perfection: it is the purest source in which to lave the soul, and in profound grief, one sends for the superhuman being for consolation, though her blame is dreaded."

"Alas, if your Majesty sends for me for this, I fear the expectation will be disappointed."

"Andrea, you forget in what awful plight you upheld me and comforted me," said the Queen.

Her hearer turned visibly paler. Seeing her totter and close her eyes from losing strength, the Queen moved to support her but she resisted and stood steady.

"If your Majesty had pity on your faithful servant, you would spare her memories which she had almost banished from her: she is a poor comforter who seeks comfort from nobody, not even heaven, from doubt that even heaven hath power to console certain sorrows."

"Then you have others to tell of than what you have entrusted to me? the time has come for you to explain, and that is why I sent for you. You love Count Charny?"

"I do," replied Andrea.

"Oh!" groaned the Queen like a wounded lioness. "I thought as much. How long since?"

"Since I first laid eyes on him."

Marie Antoinette recoiled from this statue which confessed it was animated by a spirit.

154

"And yet you said nothing?"

"You perceived it, because you loved him."

"No; but you mean that you loved him more than I, because you perceived my love. If I see it now, it is because he loves me no longer say?" and she clutched her arm.

Andrea replied not by word, or sign.

"This is enough to drive one mad," cried the royal lady. "Why not kill me outright by telling me that he loves me not."

"Count Charny's love or indifference to other women than his wife are secrets of Count Charny. They are not for me to reveal," observed Andrea.

"His secrets? I dare say he has made you his bosom friend, indeed," sneered the Queen with bitterness.

"The count has never spoken to me of his love or indifference towards your Majesty."

"Not even this morning?" She fixed a soul penetrative glance upon her.

"Not even this morning. He announced his departure to me by letter."

"Ah, he wrote to you?" exclaimed the Queen in a burst which, like King Richard's cry: "My kingdom for a horse!" implied that she would give her crown for that letter.

Andrea comprehended her absorbing desire but she wished to enjoy her anxiety for a space, like a woman. At last, drawing the letter from her corsage, warm and perfumed, she held it out to her royal mistress. The temptation was too strong, and the latter opened it and read:

"My Lady: I am leaving town on a formal order from the King. I cannot tell even you whither I go, wherefore, or how long I am to stay away: these are matters probably little in import to you, but I ought none the less to wish I were authorized to tell you.

"I had the intention to take farewell of you: but I dared not without

155

your permission——"

The Queen had learnt what she wanted to know, and was about to return the writing, but Andrea bade her read to the end as if she had a claim to command.

"I refused the last mission offered me because, poor madman! I believed that affection retained me in Paris: but I have unfortunately acquired proof to the contrary, and I accept with joy this opportunity to depart from hearts to which I am indifferent.

"If, during this journey, that happens me which befel poor Valence, all my measures are taken for you, my lady, to be the first to know of the misfortune visiting me and the liberty restored to you. Then, only, will you learn what profound admiration was born in my heart from your sublime devotion, so poorly recompensed by her to whom you sacrificed youth, beauty and bliss.

"All I beseech of heaven and you is your according me a remembrance for having too late perceived the treasure he possessed.

"With all the respect in my heart,

"George Oliver de Charny."

The reader returned the letter to Andrea, and let her hand fall inert by her side, with a sigh.

"Have I betrayed you," murmured the countess: "have I failed in the faith you put me in, for I made no promises?"

"Forgive me, for I have suffered so much," faltered Marie.

"You, suffered," exclaimed the ex-lady of honor, "do you dare to talk to me of suffering? what has happened me, then? Oh, I shall not say that I suffered, for I would not use the word another did for painting the same idea. I need a new one to sum up all griefs, pangs and pains,—you suffer? but you have not seen the man you loved indifferent to that love, and paying court on his bended knees to another woman! you have not seen your brother, jealous of this other woman whom he adored in silence as a pagan does his goddess, fight with the man you loved! you have not heard this man, wounded it was thought mortally, call out in his delirium for this other woman, whose confidential friend you were: you have not seen this other prowling in the lobbies, where you were wandering to hear the revelations of fever which prove that if a mad passion does not outlive life it may follow one to the grave-brink! you have not seen this beloved one, returning to life by a miracle of nature and science, rising from his couch to fall at the rival's feet.—— I say, rival, and one, from the standard of love being the measure of greatness of ranks. In your despair you have not gone into the nunnery at the age of twenty-five, trying to quiet at the cold crucifix your scorching love: then, one day when you hoped to have damped with tears if not extinguished the flame consuming you, you have not had this rival, once your friend, come to you in the name of the former friendship to ask you to be the wife of this very man whom you had worshipped for three years—for the sake of her salvation as a wife, her royal Majesty endangered——!

"She was to be a wife without a husband, a mere veil thrown between the crowd and another's happiness, like the shroud between the corpse and the common eye: overruled by the compulsory duty, not by mercy, for jealous love knows no pity—you sacrificed me—you accepted my immense devotion. You did not have to hear the priest ask if you took for helpmate the man who was not to be your husband: you did not feel him pass the ring over your finger as the pledge of eternal love, while it was a vain and meaningless symbol; you did not see your husband quit you at the church door within an hour of the wedding, to be the gallant of your rival! oh, madam, these three years has been of torture!"

The Queen lifted her failing hand to seek the speaker's but it was shunned.

"I promised nothing, but see what I have done," said she. "But you promised two things—not to see Count Charny, the more sacred as I had not asked it; and, by writing, to treat me as a sister, also the more sacred as I never solicited it.

"Must I recall the terms of that pledge? I burnt the paper but I remember the words; and thus you wrote:

"'Andrea: You have saved me! my honor and my life are saved by you. In the name of that reputation which costs you so dear, I vow that you may call me sister; do it, and you will not see me blush. I place this writing in your hands as pledge of my gratitude and the dower I owe you. Your heart is the noblest of boons and it will value aright the present I offer.

'MARIE ANTOINETTE.'"

"Forgive me, Andrea, I thought that he loved you."

"Did you believe it the law of the affections that when one loves a woman less he loves another woman more?"

She had undergone so much that she became cruel in her turn.

"So you too perceive his love falling off?" questioned the Queen dolefully.

Without replying Andrea watched the despairing sovereign and something like a smile was defined on her lips.

"Oh heaven, what must I do to retain this fleeting love? my life that ebbs? Oh, if you know the way, Andrea, my friend and sister, tell me, I supplicate you!" She held out both hands from which the other receded one step.

"How am I to know, who have never loved?"

"Yes, but he may love you. Some day he will come to your arms for forgiveness and to make amends for the past, asking your pardon for all he has made you suffer: suffering is quickly forgotten, God be thanked! in loving arms, pardon is soon granted to the beloved who gave pain."

"This misfortune coming—and it would be that for both of us, madam, do you forget the secret which I confided in you, how—before I became the wife of Count Charny—I was mother of a son?"

The Queen took breath.

"You mean you will do nothing to bring Charny back to you?" she asked.

158

"Nothing; no more in the future than in the past."

"You will not tell him—will not let him suspect that you love him?"

"No, unless he comes to tell me that he loves me."

"But, if he should——"

"Oh, madam," interrupted Andrea.

"Yes, you are right, Andrea, my sister and friend; and I am unjust, exacting and cruel. But when all falls away from me, friends, power and fame, I may wish that at least this passion to which I have sacrificed friendship, power and reputation, should be left to me."

"And, now," went on the lady of honor, with the glacial coldness she had laid aside only for a moment, when she spoke of the torments she had undergone, "have you anything more to ask me—or fresh orders to transmit?"

"No, nothing, I thank you. I wished to restore you my friendship but you will not accept it. Farewell; at least take my gratitude with you."

Andrea waved away this second feeling as she had the former, and making a cold and deep reverence, stole forth silently and slowly as a ghost.

"Oh, body of ice, heart of diamond and soul of fire, you are right not to wish either my friendship or my gratitude; for I feel—though the Lord forgive me! that I hate you as I never hated any one—for if he does not love you now, I foresee that he will love you some day."

She called Weber to ask if Dr. Gilbert was coming next day.

"At ten in the morning."

Pleading that she was ailing and wearied, she forbade her ladies to disturb her before ten, the only person she intended to see being Gilbert.

CHAPTER XXI. WHAT A CUT-OFF HEAD MAY COUNSEL.

WHEN Gilbert appeared before the Queen, she uttered a scream, for his ruffles and part of his coat were torn and drops of blood stained his shirt.

"I ask pardon for presenting myself to your Majesty in this attire," he said, "but your trusty servant who came to learn why I was late to the appointment, will tell you that he found me in the midst of a mob, trying to save a baker who was done to death for withholding bread. They cut the poor fellow to pieces: and to make matters worse, in parading his head on a pike it was shown to his wife who fell down and alas! has been prematurely confined."

"Poor woman," cried the Queen, "if she does not die I will see her to-morrow and, any way, her child shall be maintained out of my private purse."

"Ah, madam," exclaimed Gilbert, "why cannot all France see these tears in your eyes and hear these words from your lips!"

But almost instantly the monarch returned to master the woman. She said with a change of tone:

"And are these, sir, the fruits of your revolution? after slaying the great lords, the officials and the soldiery, the people are killing one another; is there no means of dealing out justice to these cutthroats?"

"We will try to do so; but it would be better to prevent the murders than wait and punish the murderers."

"How? the King and I ask nothing more fervently."

"All these woes come from the people having lost confidence in those set above them. Nothing of the kind would occur if they were ruled by men with the public confidence."

"You allude to this Mirabeau and Lafayette?"

"I hoped that your Majesty had sent to tell me that the King was no longer hostile to the Cabinet I proposed."

"In the first place, doctor," replied the royal lady, "you fall into a grave error shared with many more, I admit: you think that I have influence over the King. You believe that he follows my inspirations? You mistake: if any body has a sway over him, it is Lady Elizabeth; the proof is that she yesterday sent one of my servitors, Count Charny, on an errand without my knowing whither he goes or what is its aim."

"Still, if your Majesty will surmount her repugnance to Mirabeau, I can answer for bringing the King round to my views."

"Is not such repugnance based on a motive, tell me?" counterqueried the lady.

"In politics, there should be neither sympathy nor antipathy; only the meetings of principles and combinations of gains, and I ought to say that gains are surer than principles."

"Do you believe that this man who has publicly insulted me, would consent to join us?"

"He is entirely yours: when a Mirabeau turns from monarchy, it is like a horse that shies; reminded of his allegiance by whip or spur, he will resume his place in the right road."

"But he is for the Duke of Orleans?"

"So far from him is he, that on hearing of the duke going over to England when Lafayette threatened him, he said: 'They say I am in his pay! I would not have him for my lackey.'"

"That reconciles him some with me," said the lady, trying to smile: "if I could believe he might be relied on——"

"Well?"

"Perhaps I should be nearer him than the King."

"Madam, I saw him at Versailles when the mob stormed the palace: then he thought the Royal Family ought to flee but I have had a note from him this day."

He took out a slip of rough paper.

"Excuse the writing—it is on paper found in a wine saloon and written on the counter."

"Never mind that: it is in keeping with the present style of politics."

Taking the paper, the Queen read:

"This bread riot changes the face of things. A great deal can be drawn from this cut-off head. The Assembly will be frightened and call for martial law. If there be a Mirabeau-Lafayette Cabinet, Mirabeau will answer for all?"

"It is not signed," objected the Queen.

"He handed it to me himself. My advice is that he is perfectly right and that this alliance alone can save France."

"Be it so, let the gentleman put the project on paper and I will lay it before the King, as well as support it."

"Then I will go to the Assembly and see him. In two hours I shall return."

The Queen waited in impatience, always fond of plotting and agitation as she was. His answer was that Mirabeau had become the spokesman of the court.

In fact, after a hot discussion, martial law was voted by the Assembly. The crime of treason was to be tried at the Chatelet Royal Court, which meant that royalty still held three fourths of the active power.

Gilbert did not go near the Queen until the cases were tried here which would test the alliance.

The triumph was great to have them tried under the Royal party's thumb. The first trial was of three men who had killed the baker of the Assemblymen, François; two of whom were hanged on the mere accusation and public notoriety; the third was tried and sent to the gallows likewise.

Two other cases were on the docket.

Both the accused prisoners were on the court side, the contractor Augeard and Inspector General Pierre Victor Benzenval, of the Swiss Guards.

Augeard was suspected of supplying the funds for the Queen's camerailla to pay the troops gathered in July to fight the Parisians: the contractor was not much known and the people bore him no grudge so that he was acquitted without protest.

It was not so with Benzenval, who was notorious. He had commanded the Swiss regiments during the riots and the week of the attack on the Bastile. It was remembered that he had charged the crowds, who wanted to pay him out.

But the most precious orders had been sent out by the King and the court; under no pretext must Benzenval be punished. It took at least this two-fold protection to save him. He had acknowledged himself guilty by taking to flight after the Bastile fell: caught half way to the frontier, he had been brought back to the capital.

Nevertheless he was acquitted.

Amid the hooting, angry crowd, leaving the court, was a man, dressed like a plain storekeeper who familiarly laid his hand on the shoulder of a gentleman dressed better than he, and said:

"Well, what does Dr. Gilbert think of these acquittals?"

The other started, but recognized the speaker by sight as well as by the voice, and replied:

"The Master!—you ought to be asked that, not me, for you know all, present, past and future!"

"Well, I should say: The third prisoner will catch it severely, even though he be innocent."

"Why should the innocent, if coming next, be wrongfully punished?" inquired the doctor.

"For the simple reason that in this world the good pay for the bad," returned the Chief of the Invisibles with the irony natural to him.

"Good-bye, Master," said Gilbert, offering his hand; "for I have business."

"With whom? Mirabeau, Lafayette or the Queen?"

Gilbert stopped and eyed Cagliostro uneasily.

"Let me tell you that you ofttimes frighten me," he said.

"On the contrary, I want to encourage you," said the magician. "Am I not your friend? You may be sure of that: I will afford you a proof if you will come with me home. I will give you such hidden particulars of this negociation which you believe secret, that you who fancy you are managing it, will confess ignorance of it."

"Listen," said Gilbert; "perhaps you are jesting with me by one of those marvellous funds of information familiar to you; but no matter! circumstances amid which we are treading are so grave that I would accept enlightenment though from Old Harry himself. I am following you therefore whithersoever you lead me."

"Be easy, it will not be far and to a place not unknown to you; only let me hail this passing hack; the dress I came out in did not allow me to use my carriage and horses."

They got into the hackneycoach which came on at a sign.

"Where am I to drive you, master?" inquired the Jehu, to Cagliostro as though, somehow, he saw that he was the leader of the pair, though the more plainly dressed.

"Where you know," answered the Chief, making a masonic sign, "The Temple."

The driver looked at the Grand Copt with amazement.

"Excuse me, Thou Supreme, I did not know you," he said, replying with another sign.

"It is not thus with me," replied Cagliostro, with a firm and lofty voice, "innumerable as are those whom the uninitiated eyes see not, I know all from the topmost to the lowest of those who bring the bricks and hew the stones."

The coachman shut the door, got upon the box, and took the carriage at a gallop to St. Claude Street. The carriage was stopped and the door opened with a zeal which testified to the man's respect.

Cagliostro motioned for Gilbert to alight first and as he descended, he said to the jarvey:

"Any news?"

"Yes, Master," said the knight of the whip, "and I should have made my report this evening if I had not the luck to meet you."

"Speak."

"My news is not for outsiders."

"Oh, the bystander is not an outsider," returned Cagliostro, smiling.

But Gilbert moved off a little, though he could not help glancing and listening partially. He saw a smile on the hearers's face as the man told his story. He caught the name of Favras and Count Provence, before the report was over, when the magician took out a goldpiece and offered it.

"The Master knows that it is forbidden to receive pay for giving information," he objected.

"I am not paying for your report, it is plain, but for your bringing us," said the conspirator.

"That I can accept. Thank you," he said, taking the coin, "I need not work any more to-day."

He drove away, leaving Gilbert amazed at what he had witnessed, and he crossed the threshold reeling like a tipsy man.

He knew this house from having traversed it years ago under impressive circumstances; little was changed in it, even to the same servant Fritz, only he had aged sixteen years.

Ushered into a sitting room, the count bade his guest take a seat.

"I am entirely yours, doctor," said he.

The younger man forgot his present curiosity in the memories evoked by this room. Cagliostro looked at him like Mephistopheles regarding Faust in his brown studies.

"This room seems to set you thinking, doctor," he said audibly.

"It does, of the obligations I am under to you."

"Pooh, bubbles!"

"Really, you are a strange man," said Gilbert, speaking as much to himself as to the other, "and if reason allowed me to put faith in what we learn from legends, I should be inclined to take you for a magician."

"This am I for the world, Gilbert: but not for you. I have never tried to dazzle you with jugglery. You know I have always let you see the bottom of the well and if you have seen Truth come up not so scantily clothed as the painters represent her, it is because I am a Sicilian and cannot help decorating my lady-love."

"It was here, count, that you gave me a large sum of money that I might be rich in offering my hand to Andrea de Taverney, with the same ease as I might give a penny to a beggar."

"You forget the most extraordinary part of it: the beggar brought back the sum, except for a couple of coins which he spent for clothes."

"He was honest but you were generous."

"Who tells you that it was not more easy for him who handled millions to give a hundred thousand crowns than for him who was penniless to bring back so large a sum as that was to him? Besides, all depends on the man's state of mind. I was under the blow of the loss of the only woman I ever loved— my darling wife was murdered, and I believe you might have had my life for the asking."

"Do you feel grief, and experience it like other men," inquired Gilbert, eyeing him with marked astonishment.

"You speak of memories this room gives you," sighed the other. "Were I to tell you—your hair would whiten—but let it pass; leave those events in their grave. Let us speak of time present, and of that to-come if you like."

"Count, you returned to realism just now; again you turn to pretence, for you speak of the future with the voice of a conjurer asserting the power to read indecipherable hieroglyphics."

"You forget that having more means at my beck and call than other men, I see more clearly and farther than they. You shall see that the pretence is but a veil—solid are the facts beneath. Come, doctor, how is your Fusion Cabinet getting on? the Mirabeau-Lafayette Ministry?"

"It is in the skies; you are trying to learn the facts by pretending to know more than the rumors."

"I see that you are doubt incarnate, or wish not to see what you do not doubt. After telling you of things you do know I must tell of those beyond your ken. Well, you have recommended Mirabeau to the King as the only man who can save the monarchy. He will fail—all will fail, for the monarchy is doomed. You know that I will not have it saved. You have achieved your end; the two rulers will welcome your advocate: and you flatter yourself that the royal conversion is due to your irrefutable logic and irresistible arguments."

Gilbert could not help biting his lip on hearing this ironical tone.

"Have you invented a stethoscope by which you can read the heart of kings? pass the wonderful instrument on to me, count: only an enemy of mankind would want to keep it to himself alone."

"I told you I keep nothing back from you, dear doctor. You shall have my telescope and may look as you please through the small end which diminishes or the other which magnifies. The Queen gave way for two reasons: first, she met a great sorrow the night before and she must have some mental distraction; next, she is a woman and having heard Mirabeau spoken of as a tiger, she wants to see him and try to tame him. She thinks: 'It will be fine revenge to bring him to lick my feet: if some good follows for France and the crown, so much the better.' But you understand, this idea is quite secondary."

"You are building on hypothesis and I want facts."

"I see you refuse my glass and I must come back to material things: such as can be seen with the naked eye, Mirabeau's debts, for instance."

"What a chance you have to exhibit your generosity, by paying his debts as you once did Cardinal Rohan's."

"Do not reproach me with that speculation, it was one of my greatest successes. The Queen's Necklace was a pretty affair, I think, and ruined the Queen in the general eye. At the same price I would pay Mirabeau's debts. But you know that he is not looking to me for that, but to the future Generalissimo, Lafayette, who will make him caper for a beggarly fifty thousand francs, which he will not get any more than the dog gets the cake for which he has danced.

"Poor Mirabeau, how all these fools and conceited dunces make your genius pay for the follies of your youth! Yet all this is providential and heaven is obliged to proceed by human methods. All these politicians and wirepullers blame him for some virtue which is not theirs, and yet, if he dies to-morrow, the masses will award him an apotheosis, and all these pigmies, over whom he stands head and shoulders, will follow as mourners and howl: 'Woe to France which has lost her greatest orator—woe to royalty which has lost its supporter!'"

"Are you going to foretell the death of Mirabeau?" cried Gilbert, almost frightened.

"Frankly, doctor, do you see any length of life for a man whose blood stews him, whose heart swells to suffocate him and whose genius eats him up? do you believe that even such powers will not be worn out in stemming the tide of mediocrity? his enterprise is the rock of Sisyphus. For two years they have been holding him down with the cry of Immorality. As if God moulded all men in the same form, and as if the circle enlarged for a great mind should not enclose greater vices. Mirabeau will not be Premier because he owes a hundred thousand francs debt, which would be settled were he a rich contractor's son, and because he is condemned to death for having run away with an old imbecile's wife—who smothered herself in charcoal fumes for the love of a strapping military captain! What a farce the tragedy of human life is! How I should weep over it if I had not made up my mind to laugh!"

"But your prediction?" cried Gilbert.

"I tell you," said the diviner, in the prophet's tone which was his alone, and allowed no reply, "Mirabeau will wear out his life without becoming Prime Minister. So great a bar is mediocrity. Go to the Assembly to-morrow and see. Meanwhile, come with me to the Jacobins Club, for these night-birds will hold their session in an hour. Do you belong?"

"No: Danton and Desmoulins entered me at the Cordeliers. We will go after dinner."

Two hours subsequently, two man in gentlemanly black suits were set down from a plain private carriage at the door of St. Roch's church, where the throng was great. They were Dr. Gilbert and Baron Zannone, as Cagliostro chose to call himself at this epoch.

"Will you come into the nave or sit in the gallery?" asked the magician.

"I thought the nave was kept for the members?" said the other.

"Just so, but am I not a member of all societies?" returned the Arch-master laughing. "Besides, this club is but the seat of the Invisibles, and you can enter as one of the Rosicrucians. We are sixty thousand strong in France alone in three months since foundation as Jacobins, and will be four hundred thousand in a year."

"Though I am a Rose-Croix, I prefer to be in the gallery where I can see over the crowd and you can better tell me of the persons whom I descry."

The seats were roughly knocked up in tiers and a wooden staircase led up them. Cagliostro made a sign and spoke a word to two who were sitting in the already filled seats and they got up to give them their places as if they had been sent before to keep them.

The place was ill lighted in the growing gloom but it was clear that these were the best sort of the revolutionists, while the uniforms of officers of the army and navy abounded. For the common brothers held their meetings in the crypt. Here the literati and artists were in the majority.

Casting a long look around, Gilbert was encouraged by seeing that most were not so very hostile to the royal cause.

"Whom do you see here hostile to royalty?" he inquired of his guide.

"In my eyes there are but two."

"Oh, that is not many among four hundred men."

"It is quite enough when one will be the slayer of Louis XVI. and the other his successor."

"A future Brutus and a future Caesar here?" exclaimed the doctor starting.

"Oh, apostle with scales over your eyes," said Cagliostro; "you shall not only see them but touch them. Which shall I commence with?"

"By the overthrower; I respect chronology: let us have Brutus first."

"You know that men do not use the same means to accomplish a like work," said Cagliostro, animated as by inspiration. "Therefore our Brutus will not resemble the antique one."

"That makes me the more eager to see ours."

"There he is."

He pointed to a man leaning against the rostrum in such a position that his head alone was in the light. Pale and livid, this head seemed dissevered from the trunk. The eyes seemed to shine with a viper's expression, with almost scornful hatred, knowing his venom was deadly. Gilbert felt a creeping of the flesh.

170

"You were right to warn me," he said; "this is neither Brutus nor Cromwell."

"No, it is rather Cassius the pale-faced and leaned man whom the Emperor dreaded most. Do you not know him?"

"No; or rather I have seen him in the Assembly. He is one of the longest-winded speechifyers of the Left, to whom nobody listens. A pettifogger from Arras——"

"The very man."

"His name is Maximilian Robespierre."

"Just so. Look at him. You are a pupil of Lavater the physiognomist."

"I see the spite of mediocrity for genius as he watches Barnave."

"In other words you judge like the world. I grant that he cannot expect to make a hit among all these proven orators; but at least you cannot accuse him of immorality; he is the Honest Man: he never steps outside of the law, or only to act within a new law which he legally makes."

"But what is this Robespierre?" asked the other.

"You ask that as Strafford did of the future Lord Protector: 'What is this Cromwell? a brewer!' But he cut off his head, mark, you aristocrat of the Seventeenth Century!"

"Do you suggest that I run the same risk as Charles First's Minister," said Gilbert, trying to smile, but it was frozen on his lips.

"Who can tell?" replied the diviner.

"The more reason for me to inquire about him."

"Who is Robespierre? he was born in Arras, of Irish extraction, in 1758. He was the best pupil in the Jesuits' College and won a purse on which he came to study at Paris. It was at the same college where your young Sebastian had an experience. Other boys went out sometimes from those sombre aisles which bleach the pallid, and had holidays with their families and friends;

171

young Robespierre was cooped up and breathed the bad air of loneliness, sadness and tedium; three bad things which rob the mind of its bloom and blight the heart with envy and hatred. The boy became a wilted young man. His benefactor had him appointed judge, but his tender heart would not let him dispose of the life of a man; he resigned and became a lawyer. He took up the case of peasants disputing with the Bishop of Arras and won their just claim; the grateful boors sent him up to the Assembly. There he stood between the clergy's profound hatred for the lawyer who had dared speak against their bishop and the scorn of the nobles for the scholar reared by charity."

"What is he doing?"

"Nothing for others but much for the Revolution. If it did not enter into my views that he should be kept poor, I would give him a million francs to-morrow. Not that I should buy him, for he is joked with as the Incorruptible! Our noble debaters have settled that he shall be the butt of the House, for all assemblies must have one. Only one of his colleagues understands and values him—it is Mirabeau. He told me the other day, 'that man will go far for he believes what he says!'"

"This grows serious," muttered Gilbert.

"He comes here for he gets an audience. The Jacobin is a young minotaur: suckling a calf, he will devour a nation in a while. I promised to show you an instrument for lopping off heads, did I not? Well, Robespierre will give it more work than all those here."

"Really, you are funereal, count," said Gilbert; "if your Caesar does not compensate for your Brutus, I may forget what I came here for."

"You see my future Emperor yonder, talking with the tragic actor Talma, and with another whom he does not know but who will have a great influence over him. Keep this befriender's name in mind—Barras, and recall it one of these days."

"I do not know how right you are, but you choose your typical characters well," said Gilbert; "this Caesar of yours has the brow to wear a crown and his eyes—but I cannot catch the expression——"

172

"Because his sight is diverted inwards—such eyes study the future, doctor."

"What is he saying to Barras?"

"That he would have held the Bastile if he were defending it."

"He is not a patriot, then?"

"Such as he are nothing before they are all in all."

"You seem to stick to your idea about this petty officer?"

"Gilbert," said the soothsayer, extending his hand towards Robespierre, "as truly as that man will re-erect the scaffold of Charles Stuart, so truly will 'this one'"—he indicated the lieutenant of the line regiment—"will re-erect the throne of Charlemagne."

"Then our struggle for liberty is useless," said Gilbert discouraged.

"Who tells you that he may not do as much for us on his throne as the other on his scaffold?"

"Will he be the Titus, or Marcus Aurelius, the god of peace consoling us for the age of bronze?"

"He will be Alexander and Hannibal in one. Born amid war, he will thrive in war-fare and go down in warring. I defy you to calculate how much blood the clergy and nobles have made Robespierre lose by his fits of spite against them; take all that these nobles and priests will lose, multiply upon multiplications, and you will not attain the sea of blood this man will shed, with his armies of five hundred thousand men and his three days' battles in which hundreds of cannon-shots will be fired."

"And what will be the outcome of all this turmoil—all this chaos?"

"The outcome of all genesis, Gilbert. We are charged to bury this Old World. Our children will spring up in a new one. This man is but the giant who guards the door. Like Louis XIV., Leo X. and Agustus, he will give his name to the era unfolding."

173

"What is his name?" inquired Gilbert, subjugated by Cagliostro's convinced manner.

"His name is Buonaparte; but he will be hailed in History as Napoleon. Others will follow of his name, but they will be shadows—the dynasty of the first Charlemagne lasted two hundred years; of this second one, a tithe: did I not tell you that in a hundred years the Republic will have the empire of France?"

Gilbert bowed his head. He did not notice that the debates were opened. An hour passed when he felt a powerful hand grip his shoulder.

He turned: Cagliostro had disappeared and Mirabeau stood in his place—after the eagle, the lion.

Mirabeau's face was convulsed with rage as he roared in a dull voice:

"We are flouted, deceived, betrayed! the court will not have me and you have been taken for a dupe as I for a fool. On my moving in the House that the Cabinet Ministers should be invited to be present at the Assembly sessions, three friends of the King proposed that no member of the House should be a minister. This laboriously managed combination dissolves at a breath from the King; But," concluded Mirabeau, like Ajax, shaking his mighty fist at the sky, "by my name, I will pay them for this, and if their breath can shake a minister, mine shall overthrow the throne. I shall go to the Assembly and fight to the uttermost; I am one of those who blow up the fort and perish under the ruins."

He rushed away, more terrible and handsomer for the divine streak which lightning had impressed on his brow.

Gilbert did not go to the House to witness his companion's defeat—one very like a victory. He was musing at home over Cagliostro's strange predictions. How could this man foresee what would be Robespierre and Napoleon? I ask those who put this question to me how they explain Mdlle. Lenormand's prediction to the Empress Josephine? One often meets inexplicable things; doubt was invented to comfort those who cannot explain them but will not believe them.

174

CHAPTER XXII. THE SMILE AND THE NOD.

AS Cagliostro had said and Mirabeau surmised, the King had upset the scheme.

Without much regret the Queen saw the constitutional platform fall which had wounded her pride. The King's policy was to gain time and profit by circumstances; besides he had two chances of getting away into some stronghold, which was his favorite plan. These two plans, we know, were his brother Provence's, managed by Favras; the other his own, managed by Charny.

The latter reached Metz in a couple of days where the faithful royalist Bouille did not doubt him, but resolved to send his son Louis to Paris to be more exactly informed on the matter. Charny remained as a kind of hostage.

Count Louis Bouille arrived about the middle of November. At this period the King was guarded closely by Lafayette whose cousin the young count was.

To keep him in ignorance of Charny's negociations, the latter worked to be presented to the King by his kinsman.

Providence answered the envoy's prayer for Lafayette, who had been informed of his coming but swallowed his excuse that it was on a visit to a sweetheart in Paris, offered to take him with him on his morning call on the monarch.

All the palace doors opened to the general. The sentinels presented arms and the footmen bowed, so that Count Louis could see that his relative was the real King of Paris.

The King was in his forge so that the visitors had to see the Queen first.

Bouille had not seen her for three years. The sight of her at thirty-four, a prisoner, slandered, threatened, and hated, made a deep impression on the chivalric heart of the young noble.

She remembered him at a glance and with the same was sure this was a friendly face. Without busying about General Lafayette she gave her hand for the young man to kiss, which was a fault such as she plentifully committed; without this favor she had won Louis Bouille, and by doing him it before the general she slighted the latter who had never been so gratified; she wounded the very man she most wanted as a friend.

Hence with a faltering in the voice but with the courtesy never leaving him, Lafayette said:

"Faith, my dear cousin, you want me to present you to the Queen: but it seems to me that you were better fitted to present me."

The Queen was so enraptured at meeting a friend on whom she could rely, and as a woman so proud of the effect produced on the young nobleman, that she turned round on the general with one of the beams of youth which she had feared forever extinct.

"General," she said with one of the smiles of her sunnier days, "Count Bouille is not a severe republican like you: he comes from Metz, not from America; he does not come to bother about Constitutions but to present his homage. Do not be astonished at the favor shown him by a nearly dethroned Queen, which this country squire may esteem a boon———"

She completed her sentence by a playful smile as much as to say: "You are a Scipio and think nothing of such nonsense."

"It is a pity for me, and a great misfortune for your Majesty," returned Lafayette, "that I pass without my respect and devotion being noticed."

The Queen looked at him with her clear, searching eye. This was not the first time that he had spoken in this strain and set her thinking: but unfortunately, as he had said, she entertained an instinctive repugnance for him.

"Come, general, be generous and pardon me, my outburst of kindness towards this excellent Bouille family, which loves me with a whole heart and of which this youth is the chain of contact. I see his whole family in him, coming to kiss my hand. Let us shake hands, as the American and English do, and be good friends."

The marquis touched the hand coldly.

"I regret that you do not bear in mind that I am French. The night of the attack on the Royal Family at Versailles ought to remind you."

"You are right, general," responded the lady, making an effort and shaking his hand. "I am ungrateful. Any news?"

Lafayette had a little revenge to take.

"No; merely an incident in the House. An old man of one hundred and twenty was brought to the bar by five generations of descendants to thank the Representatives for having made him free. Think of one who was born a serf under Louis XIV. and eighty years after."

"Very touching," retorted the Queen; "but I could not well be there as I was succoring the widow and child of the baker murdered for supplying bread to the Assembly."

"Madam, we could not foresee that atrocity but we have punished the offenders."

"That will do her no good, as she is maddened and may give birth to a still-born babe; if it should live, do you see any inconvenience to standing godmother to it at the Cathedral of Notre Dame?"

"None: and I take this opportunity of meeting your allusion, before my kinsman, to your pretended captivity. Nothing prevents your going to church or elsewhere, and the King may go hunting and out riding, as much as he likes."

The Queen smiled, for this permission might be useful as far as it went.

"Good-bye, count," she said to Bouille; "the Princess of Lamballe receives for me and you will be welcome any evening with your illustrious kinsman."

"I shall profit by the invitation," said Lafayette, "sure that I should be oftener seen there and elsewhere by your Majesty if the request had not been heretofore omitted."

The Queen dismissed them with a smile and a nod, and they went out, the one with more bitterness because of the nod, the other with more adherence because of the smile.

CHAPTER XXIII. THE ROYAL LOCKSMITH.

AS the King had undertaken a very important piece of locksmith work, he sent his valet Hue to beg General Lafayette to come into his smithy.

It was on the second floor above his bedroom, with inner and outer stairs.

Since morning he had been hammering away at the work for which Master Gamain gave him praise and so much regret that the politicians should take him away from it to trouble about foreign countries.

Perhaps he wanted to show the Commander of the National Guard that however weak as a monarch, he was mighty as a Tubal Cain.

On the road Count Louis had time to meditate; and he concluded that the Queen knew nothing of his errand. He would have to study the King's reception and see if he did not give some sign of better understanding what brought him to Paris than his cousin the marquis.

The valet did not know Bouille so that he only announced the general.

"Ah, it is you, marquis," said the King, turning. "I must ask pardon for calling you up here, but the smith assures you that you are welcome in his forge. A charcoal-burner once said to my ancestor Henry IV.: 'Jack is king in his own castle.' But you are master in the smithy as in the palace."

Louis spoke much in the same way as Marie Antoinette.

"Sire, under whatever circumstances I present myself to your Majesty," said Lafayette, "and whatever costume your Majesty is in, the King will be ever the sovereign and I the faithful subject and devoted servant."

"I do not doubt that, my lord; but you are not alone. Have you changed your aid-de-camp?"

"This young officer, Sire, whom I ask leave to introduce, is my cousin, Count Louis Bouille, captain in the Provence Dragoons."

"Oh, son of Marquis Bouille, commander of Metz?" said the King, with a slight start not escaping the young man.

"The same, Sire," he spoke up quickly.

"Excuse me not knowing you, but I have short sight. Have you been long in town?"

"I left Metz five days ago; and being here without official furlough but under special permission from my father, I solicited my kinsman the marquis for the honor of presentation to your Majesty."

"You were very right, my lord, for nobody could so well present you at any hour, and from no one could the introduction come more agreeably."

The words "at any hour" meant that Lafayette had the public and private entry to the King. The few words from the sovereign put the young count on his guard. The question about his coming signified that he wanted to know if Charny had seen his father.

Meanwhile Lafayette was looking round curiously where few penetrated; he admired the regularity with which the tools were laid out. He blew the bellows as the apprentice.

"So your Majesty has undertaken an important work, eh?" queried Lafayette, embarrassed how to talk to a King who was in a smutty apron, with tucked up sleeves and had a file in his hand.

"Yes, general, I have set to making our magnus opus a lock. I tell you just what I am doing or we shall have Surgeon Marat saying that I am forging the fetters of France. Tell him it is not so, if you lay hold of him. I suppose you are not a smith, Bouille?"

"At least I was bound apprentice, and to a locksmith, too."

"I remember, your nurse's husband was a smith and your father, although not much of a student of Rousseau acted on his advice in 'Emile' that everybody should learn a craft, and bound you to the workbench."

"Exactly; so that if your Majesty wanted a boy——"

"An apprentice would not be so useful to me as a master," returned the King. "I am afraid I have ventured on too hard a job. Oh, that I had my teacher Gamain, who used to say he was a crafts-master above the masters."

"Is he dead, my lord?"

"No," replied the King, giving the young gentleman a glance for him to be heedful; "he lives in Versailles, but the dear fellow does not dare come and see me at the Tuileries for fear he will get an ill name. All my friends have gone away, to London, Turin or Coblentz. Still, my dear general, if you do not see any inconvenience in the old fellow coming with one of his boys to lend me a hand, I might ask him to drop in some day."

"Your Majesty ought to know perfectly that he can see and send for anybody."

"Yes, on condition that you sentries search them as the revenue officers do those suspected of smuggling; poor Gamain will believe he is to be hanged, drawn and quartered if they found his bag of tools on him and took his three-cornered file for a stiletto!"

"Sire, I do not know how to excuse myself to your Majesty, but I am answerable for your person to the Powers of Europe, and I cannot take too many precautions for that precious life to be protected. As for the honest fellow of whom we are speaking, the King can give what orders he pleases."

"Very well; thank you, marquis; I might want him in a week or ten days—him and his 'prentice," he added, with a glance at Bouille; "I could notify him by my valet Durey, who is a friend of his."

"He has only to call to be shown up to the King; his name will suffice. Lord preserve me from getting the title of your jailer, Sire; never was the monarch more free; and I have even desired your Majesty to resume hunting and riding out."

"Thank you, but no more hunts for me! Besides, you see I have something to keep me in doors, in my head. As for traveling, that is another matter; the last trip from Versailles to Paris cured me of the desire to travel, in such a large party at all events."

He threw a glance to Bouille who ventured to blink to show that he understood.

"Are you soon going back to your father?" inquired the King of the latter.

"Sire, I am leaving Paris in a couple of days to pay a visit to my grandmother, living in Versailles; I am bound to pay my respects. Then I am charged by my father to attend to a rather important family matter, for which I expect to see the person who will give me the directions in about a week. So I shall hardly be with my father before the first week in December, unless the King has particular reasons for me to see him sooner."

"No, my lord, take your time; go to Versailles and transact your business and when done, go and tell the marquis, that I do not forget him as one of my faithful lieges, and that I will speak of him one of these days to General Lafayette for him to advance him."

Lafayette smiled faintly at this allusion to his omnipotence.

"Sire," he said, "I should have long ago recommended Marquis Bouille to your Majesty had he not been my kinsman. The fear of raising the cry that I am looking after my family alone prevented me doing him this justice."

"This chimes in nicely, then; we will speak of this matter again."

"The King will kindly allow me to say that my father would consider any change of a post a disgrace that robbed him of the chance to serve your Majesty particularly."

"Oh, that is fully understood, count," responded Louis the King, "and Marquis Bouille shall not be moved without it being according to his desires and mine. Let General Lafayette and I manage this, and you run to your pleasure-making without altogether forgetting business. Good bye, gentlemen!"

He dismissed them with a majestic manner in singular contrast with the vulgar attire.

"Come, come," he said to himself, when the door was shut. "I believe the young blade has comprehended me, and that in a week or so we shall have Master Gamain coming to aid me, with his 'prentice."

CHAPTER XXIV. HAPPY FAMILY.

ON the evening of this same day, about five, a scene passed in the third and top flat of a dirty old tumbledown house in Juiverie Street which we would like our readers to behold.

The interior of the sitting-room denoted poverty, and it was inhabited by three persons, a man, a woman, and a boy.

The man looked to be over fifty; he was wearing an old uniform of a French Guards sergeant, a habit venerated since these troops sided with the people in the riots and exchanged shots with the German dragoons.

He was dealing out playing cards and trying to find an infallible means of winning; a card by his side, pricked full of pinholes, showed that he was keeping tally of the runs.

The woman was four-and-thirty and appeared forty; she wore an old silk dress; her poverty was the more dreadful as she exhibited tokens of splendor; her hair was built up in a knot over a brass comb once gilded: and her hands were scrupulously cared for with the nails properly trimmed in an aristocratic style. The slippers on her feet, over openwork stockings, had been worked with gold and silver.

Her face might pass in candlelight for about thirty; but, without paint and powder it looked five years older than reality.

Its resemblance to Queen Marie Antoinette's was still so marked that one tried to recall it in the dusty clouds thrown up by royal horses around the window of a royal coach.

The boy was five years of age; his hair curled like a cherub's; his cheeks were round as an apple; he had his mother's diabolical eyes, and the sensual mouth of his father—in short, the idleness and whims of the pair.

He wore a faded pearl velvet suit and while munching a hunk of cake sandwiched with preserves, he frayed out the ends of an old tricolored scarf inside a pearl gray felt hat.

The family was illuminated by a candle with a large "thief in the gutter," stuck in a bottle for holder, which light fell on the man and left most of the room in darkness.

"Mamma," the child broke the silence by saying, as he threw the end of the cake on the mattress which served as bed, "I am tired of that kind of cake—faugh! I want a stick of red barley sugar candy."

"Dear little Toussaint," said the woman. "Do you hear that, Beausire?"

As the gamester was absorbed in his calculations, she lifted her foot within snatch of her hand and taking off the slipper, cast it to his nose.

"What is the matter?" he demanded, with plain ill-humor.

"Toussaint wants some candy, being tired of cheap cake."

"He shall have it to-morrow."

"I want it to-day—this evening—right now!" yelled the innocent in a tearful voice which threatened stormy weather.

"Toussaint, my boy, I advise you to give us quiet or papa will take you in hand," said the parent.

The boy yelled again but more from deviltry than from fear.

"You drunken sot, you just touch my darling, and I will attend to you," said the mother, stretching out the white hand towards the bully which her care of the nails made to become a claw at need.

"Who the deuse wants to touch the imp? you know it is only my style of speaking, my dear Oliva, and that though I may dust your skirt now and then I have always respected the kid's jacket. Tut, tut, come and embrace your poor Beausire who will be rich as a King in a week; come, my little Nicole."

"When you are rich as a king, it will be another matter: but up to that time no fooling."

"But I tell you that it is as safe as if I had a million. You might be kind

185

for a little while. Go and get credit of the baker."

"A man rolling in millions wants a baker to let him have a loaf on trust, ha, ha!"

"I want some red barely sugar," howled the child.

"Come, you king with the millions, give some sugar sticks to your prince."

Beausire started to put his hand to his fob but stopped half way.

"You know I gave you my last piece yesterday."

"Then, if you have the money," said the child to the woman whom Beausire called indifferently Nicole or Oliva, "give me a penny to buy candy."

"There are two cents, you naughty boy, and mind you do not fall in sliding down the bannisters."

"Thank you, dear mother," said the boy, capering for joy and holding out his hand.

"Come here till I set your hat on and adjust your sash: it must not be said that Captain Beausire let his son race about the streets in disorder—though it is all the same to him, the heartless fellow! I should die of shame!"

At the risk of whatever the neighbors might say against the heir to the Beausire name, the boy would have dispensed with the hat and band, of which he recognized the use before the other urchins did the freshness and beauty. But as the arrangement of his dress was a condition of the gift, the young Hector had to yield to it.

He consoled himself by taunting his father with the coin by thrusting it up under his nose; absorbed in his figuring the parent merely smiled at the pretty freak.

Soon they heard his timid step, though quickened by gluttony, descending the stairs.

"Now then, Captain Beausire," snapped the woman after a pause, "your wits must lift us out of this miserable position, or else I must have recourse to mine."

She spoke with a toss of the head as much as to say: "A lady of my lovely face never dies of starvation, never fear!"

"Just what I am busy about, my little Nicole," responded Beausire.

"By shuffling the cards?"

"Did I not tell you that I have found the infallible coup?"

"At it again, eh? Captain Beausire, I warn you that I am going to hunt up my old acquaintances and see if one of them cannot have you shut up in the madhouse. Dear, dear, if Lord Richelieu were not dead, if Cardinal Rohan were not ruined, if Lady Lamotte Valois were not in London dodging the sheriff's officers——"

"What are you talking about?"

"I should find means and not be obliged to share the misery of an old swashbuckler like this one."

With a queenly flirt of the hand Oliva alias Nicole Legay, disdainfully indicated the gambler.

"But I keep telling you that I shall be rich to-morrow," he repeated, himself at any rate convinced.

"Show me the first gold piece of your million and I shall believe the rest."

"You will see ten gold pieces this evening—the very sum promised me. You can have five to buy a silk dress and a velvet suit for the youngster: with the balance I will bring you the million I promised."

"You unhappy fellow, you mean to gamble again?"

"But I tell you again that I have lit on an infallible sequence."

"Own brother to the one with which you threw away the sixty thousand

The Hero of the People

livres from the amount you stole at the Portuguese Ambassador's?"

"Money got over the devil's back goes under his belly," replied Beausire sententiously. "I always did think that the way I got that cash brought bad luck."

"Is this fresh lot coming from an inheritance? have you an uncle who has died in the Indies or America and left you the ten louis?"

"Nicole Legay," rejoined Beausire with a lofty air, "these ten will be earned not only honestly but honorably, for a cause which interests me as well as the rest of the nobility of France."

"So you are a nobleman, Friend Beausire?" jeered the lady.

"You may say so: we have it stated so in the birth entry on the register of St. Paul's, and signed by your servitor, Jean Baptiste Toussaint de Beausire, on the day when I gave my name to our boy——-"

"A handsome present that was," gibed Nicole.

"And my estate," added the so-called captain emphatically.

"If kind heaven does not send him something more solid," interposed Nicole, shaking her head, "the poor little dear is sure to live on air and die in the poorhouse."

"Really, Nicole, this is too much to endure—you are never contented."

"Endure? good gracious, who wants you to endure?" exclaimed the reduced gentlewoman, breaking down the dam to her long-restrained ire: "Thank God, I am not worried about myself or my little pet, and this very night I shall go forth and seek my fortune."

She rose and took three steps towards the door, but he strode in between them and opened his arms to bar the way.

"You naughty creature, did I not tell you that my fortune——-"

"Go on," said Nicole.

"Is coming home to-night: though the coup were a mistake—which is

188

impossible, it would only be five louis lost."

"There are times when a few pieces of money are a fortune, sir. But you would not know that, who have squandered a pile of gold as high as this house."

"That proves my merit: I made it at the cards, and if I made some once I shall make more another time: besides, there is a special providence for— smart rogues."

"That is a fine thing to rely on!"

"Do you not believe in Providence? are you an atheist, Nicole? of the school of Voltaire who denies all that sort of thing?"

"Beausire, no matter what I am, you are a fool."

"Springing from the lower class, as you do, it is not surprising that you nourish such notions. I warn you that they do not appertain to my caste and political opinions."

"You are a saucebox," returned the beauty of the past.

"But I have faith. If anyone were to say, 'Beausire, your son who has gone out to buy a sugar stick, will return with a lump of gold,' I should answer: 'Very likely, if it be the will of Allah!' as a Turkish gentleman of my acquaintance says."

"Beausire, you are an idiot," said Nicole, but she had hardly spoken the words before young Toussaint's voice was heard on the stairs calling:

"Oh, papa—mamma!"

"What is the matter?" cried Nicole, opening the door with true maternal solicitude. "Come, my darling, come."

The voice drew near like the ventriloquist doing the trick of the man in the cellar.

"I should not be astonished if he had lit on the streak of good luck I feel promised," said the gambler.

The boy rushed into the room, holding a sugarstick in his mouth, hugging under his left arm a bag of sugarplums, and showing in his right hand a gold coin which shone in the candle glimmer like the North Star.

"Goodness of heaven, what has occurred?" cried Nicole, slamming the door to.

She covered his gluey face with kisses—mothers never being disgusted, from their caresses seeming to purify everything.

"The matter is a genuine louis of gold, worth full value of twenty-four livres," said Beausire, skillfully obtaining the piece.

"Where did you pick that up that I may go for the others, my duck?" he inquired.

"I never found it, papa: it was give to me," replied the boy. "A kind gentleman give it me."

Ready as Beausire to ask who this donor was, Nicole was prudent from experience on account of Captain Beausire's jealousy. She confined herself to repeating:

"A gentleman?"

"Yes, mamma dear," rejoined the child, crunching the barley-sugar between his teeth: "a gentleman who came into the grocer's store where I was, and he says: 'God bless me, but, master, do I not behold a young gentleman whose name is De Beausire, whom you have the honor of attending to at the present time?'"

Beausire perked up and Nicole shrugged her shoulders.

"What did the grocer say to that, eh?" demanded the card-sharper.

"Master Grocer says: 'I don't know whether he is a gentleman or not, but his name is Beausire,' 'Does he live by here?' went on the gentleman. 'Top-floor, next house on the left.' 'Give anything the young master wants to him—I will foot the bill,' said the gentleman. Then he gave me the money saying: 'There a louis for you, young sir: when you have eaten your candy, that will buy you more. He put the money in my hand; the grocer stuck this bag under my arm and I came away awfully glad. Oh, where is my money-piece?"

Not having seen Beausire's disappearing trick, he began to look all round for the louis.

"You clumsy little blockhead, you have lost it," said the captain.

"No, I never!" yelled the child.

The dispute would have become warm but for the interruption which came to put an end to it.

The door opened slowly and a bland voice made these words audible:

"How do you do, Mistress Nicole? good evening, Captain Beausire! How are you, little Toussaint?"

All turned: on the threshold was an elegantly attired man, smiling on the family group.

"Oh, here's the gentleman who gave me the candy," cried young Toussaint.

"Count Cagliostro," exclaimed Beausire and the lady at the same time.

"That is a winning little boy, and I think you ought to be happy at being a parent, Captain Beausire," said the intruder.

He advanced and with one scrutinizing glance saw that the couple were reduced to the last penny.

The child was the first to break the silence because he had nothing on his conscience.

"Oh, kind sir, I have lost the shining piece," said he.

Nicole opened her mouth to state the case but she reflected that silence might lead to a repetition of the godsend and she would inherit it; her expectation was not erroneous.

"Lost your louis, have you, my poor boy?" said Cagliostro, "well, here are two; try not to lose them."

Pulling out a purse of which the plumpness kindled Beausire's greedy glances, he dropped two coins into Toussaint's little sticky paw.

"Look, mamma," said he, running to Nicole; "here's one for you and one for me."

While the child shared his windfall with his mother, the new-comer remarked the tenacity with which the former-soldier watched his purse and tried to estimate the contents before it was pocketted again. On seeing it disappear, he sighed.

"Still glum, captain?" said the visitor.

"And you, count, always rich?"

"Pooh! you are one of the finest philosophers I have ever known, as well at the present as in antiquity, and you are bound to know the axiom to which man does honor in all ages. 'Riches are not contentment.' I have known you to be rich, relatively."

"That's so: I have owned as much as a hundred thousand francs."

"It is possible; only when I met you again, you had spent nearly forty thousand of it so as to have but sixty, but that is a round sum for a corporal in the army."

"What is that to the sums you dispose of?" he sighed.

"I am only the banker, the trustee, Captain Beausire, and if I were obliged to settle up I daresay you could play St. Martin and I the beggar who would be glad to have half your cloak. But, my dear Beausire, do you not remember the circumstances of our last meeting? As I said, just now, you had sixty thousand left of the hundred thousand: were you happier than now?"

The ex-corporal heaved a retrospective sigh which might pass for a moan.

"Would you exchange your present position though you possessed nothing but one poor louis you 'nicked' from young Toussaint?"

"My lord!"

"Do not let us get warm, sir: we quarrelled once and you were obliged to go out and pick up your sword which I threw out of the window. You will remember?" went on the count, seeing that the man made no reply: "it is a good thing to have a memory. I ask you again would you change your actual position, though down to the solitary louis you 'extracted' from young Toussaint"—this time the allegation passed without protest—"for the precarious scrape from which I relieved you?"

"No, my lord, you are right—I should not change. At that epoch, alas! I was parted from my darling Nicole."

"To say nothing of being hunted by the police, on account of your robbing the Portuguese Embassy. What the mischief has become of that case, a villainous one, as I remember it, Captain B.?"

"It has been dropped, my lord," was the reply.

"So much the better: though I would not reckon on its not being picked up again. The police are awful for raking up past grievances, and the ruling powers might want to be on good terms with Portugal. However, that apart, in spite of the hard lines to which you are reduced, you are happy. If you had a thousand louis, your felicity would be complete, eh?"

Nicole's eyes glittered and her partner's flashed flames.

"Lord be good to us," cried the latter: "with half I would buy a lot in the country and live a rural life on the rest like a country squire!"

"Like Cincinnatus!"

"While Nicole would educate the boy."

"Like Cornelia! Death of my life, Captain Beausire! not only would this be exemplary but touching: do you hope to earn as much as that in the piece of business you have in hand?"

"What business?" queried the other, starting.

"That you are carrying on as sergeant of the Guards; for which you are to meet a man, this evening, under the Palais Royal arcades."

"Oh, my lord," moaned Beausire, turning pale as a corpse and wringing his hands. "Do not destroy me!"

"Why, you are going distracted now? Am I the Chief of Police to ruin you?"

"There, I told you, you are getting into a pretty pickle," exclaimed Nicole. "I know nothing about it, my lord, but whenever he hides any game from me, I know it is a bad one."

"But you are wrong, my dear lady, for this is an excellent speculation."

"Is it not?" cried the gambler. "The count, as a nobleman, understands that all the nobility are in this scheme——"

"For it to succeed. It must be allowed though, that the people are interested in its failure. If you will believe me, captain—you understand that a friend is giving advice—you will take no part in it for the peers or the people. Better act for yourself."

"Certainly, for yourself," said Nicole. "Blest if you have not toiled long enough for others: so that it is high time you looked after Number One."

"You hear the lady, who speaks like a born orator. Bear this in mind, Friend Beausire, all spec's have a good and a bad side, one for the winners, one for the losers: no affair however good, can benefit everybody; the whole trouble is to hit on the right side."

"And you do not think I am there, eh?"

"Not at all; I would even add, if you are willful—for you know I dabble in telling fortunes—that you will not only risk your honor, and the fortune you seek—but your life. You will most likely be hanged!"

"They do not hang noblemen," objected Beausire, wiping the perspiration streaming from his brow.

"That is so: but to avoid the gallows-tree and have your head cut off, you would have to prove your family-tree; it would take so long that the court would lose patience, and string you up for the time being—leaving your widow to demand compensation if you turned out to have deserved decapitation. Still you may say that it does not matter, as it is the crime that casts shame and not the scaffold, to quote a poet. Still again, I dare say you are not so attached to your opinions that you would lay down your life for them; I understand this. Deuse take us, but we have only one life, as another poet says, not so great as the other, but as truthful."

"My lord," faltered the ex-guardsman, "I have remarked in my too brief acquaintance with your lordship, that you have a way of speaking of some things which would make the hair of a more timid man than me bristle on his head."

"Hang me if that is my intention," responded Cagliostro; "Besides you are not a timid man."

"No: yet there are circumstances," began Beausire.

"I understand; such as when one has the jail for theft behind one and the gallows for high treason before one—for I suppose they give that name to the crime of kidnapping the King."

"My lord," cried Beausire, terrified.

"Wretch, is it on kidnapping that you build your fortune?" demanded Oliva.

"Oh, he was not wrong to dwell in golden dreams, my dear lady; only, as I have already said, each affair has a dark side and a bright one and Beausire has the misfortune to take the dark one; all he has to do is to shift."

"If there is time, what must I do?" asked the bully.

"Suppose one thing," said the gentleman; "that your conspiracy fails. Suppose that the accomplices of the masked man and the one in the brown cloak are arrested; we may suppose anything in these times—suppose they are doomed to death! Suppose—for Augeard and Bezenval have been acquitted, so that anything unlikely may come round nowadays—suppose that you are one of these accomplices; you have the halter round your neck, when—say what they like—a man always shows a little of the white feather about then——"

"Do have done, my lord! I entreat you, for I seem to feel the rope throttling me!"

"That is not astonishing as I am supposing it is round your neck! Suppose, then, that they say to you: 'Poor old Beausire, this is your own fault. Not only might you have dodged this Old Bony who clutches you in his claws, but gain a thousand louis to buy the pretty cottage under the green trees where you long to live with ever-lovely Oliva and merry little Toussaint, with the balance of what was partly spent for the purchase of your homestead. You might live, as you said, like a squire, in high boots in the winter and easy shoes the rest of the year; while, instead of this delicious lookout, you have the Execution-place, planted with two or three one or two-armed trees, of which the highest holds out its ugly branch unto you. Faugh! my poor Captain Beausire, what a hideous prospect!'"

"But how am I to elude it—how make the thousand to ensure my peace and that of dear Nicole and little Toussaint?"

"Your good angel would say: 'Why not apply to the Count of Cagliostro, a rich nobleman who is in town for his pleasure and who is weary of nothing to do. Go to him and tell him——"

"But I do not know where he lives! I did not even know he is in town; I did not know he was still alive!" protested Beausire.

"He lives ever. It is because you would not know these facts that he comes to you, my dear Beausire, so that you will have no excuse. You have merely to say to him: 'Count, I know how fond you are of hearing the news. I have some fresh for you. The King's brother is conspiring with Marquis Favras. I speak from full knowledge as I am the right-hand man of the marquis. The aim of the plot is to take the King away to Peronne. If your lordship likes to be amused, I will tell him step by step how the moves are played.' Thereupon the count, who is a generous lord, would reply: 'If you will really do this,

Captain Beausire, as all laborers are worthy of their hire, I put aside twenty-four thousand livres for a charitable act; but I will balk myself in this whim, and you shall have them on the day when you come and tell me either that the King shall be taken off or Marquis Favras captured—in the same way as you are given these ten louis—not as hand-money or as an advance, or a loan, but as a pure gift."

Like an actor rehearsing with the "properties," Cagliostro pulled out the weighty purse, stuck in finger and thumb and with a dexterity bearing witness to his experience in such actions, whipped out just ten pieces, neither more nor less, which Beausire—we must do him justice—thrust out his hand with alacrity to receive.

"Excuse me, captain," said the other, gently fencing off the hand, "we are only playing at Supposes."

"Yes, but through suppositions one arrives at the fact," responded the cardplayer, whose eyes glowed like burning coals.

"Have we reached this point?"

Beausire hesitated; let us hasten to say that it was not honor, fidelity to plighted word, or a pricked conscience which caused the wavering. Did our readers know Beausire, they would not want this denial. It was the simple fear that the count would not keep his word.

"I see what you are passing through," said the tempter.

"Ay, my lord, I shrink from betraying the trust a gentleman puts in me," replied the adventurer. "It is very hard," he seemed to say as he raised his eyes heavenward.

"Nay, it is not that, and this is another proof of the old saw that 'No man knows himself'," said the count. "You are afraid that I will not pay you the sum stated. The objection is quite natural; but I shall give security."

"My lord certainly need not."

"Personal security, Madam Legay."

"Oh, if the count promises, it is as good as done," said the lady.

"You see, sir, what one gains by scrupulously keeping one's promises. One day when the lady was in the same quandary as yourself, I mean the police were hunting after her, I offered her an asylum in my residence. The lady hesitated, fearing that I was no Joseph—unless so christened. I gave her my word to respect her, and this is true, eh?"

"I swear it, on my little Toussaint," said Oliva-Nicole.

"So you believe that I will pay the sum mentioned on the day when the King shall have been abducted or Marquis Favras arrested, to say nothing of my serving the running knot strangling him a while ago. For this affair, at all events, there shall be no halter or gibbet, for I cannot bind myself any farther. You understand: The man who is born to be—ahem!"

"My lord, it is as if the courts had awarded us the money," said the woman.

"Well, my beauty," said Cagliostro, putting the ten gold pieces on the table in a row, "just imbue the captain with this belief of yours."

He waved his hand for the gambler to confer with his partner. Their parley lasted only five minutes, but it was most lively. Meanwhile Cagliostro looked at the cards and the one by which tally was kept.

"I know the run," he observed, "it is that invented by John Law who floated the Mississippi Bubble. I lost a million on it."

This remark seemed to give fresh activity to the dialogue of Beausire and his light-o-love. At last Beausire was decided; he came forward to offer his hand to Cagliostro like a horse-dealer about to strike a bargain. But the other frowned.

"Captain, between gentlemen the parole suffices. Give me yours."

"On the faith of Beausire, it shall be done."

"That is enough for me," said the other, drawing out a diamond-studded watch on which was a portrait of Frederick the Great. "It is now a quarter to nine. At nine precisely you are expected under the Royale Place arcades, near Sully House. Take these ten pieces, pocket them, put on your coat and buckle on your sword—and do not keep them waiting."

"Where am I to see your lordship next?" inquired Beausire, obeying the instructions, without asking reiteration.

"In St. Jean's Cemetery, if you please. When we have such deadly matters to discuss the company of the dead is better than the living. Come when you are free; the first to arrive waits for the other. I have now to chat with the lady."

The captain stood on one foot.

"Be easy; I did not make bold when she was a single woman; I have the more reason to respect her since she is a mother of a family. Be off, captain."

Beausire threw a glance at his wife, by courtesy, at all events, tenderly hugged little Toussaint, saluted the patron with respect mixed with disquiet, and left the house just as Notre Dame clock bell was striking the three-quarters after eight.

CHAPTER XXV. DOWN AMONG THE DEAD

IT was nearly midnight when a man hesitatingly walked up to the iron gateway of St. Jean's burying-ground, in Croix Blanche Street.

As midnight boomed, he saw a spectre cross the grounds under the yews and cypresses, and, approaching the grating, turn a key harshly in the gatelock to show that, if he were a ghost and had the leave to quit his grave, he also had that to go beyond the cemetery altogether.

"Do you not recognize me, Captain B.?" queried the jesting voice of Cagliostro, "or did you forget our appointment?"

"I am glad it is you," said the man in the French Guards sergeant dress, breathing as if his heart were relieved of great weight. "These devilish streets are so dark and deserted that I do not know but it is better to run up against any body than not to meet a soul."

"Pshaw," returned the magician, "the idea of your fearing any thing at any hour of the day or night! You will never make me believe that of a man like you who would go anywhere with a sword by his side. However, step on this side of the railings, and you will be tranquil, my dear Captain Beausire, for you will meet no one but me."

Beausire acted on the invitation, and the key grated again in the lock, to fasten the gate behind him.

"Keep to this little path," continued Cagliostro, "and at twenty paces you will come upon a little broken altar, on the steps of which we can nicely manage our little business."

"Where the mischief do you see any path?" he grumbled, after starting with a good will. "I meet nothing but nettles tearing my ankles and grass up to my knees."

"I own that this cemetery is as badly kept as any I know of; but it is not astonishing, for here are buried only the condemned prisoners executed in the City, and no one plants flowers for such poor fellows. Still we have some undeniable celebrities here, my dear Beausire. If it were daylight I would show you where lies Bouteville Montmorency, decapitated for having fought a duel; the Knight of Rohan who suffered the same fate for conspiring against the Government; Count Horn broken on the wheel for murdering a Jew; Damiens who tried to kill Louis XVI., and lots more. Oh, you are wrong to defame St. Jean's; it is badly kept but it well keeps its famous ones."

Beausire followed the guide so closely that he locked steps with him like a soldier in the second rank with the predecessor so that when the latter stopped suddenly he ran up against him.

"Ah! this is a fresh one; the grave of your comrade Fleurdepine, one of the murderers of François the Assemblymen's baker, who was hanged a week ago by sentence at the Chatelet; this ought to interest you, as he was, like you, a corporal, a sergeant by his own promotion, and a crimp—I mean a recruiter."

The hearer's teeth chattered; the thistles he walked among seemed so many skeleton fingers stretched up to trip him, and make him understand that this is the place where he would have his everlasting sleep.

"Well, we have arrived," said the cicerone, stopping at a mound of ruins.

Sitting down on a stone he pointed out another to his companion, as if placed for a conversation. It was time, for the ex-soldier's knees were knocking together so that he fell rather than sat on the elevation.

"Now that we are comfortable for a chat," went on the magician, "let us know what went on under the Royale Place arches. The meeting must have been interesting?"

"To tell the truth, count, I am so upset that I really believe you will get a clearer account by questioning me."

"Be it so, I am easy going, and the shape of news little matters provided I get it. How many of you met at the arches?"

"Six, including myself."

"I wonder if they were the persons I conjecture to be there? Primo, you, no doubt."

Beausire groaned as though he wished there could be doubt on that head.

"You do me much honor in commencing by me, for there were very great grandees compared with me."

"My dear boy, I follow the Gospel: 'The first shall be last.' If the first are to be last, why, the last will naturally lead. So I begin with you, according to Scripture. Then there would be your comrade Tourcaty, an old recruiting officer who is charged to raise the Brabant Legion?"

"Yes, we had Tourcaty."

"Then, there would be that sound royalist Marquie, once sergeant in the French Guards, now sub-lieutenant in a regiment of the centre line. Favras, of course? the Masked Man? Any particulars to furnish about the Masked Man?"

The traitor looked at the inquirer so fixedly that his eyes seemed to kindle in the dark.

"Why, is it not—" but he stopped as if fearing to commit a sacrilege if he went farther.

"What's this? have you a knot in your tongue? Take care of being tongue-tied. Knots in the tongue lead to knots round the neck, and as they are slip ones, they are the worst kind."

"Well, is it not the King's b-b-brother?" stammered the other.

"Nonsense, my dear Beausire, it is conceivable that Favras, who wants it believed that he clasps hands with a royal prince in the plot, should give out that the Mask hides the King's brother, Provence, but you and your mate, Tourcaty, recruiting-sergeants, are men used to measure men by their height in inches and lines, and it is not likely you would be cheated that way."

"No, it is not likely," agreed the soldier.

"The King's brother is five feet three and seven lines," pursued the magician, "while the Masked Man is nearly five feet six."

"To a T.," said the traitor, "that occurred to me; but who can it be if not the King's brother?"

"Excuse me, I should be proud and happy to teach you something," retorted Cagliostro: "but I came here to be taught by you."

"But if your lordship knows who this man is," said the ex-corporal, becoming more at home, "might I ask his name?"

"A name is a serious thing to divulge," responded the strange man: "and really I prefer you should guess. Do you know the story of Œdipus and the Sphinx?"

"I went to see a tragedy of that title and fell asleep, unfortunately, in the fourth act."

"Plague take me, but you ought not to call that a misfortune!"

"But I lose by it now."

"Not to go into details, suffice it that Œdipus, whom I knew as a boy at one royal court and as a man at another, was predicted to be the murderer of his father and the husband of his mother. Believing King Polybius this father, he departed from his realm, but would not take a hint from me about the road. The result was that he met his own sire on the road where, as neither would turn out, a fight ensued in which he slew his father. Some time after he met the Sphinx. It was a monster with a woman's head on a lion's body which I regret never to have seen, as it was a thousand years after her death that I travelled that road. She had the habit of putting riddles to the wayfarers and eating those who could not read them aright. To my friend Œdipus she put the following:

"'What animal goes upon four legs at morning, two at noon and three at night?'"

"Œdipus answered off-hand: 'Man, who in the morning of life as a child crawls on all fours; as an adult walks upright; as an old man hobbles with a stick.'"

"That is so," exclaimed Beausire: "it crossed the sphinx!"

"She threw herself down a precipice and the winner went on to where he married his father's widow to accomplish the prophecy."

"But what analogy between the Sphinx and the Masked Man?"

"A close one. I propose an enigma; only I am not cruel like the Sphinx and will not devour you if you fail to guess. Listen: Which lord at the court is grandson of his father, brother of his mother and uncle of his sisters?"

"The devil!" burst forth Beausire, falling into a reverie. "Can you not also help me out here, my lord?"

"Let us turn from pagan story to sacred history, then. Do you know the tale of Lot?"

"Lot and the Pillar of Salt, and his daughters?"

"The same."

"Of course, I do. Wait a bit, do they not say that old King Louis XIV, and his daughter the Lady Adeliade———"

"You are getting warm, captain———"

"In that case the Masked Man would be Count Louis Narbonne!"

"Now that we are no longer in doubt about this conspirator, let us finish with the aim of the plot. The object is to carry off the King? And take him to Peronne? what means have you?"

"For money we have two millions cash———"

"Lent by a Genoese banker? I know him. Any other funds?"

"I know of none."

"So much for the money: now for the men."

"General Lafayette has authorized the raising of a legion to fly to the help of Brabant revolting against the Empire."

"Under cover of which you form a royalist legion? I see the hand of Lafayette in this," muttered Cagliostro. "But you will want more than a legion to carry out this plan—an army."

"Oh, we have the army. Two hundred horsemen are gathered at Versailles ready to start at the appointed hour: they can arrive in three columns at Paris by two in the morning. The first gets in to kill General Lafayette: the second to settle old Necker; the third will do for Mayor Baily."

"Good!" exclaimed the listener.

"This done, the cannons are spiked, and all rally on the Champs Elysées, and march on the Tuileries where our friends will be masters."

"What about the National Guards there?"

"The Brabant Column attends to them: it joins with it part of the Guards which has been bought over: four hundred Swiss, three hundred country friends, and so on. These will have taken possession of all the gates by help within. We rush in on the King, saying: 'Sire, the St. Antoine ward is in insurrection; a carriage is ready—you must be off!' if he consents, all right: if he resists, we hustle him out and drive him to St. Denis."

"Capital!"

"There we find twenty thousand infantry, with all the country royalists, well armed, in great force, who conduct the King to Peronne."

"Better and better. What do you do there?'

"The gathering there brings our whole array up to one hundred and fifty thousand men."

"A very pretty figure," commented the Chief of the Invisibles.

"With the mass we march on Paris, cutting off supplies above and below on the river. Famished Paris capitulates; the Assembly is kicked to pieces, and the King enjoys his own again on the throne of his fathers."

"Amen!" sang Cagliostro. "My dear Beausire," he went on, rising, "your conversation is most agreeable; but as they say of the greatest orators, when they have spoken all that is in them, nothing more is to be got. You are done?"

"Yes, my lord, for the moment."

"Then, good-night: when you want another ten louis call for them at my home, at Bellevue."

"At the Count of Cagliostro's?"

"No; they would not know who you meant. Ask for Baron Zannone."

"But that is the banker who cashed up the two millions on the King's brother's notes!" ejaculated Beausire.

"That is not unlikely; only I do such a large business that I have confounded it with the others. That is why it was not clear in my mind but now you remind me, I believe I did something of the kind."

Beausire went his way, stupefied that a banker could forget a matter of two millions, and beginning to believe that he was quite right in siding with the lender rather than with the borrower. He bowed lowly while the count favored him with a slight nod at the cemetery gateway.

CHAPTER XXVI. GAMAIN PROVES HE IS THE MASTER.

THE reader will not be much surprised, after the permission Lafayette gave for the King to have his locksmith call to relieve him of a trouble in lockmaking, that Gamain should present himself at the palace with his apprentice who gave the name of Louis Lecomte.

Though there was nothing in the pair aristocratic, King Louis ran to the forge door on hearing the announcement and bade them enter.

"Here I am," returned Gamain, with the familiarity of a crony.

Whether he was less used to royal company, or endowed by more respect for crowned heads under whatever attire they appeared, the boy kept on the sill, at a space from his master, with his cap in his hand near the door closed by the valet behind both.

He may have been better placed there to catch the gleam of glee in the King's dull eye, and to give unseen a respectful nod.

"Glad to see you, my old Gamain," said Louis; "I really did not look for you—I thought you had forgotten old times."

"And that is why you have taken on a 'prentice," said Gamain. "You did right enough to have help when I was not on hand, but unfortunately an apprentice is not a master."

"How could I help it? I was assured that you did not care to come near me from fear of injuring yourself."

"Faith, it was not hard to learn at Versailles that it was not healthy to be friend of yours—as witness that brace of your Lifeguardsman whom they cut off the heads of! ay, and by the same token had the Queen's barber Leonard dress them in the latest fashion, which I saw in a saloon at Secres."

A cloud passed over the royal brow and the apprentice hung his head.

"But folks say that you are getting on nicely since you came back to town, and that you can make the Parisians do anything you like; not that it is astonishing, for the Parisians are ninnies and the Queen is such a weedler when she likes to be."

Louis made no remark, but his cheeks were colored. The young man seemed pained by the locksmith's familiarity. After wiping his forehead with a handkerchief, rather fine for a locksmith's help, he approached the King to whom he said:

"Does your Majesty allow me to tell how we have Master Gamain here and how I am in your employment?"

"Yes, my dear Louis," said the King.

"That is the style! 'My dear Louis!' as long as your arm. To a fortnight's acquaintance, a workman, a 'prentice! why, what are you going to call me, who has known you these five and twenty years? who put the file in your fist? who am the master? this is the advantage of having white hands and a glib tongue."

"I will call you 'My good Gamain' if you like. I speak to the lad affectionately because I owe to him the joy of seeing my old master again: not because he speaks prettily or keeps his hands smooth, for you know I think nothing of these fine ways—but I like him for proving it was false what they said about my never seeing you any more."

"Well, it was not me that held back, but that wife of mine. She was always saying: 'Gamain, you have bad acquaintances, those who fly too high for you. It is not good to hobnob with aristocrats nowadays. We have a little property—look after it. Let us rear our young ones: and let the Dauphin learn locksmithing from others than you, if he wants to, like his father before him. There are plenty of smiths in France.'"

Louis glanced at the apprentice, and stifling a sigh, partly sad and partly rallying, said:

"No doubt, but there are few like you."

"Just what I said to the master when I called on him," said the young man, "I told him the King was making a hidden-bolt lock; and that he had got along very well till he came to the sliding bolt itself——"

"I should think so," interrupted Gamain: "bless you, the bolt is the backbone of a lock. It is not given to everybody to get over that difficulty."

"No, nor mine in passing the examination you put me through to be convinced I came from the King," replied the young man, laughing. "You said it was a trap laid by your enemies; but the twenty-five yellow boys sent by his Majesty convinced you. So off we started, and here we are."

"And welcome," said the royal smith, thanking the speaker with a glance; "and now, Master Gamain, as you appear in a hurry, let us tackle the job."

"You have hit it. I promised the mistress that I should be home by evening. Let us see this puzzler of a lock."

The King put in his hands a lock three-parts finished.

"Lord help us," said the man, grinning: "this is not a secret bolt but a trunk lock. You have three wards on it and the second ought to catch while the first is released by the key."

He was using the key as he spoke and the others contemplated his demonstration with awe for his learning.

"But the second ward catches, like the Assembly when you want it to do something your way and says: 'I won't budge.'"

"But there must be some way of getting over the fix," said the King.

"Of course; it would be a day's work to an ordinary workman but I will knock it off in a couple of hours. Only," said he, with the suspicious air of an artisan jealous of the secrets of the craft; "I want no fussing round me."

What Gamain desired was the yearning of the King. His loneliness would allow him a dialogue apart with the Apprentice.

"But you may need something?"

"I will set the footman trotting."

The King went himself to the door to acquaint François with the arrangement, and then led away the apprentice, Louis Lecomte, in whom the reader will have recognized Louis Bouille.

They went by a secret stairway into the royal study, where a table was covered by a large map of France, showing the King had been studying the route of the flight.

"Now that we are alone, count," said he, "let me compliment you on your skill and thank you for your dedication of services to me."

"And I ask to be excused for my apparel and the language I have had to use before you."

"You speak like a brave gentleman and your apparel covers a loyal heart in any case. But we have no time to lose. Even the Queen is ignorant of your presence here; nobody is listening; so to the point."

"Did not your Majesty send us a naval officer, the count of Charny, who brought a letter——"

"Insignificant," interrupted the monarch, "a mere introduction to a verbal communication."

"He fulfilled it and it was to make its performance certain that my father sent me to town to try to have an interview alone with your Majesty. The King can have the certainty of leaving France. My father is proud and happy of the honor done him."

"Now for the principal point; what says he of the project?"

"That it is hazardous and requires great precautions but is not impossible."

"Firstly, will not your father want the command over the adjoining districts?"

"It is his advice, but he would not like it to be thought personal ambition——"

"Pooh, do I not know his disinterestedness? did he explain about the best road to take?"

"In the first place he fears one thing: that many projects of flight have been proposed and that all these getting entangled, this one will meet some block which will be ascribed to fatality, when it will be the spite or the rashness of the other parties."

"I promise, my dear Louis, to let the parties intrigue around me; it is their want and a necessity of my position. While they are following these threads which will end in nothing but leading them astray we will follow our own route with no other confidants, with more security from our greater secresy. But I do not want to leave the kingdom altogether. It is hard for a sovereign to get back if he does so. I have decided on Montmedy as the place of retirement, which is in the centre of your father's command and at a suitable distance."

"Has your Majesty planned out the flight or is this but a sketch?" queried the count.

"Nothing is settled," replied Louis, "and all depends on circumstances. If I see the Queen and the Family running fresh dangers from the ruffians I will take an irrevocable decision."

"My father thinks the dangers of the journey will be diminished by dividing the passengers."

"Yes, but it is useless to discuss this point. In a solemn hour the Queen and I resolved to go together or not at all."

The envoy bowed.

"At the meet moment the King has but to issue the orders to have them executed," he said. "Now, for the route. There are three ways to Montmedy."

"I have marked them on the map. The best is through Reims, but I was consecrated there and would be recognized by many. I choose the Chalons Road via Vacennes and going round Verdun. Let the regiments be posted in the petty towns between Chalons and Montmedy: I see no inconvenience in the first detachment awaiting me in the former place."

"Sire, the location of the regiments will have to be settled. By the way, the King should know that there is no posting-house at Varennes."

"I am glad you are so well informed," observed the King, merrily; "it shows you have deeply studied the plans. But do not worry about such matters. Charny is my engineer, who has drawn up the maps and he will see to the supply of horses."

"And now, Sire, that all is arranged on the main lines," said the young conspirator, "will your Majesty allow me to quote some lines from an Italian author, which my father thought appropriate to the situation? They are:

"Delay is always prejudicial, and there is no wholly favorable time in any business; hence if one were to wait for a perfect chance, nothing would ever be done, or if done be bungled."

"That is Machiavelli," said the King. "I will remember the advice of that secretary to the Magnificent Republic of Venice. But hush! I hear steps—it is Gamain; let us go to meet him so that he may not think we were busy about something else than the cupboard the lock is for."

He opened the secret door, in time, for the master locksmith was there, with the lock in his hand and a grin on his face.

CHAPTER XXVII. THE FRIEND OF THE FALLEN.

AT eight that same evening, a workingman, holding his hand to his waistcoat pocket as though it contained money in larger quantity than usual, staggered out of the Tuileries Palace and meandered along the road to the Soapworks Wharfside. It was there a strolling ground with drinking resorts along the line. On Sundays and holidays, it was thronged; on other days lonesome.

This man passed the wine-stores with much difficulty but for a period temperance triumphed; but when it came to the twentieth saloon on the route, it was too much, and he entered the next one for—only one glass.

The demon of drink, against whom he had valiantly struggled, seemed embodied in a stranger who followed him closely and even went into the saloon with him, sitting opposite and apparently watching him succumb with glee.

Five seconds after the workman had resumed his road, this watcher was on his track.

But how can the drinkingman stop going downhill when he has taken a whet, and perceives with the amazement of the toper that nothing makes one so thirsty as taking a drink? Scarcely had he tottered a hundred paces before his thirst was so sharp that he had to slack it once more.

The result of these lapses from the path he had previously trod was that he reached deviously the highway beyond the Passy bars, where he felicitated himself on the road being tolerably free from temples of the God of Wine.

In his gladness he set up singing. Unfortunately the delight was ephemeral and the song of short duration.

He fell to muttering and then talking to himself, and the soliloquy was in the form of imprecations on unknown persecutors of whom the unsteady sot complained.

"Oh, the scoundrel! to give an old friend, a master, doctored wine—ugh! So, just let him send again for me to fix his locks, let him send his traitor of a workmate who gives me the go-by and I will tell him: 'It won't work this trip! let your Majesty fix up your own locks.' We shall see then if a lock is to be turned out as sleek as a decree. Oh, I'll give you all you want of locks, with three wards, confound the villain! the wine was salted, peppered—by heaven, it was poisoned! Hope I may be saved, but the wine was poisoned!"

So howling, overcome by the force of the poison, of course, the unfortunate victim laid himself at full length, not for the first time, on the road, mercifully carpetted thickly with mud.

On other occasions the drunkard had scrambled up alone; difficult to do but he had got through the difficulty with honor; but this third time, after desperate efforts, he had to confess that the task was beyond him. With a sigh, much resembling a groan, he seemed decided to sleep for this night on the bosom of our common Mother Earth.

No doubt the follower had waited for this period of doubt, disheartenment and weakness, for he approached him warily, went all round fallen greatness, and calling a hack, said to the driver:

"Old man, here's my friend who has shipped too heavy a cargo. Take this piece for yourself, help me to put the poor fellow in the straw of your coach where he will not soil the elegant cushions, and take him to your wine saloon at Sevres Bridge. I will get up beside you."

There was nothing surprising that the customer should sit up with the driver, as he appeared to be one of his sort. So, with the touching confidence men of the lower classes have for one another, the jarvey said:

"All right, but let us have a look at the silver, see!"

"Here you are, old brother," ventured the man without being in the least offended and handing over a six-livre crownpiece.

"But will there be a little bit beyond the fare for myself, my master?" inquired the coachman, mollified by the money.

"That depends how we get along. Let us get the poor chap in; shut the blinds, try to keep your pair of skeletons on their hoofs, and we will see when we get to Sevres, how you conducted us!"

"Now, I call this speaking to the purpose," returned the knight of the whip. "Take it easy, master! A nod is as good as a wink. Get upon the box and keep my Arabian steeds from bolting up the road; no jokes, they feel the want of a supper and are chafing to race home to the stables. I will manage the rest."

The generous stranger did as he was bid; the driver, with all the delicacy of which he was susceptible, dragged the sot up by the arms, jabbed him down between the seats, slammed the door, drew down the blinds, mounted the box again, and whipped up the barbs. With the funeral gait of night hack-horses they stumbled through the village of Point-du-Jour and reached the Sevres Saloon in an hour.

The house was shut up for the night, but the new-comer jumped down and applied such blows of the fist to the door that the inhabitants, however fond of slumber, could not enjoy it long under so much racket. The host, who was alone, finally got up in his night dress, to see the rioter and promised to pack him off smartly if the game were not worth the candle.

Apparently though the value of the game was clear, for, at the first whisper by the irreverent arouser to the landlord, he plucked off his cotton nightcap and made bows which his scanty costume rendered singularly grotesque. He hastened to pilot the coachman, lugging Gamain, into the little taproom where he had once filled himself with his favorite burgundy.

As the driver and his steeds had done their best, the stranger gave the former a piece of money as extra.

Then seeing that Master Gamain was stuck up in a chair, with his head on the table before him, he hastened to have the host bring him two bottles of wine and a decanter of water, and opened the windows and blinds to change the mephitic air which the common people like to breathe in such resorts.

After bringing the wine, with alacrity, and the water, with reluctance, the host respectfully retired and left the stranger with the drunkard.

Having renewed the air, as stated, the former clapped smelling salts to Gamain's nose which ceased to snore and gave a sneeze. This awakened him a little from that disgusting sleep of drunkards the sight of which would cure them—if by a miracle, they could see what they look like at such periods.

Gamain opened his eyes widely, and muttered some words, unintelligible for anybody but the philologist who distinguished by his profound attention these words:

"The scoundrel—he—poisoned—poisoned wine——"

The good Samaritan seemed to see with satisfaction that his ward was under the same impression: he gave him another sniff of the hartstorn which permitted the son of Noah to complete the sense of his phrase in an accusation pointing to an abuse of trust and wanton heartlessness.

"To poison a friend—an old friend!"

"That's so—it is horrible," observed the other.

"Infamous," faltered Gamain.

"What a good thing I was handy to give you an antidote," suggested the hearer.

"It was lucky," said the locksmith.

"But as one dose is not enough, have another," said the stranger, putting a few drops from the smelling bottle in a glass of water; it was ammonia and the man had hardly swallowed the compound than he opened his eyes immeasurably and gurgled between two sneezes:

"Ah, monster, what are you giving us there? augh, augh!"

"My dear fellow, I am giving you stuff that will save your life," returned the kind friend.

"If it is physic, that is all right," said Gamain: "but it is a beastly failure if you call it a drink."

216

The stranger profited by his sneezing again and twitching his features, shut the blinds though not the windows.

Looking round him the master locksmith recognized with the profound gratitude of drinking men for old haunts, the saloon where he had feasted before. In his frequent trip to town from Versailles, he had not seldom halted here. It might be thought necessary, as the house was halfway.

This gratitude produced its effect: it gave him a great confidence to find himself on friendly ground.

"Hurrah, it looks as though I were halfway home anyway," he exclaimed.

"Yes, thanks to me," said the stranger.

"Thanks to you? why, who are you?" stammered Gamain, looking from still life to animated things.

"My dear Gamain, your question shows that you have a poor memory."

"Hold on," said the smith, giving him more attention: "it strikes me that I have seen you before."

"You don't say so? that is a blessed thing."

"Ay, but where—that is the rub."

"Look around you, then; something may remind you; or had you better have some more of the counterbane to refresh you?"

"No, thank 'ee, I have had enough of that remedy," said Gamain, stretching his arms out. "I am so nearly brought round that I will do without it. Where did I see you? why, in this very spot, of course. And when? the day I was coming back from doing a special job at Paris—I seem to be in for this sort of thing," added he, chuckling.

"Very well: but who am I?"

"A jolly honest mate who paid for the liquor. Shake hands!"

"Good, good, you remember now."

"With all the more pleasure as it is but a step from Master locksmith to master gunsmith," said the other.

"Ah, good, good, I remember now. Yes, it was the sixth of October, when the King went to Paris: we talked about him."

"And I found your conversation interesting, Master Gamain; so that, as your memory comes home and I want to enjoy it again, I should like to know, if I am not too inquisitive, what the deuse you were doing across the road where a vehicle might have cut you in two? Have you sorrows, old blade, and had you screwed up your mind to suicide?"

"Faith, no! What was I doing flat across the road, eh? Was I in the road?"

"Look at your clothes."

"Whew!" whistled Gamain after the inspection. "Mother Gamain will kick up a hullabaloo for she said yesterday: 'Don't put on your new coat; any old thing will do for the Tuileries.'"

"Hello? been to the Tuileries? were you coming from the Tuileries when I picked you up?" asked the kind soul.

"Why, yes, that's about the size of it," responded Gamain, scratching his head and trying to collect his entangled ideas; "certainly I was coming home from the Tuileries. Why not? It is no mystery that I am master locksmith to Master Veto."

"Who is he?"

"Why, have you come from China? not to know old Veto?"

"What do you want? I am obliged to stick to my trade, and that is not politics."

"You are blamed lucky! I have to mix up with these high folk—more's the pity! or rather, they force me to mix with them. It will be my ruin." He sighed as he looked up to heaven.

"Pshaw! were you called to Paris again to do another piece of work in the style of that other one?" asked the friend.

"But this time I was not blindfolded but taken with my eyes open."

"So that you knew it was the Tuileries this time?"

"The Tuileries? who said anything about the Tuileries?"

"Why, you, of course, just now. How would I know where you had been carousing had you not told me?"

"That is true," muttered Gamain to himself; "how should he, unless I told him? Perhaps," he said aloud, "I was wrong to let you know; but you are not like the rest. Besides I am not going to deny that I was at the Tuileries."

"And you did some work for the King, for which he gave you twenty five louis," went on the other.

"Indeed, I had twenty-five shiners in my pouch," said Gamain.

"Then, you have got them now, my friend."

The smith quickly plunged his hand into his pocket and pulled it out full of gold mixed with small change in silver and bronze.

"To think that I had forgot it! twenty-five is a good bit, too—and it is right to the 'broken' louis—one does not pick up such a lot under the horse's foot. Thank God the account is correct." And he breathed more freely.

"My dear Master Gamain, I told you I found you on the King's highway, not twenty paces from a heavy wagon which would have cut you in twain. I shouted for the carrier to pull up; I called a passing cab; I unhooked one of the lamps and as I looked at you by its light, I caught sight of a gold piece on the ground; as they were near your pocket, I judged that you had dropped them. I put my finger in the pocket and as there were a score of their brothers in bed there I guessed that these were of the same brood. Thereupon the hack driver shook his head. 'I ain't going to take this fare,' said he: 'he is too rich for his dress. Twenty louis in gold in a cotton waistcoat suggests that the gallows will be his end.' 'What,' says I, 'do you take him for a thief?' The word struck you, for you says. 'Thief? you are another!' says you. 'So you must be a prig,' returned the coachman, 'or how would the likes of you have a pocket gold-lined, say?'

"'I have money because my pupil the King of France gave it me,' said you. By these words I thought I recognized you, and clasping the lamp to your nose, I cried: 'Bless us and save us: all is clear; this is Master Gamain, master locksmith at Versailles. He has been working in the royal forge and the King has given him twenty-five mint-drops for his trouble. All right: I will answer for him.' From the moment that I answered for you, the driver raised no objections. I replaced the coins in your pocket; we laid you snugly in the hack; and we set you down in this retreat so that you have nothing to complain of except that your 'prentice left you in the lurch."

"Did I speak of my 'prentice? that he left me in the lurch?" questioned Gamain, more and more astonished.

"Why, hang it all, are you going back on what you said? Did you not growl that it was all the fault of—of—dash me if I can remember the name you used."

"Louis Lecomte?"

"I guess that was it. Did you not say: 'Louis Lecomte is in fault! for he promised to see me safe home and at the last moment he dropped me like a hot roll?'"

"I daresay I did so, for it is the blessed truth."

"Then, why do you deny the truth? let me tell you, that with another than me, such chatter would be dangerous?"

"But with you, one is safe, eh? with a regular friend," said the smith, coaxingly.

"Lord, you have lots of trust in your friend. You say yes and you say no; you wiggle and waver so that none knows how to have you. It is like your fable t'other day about the secret door that a nobleman had you fit on the strict quiet."

"Then you will not believe this tale either, for it also hangs upon a door."

"In the palace?"

"In the King's palace. Only instead of its being a clothes-press door, or rather that of a safe in the wall, it is a cupboard door this time."

"Are you gaming me that the King, while he certainly dabbles in locksmithery, sent for you to do up a door?"

"He did, though. Poor fellow, he thought he was smart enough to get on without me, and began to make a lock. 'What good is Gamain anyhow?' but he got mixed up with the works in the lock and had to fall back on Gamain after all."

"So you were hunted up by one of his trusty flunkeys, Hue, or Durey or Weber, eh?"

"That is just where you make a mistake. He has taken a green hand on to help him, who is as much of an amateur as himself; a young sprig who popped in upon me one morning at Versailles, and says he: 'Look here, Daddy Gamain, the King and me tried to make a lock, and by Jove we have made a muddle of it. The old thing won't work! 'What have I to do with it?' I wanted to know. 'You are wanted to set it right,' says he, and as I said that it was a plant and he did not come from the King, he slaps some gold on the bench and says: 'Is not this earnest enough? here are twenty-five louis which the King sends you to remove any doubts.' He gave me them, too."

"So these are what you are sporting round with you?"

"No: these are another lot. These were for traveling expenses and a sort of a payment on account!"

"Fifty louis for filing up an old lock? there is a snake in the grass, Friend Gamain."

"Just what I said to myself: particularly as the 'prentice does not seem a regular craftsman but dodged my question about work and where you stop when you are on tramp in France, as well as who is Mother Marianne."

"But you are not the man to be taken in when you see a boy at work."

221

"I do not say so much as that. The lad plied the file and the chisel handily. I have seen him cut a rod of iron through velean at a blow, and put a hole in a band with a rattail file as if using a gimlet on a lath. But there is more theory than practice about his style: he no sooner finishes the job than he washed his hands, and what hands? so white that never did a locksmith boast the like. You don't see me scrubbing my hands till they are white!"

With pride he showed his grubby, black and callous hands which indeed seemed to defy all the cosmetics and skin-bleaches in the world.

"But in short what did you do when you got to the King's?" asked the other, bringing the man to the point most interesting to him.

"It looked as though we were expected: in the forge the King showed me a lock commenced not badly, but he had got in a corner. It was one with three wards, d'ye see, which few locksmiths can grapple with and royal ones least of all. I looked at it and saw where the key caught. 'All right,' I says; 'let me alone with it for an hour and it will work as if greased.' 'Go ahead,' said the King, 'consider yourself at home; call for anything you like while we get the cupboard ready on which the lock goes.' On which he went out with the imp of a 'prentice."

"By the main stairs?" queried the gunsmith carelessly.

"No: by a secret one leading to his study. When I got through, I had done something, too; I said to myself: 'It is all bosh about this here cupboard; they are laying their heads together for some mischief.' So I crept down softly and opening the study door, I got a glimpse of what they were up to."

"And what were they up to?" inquired the gunsmith.

"Well, I did not catch them in the act, for they must have heard me coming, for I have not the light step of a dancer. They pretended to be up and coming to me, and the King said, 'Oh this is you, and you have finished? Come along for I have something else for you to do.' So he hurried me through the study, but not so fast that I did not spy spread out on a table a big map which I believe to be France on account of a lily-flower printed in one corner. From the midst three rows of pins ran out to the edges like files

222

of soldiers, for they were stuck in at regular spaces."

"Really, you are wonderfully sharp," said the stranger in affected admiration: "So you believe that instead of bothering about their cupboard, they were busy with this map?"

"I am sure of it: the pins had wax heads of different colors, black, blue and red; and the King was using a red one to pick his teeth with, without thinking what he was about."

"Gamain, if I discovered some new kind of gun, hang me if I would let you come into my workshop, even to pass through it, or I would bandage your eyes as on the day you were taken to the great nobleman's house though you did perceive that the house had ten steps to the stoop and that it fronted on the main avenue."

"Wait a bit," said the smith, enchanted at the eulogies; "you have not heard all—there is really a safe in the wall."

"What wall?"

"Of the inner corridor running from the royal alcove to the young prince's room."

"What you say is very queer. And was this safe open?"

"Is it likely? I squinted round in all ways but it was no use my asking myself: 'Where on earth is this secret press?' Then the King gave me a look and says he: 'Gamain, I have always had trust in you. So I would not let anybody but you know the secret.' While speaking, the King lifted a panel, while the boy held a light, for the corridor has no windows, and showed me a two foot round hole. Seeing my astonishment, he winked to our companion and said: 'Do you see that hole, my friend; I made it to keep money in; this young fellow helped me during the four or five days he has been staying in the palace. Now we want the lock put on the panel so that it will be hidden and not interfere with its sliding. Do you want an aid, in which case this young man will help you? or can you do without? if so I will set him to work elsewhere. 'Tut,' I said, 'you know that I like to go alone when I am the job.

223

It is four hour's work for a good hand but I am a master and will be through in three. Go and attend to your work, young fellow; and your Majesty may stick to his. And in three hours fetch along anything you want kept in this meat-safe.'

"We may believe the young chap had other fish to fry, for I saw nothing more of him: but when the time was up, the King came back. 'U. P., it is all UP!' said I, and I made him see that the door slid without the lock being in the way as neat as the Automatons of Vaucanson. 'Good,' said he; 'just help me count the cash I am going to bestow here.' A valet brought four fine bags of coin and we reckoned a million a-piece; there were twenty-and-five over. 'There you are, Gamain,' said the King, 'Take them for your trouble!' as though it was not disgraceful to give an old mate a beggarly twenty-five—a man with five children, and he has been handling two millions! What do you think of that?"

"The truth is that this is mean," said the other, shrugging his shoulders.

"Wait, this is not all. I put the coin in my pocket and said. 'I thank your Majesty: but Lord love you, I have not had sup or bite since morning and I am ready to burst!' I had barely finished before the Queen walked in by a secret door, so that she was on the top of us without saying Lookout! She had a platter in her hand with a cake and a glass on it.

"'My dear Gamain, as you are hungry and thirsty, try our wine and cake!' 'Sorry to trouble you, Royal Madam,' I said, but just think of a drop like that and a mouthful of wine like that fancy cake for a man. What do you expect sensible in that line from a Queen, though? it is plain that such folks are never really hungry and athirst. A glass of wine—oh, dear!"

"So you refused it?"

"It would have been better if I had; but I drank. As for the cake I rolled it up in my handkerchief, saying 'What is no good for the father will do for the children.' Then I thanked his Majesty, as though it were worth thanks, and I started off, saying that they will not catch me in their old palace in a hurry again."

"And why do you say you had better have refused the drink?"

"Because they had put poison in it! Hardly had I got over the bridge before I was seized by thirst, such a raging thirst that between the liquor saloons and the river, I balanced myself. I could tell it was queer stuff they gave me for the more I took the thirstier I was. This kept on with my trying to correct that dose till I lost my senses. They may be easy on this score: if ever they come to me for a good character, I will say they gave me twenty-five louis for four hours' work and counting a million, and for fear I should tell where they keep their treasure, they poisoned me like a dog!"

"And I, my dear Gamain," said the hearer, rising as though he had all the information he wanted: "I will support your evidence by swearing that I saved you with the antidote."

"That is why we are sworn comrades till death do us part," exclaimed the smith, grasping the speaker's hands.

Refusing with Spartan sobriety the wine which his friend offered him for the third or fourth time—for the amoniacal dose had sobered him as well as disgusted him with drink for a time, Gamain took the road for Versailles where he arrived safely at two in the morning with the King's coin in his pocket and the Queen's cake in another.

Left behind in the saloon, the pretended gunsmith drew out a set of tablets mounted in diamonds and gold, and wrote with fluid-ink pencil these two notes:

"An iron safe behind the King's alcove, in the unlighted passage leading to the prince's rooms. Make sure whether Louis Lecomte, locksmith's boy, is not really Count Louis, son of Marquis Bouille, arrived eleven days ago from Metz."

CHAPTER XXVIII. THE FIRST GUILLOTINE.

ON Christmas Eve, a party was given at the Princess Lamballe's, which the Queen's presiding over made it really her own reception.

Isidore Charny had returned from Italy that morning and he had found King and Queen very kind to him. Two reasons influenced the latter: one his being the brother of Count Charny, which was a charm in his absence, and his bringing back news from the fugitive princes which suited her wishes.

They backed the Favras scheme and urged her to flee for Turin.

He left her only to go and acquaint Favras with the encouragement. The Queen had said nothing positive about the flight: but he took enough to the conspirator to fill him with joy. For the rest, the cash was in hand, the men notified to stand ready, and the King would only have to nod to have the whole plot set in motion.

The silence of the royal couple was the only thing which worried him. The Queen broke this by sending Isidore, and vague as were the words he repeated, they acquired weight from coming out of a royal mouth.

At nine the young viscount went to Lady Lamballe's.

Count Provence was uneasy; Count Louis Narbonne walked about with the ease of a man quite at home among princes. Isidore was not known to any of the circle of the princes' bosom friends, but his well-known name and the partiality accorded him by the princess led to all hands being held out to him.

Besides, he brought news from the foreign refuge where so many had relatives.

When he had delivered his budget, the conversation returned to its former channel; the young men were laughing about a machine for executing criminals which Dr. Guillotin had shown in a full size working model and had proposed to the National Assembly.

When an usher announced the King, and another the Queen, of course all the merriment and chatter ceased.

The more the revolutionary spirit stripped majesty of its eternals the more the true royalists vied with each other to pour evidences of respect upon the august chiefs. 1789 saw great ingratitude, but 1793 great devotion.

To talk over the Favras scheme in secret a whist party was made up of the two rulers, Provence and Charny for the fourth hand. Respect isolated the table.

"Brother," said the Queen, "Lord Charny, who comes from Turin, says that our kinsfolk there are begging us to join them."

The King gave a stamp with impatience.

"I entreat you to listen," whispered Lady Elizabeth, who sat on a stool.

"Listen to what?"

"That Lord Charny has also seen the Marquis Favras since he came home, a gentleman whose lealty we know, and he says that the King has but to say a word," went on the Queen, "or make a sign, and this very night, you will be at Peronne."

The King kept still. His brother twisted a jack of hearts all to rags.

"Repeat this as the marquis put it," said he to Isidore.

"Your Majesty, thanks to measures taken by Marquis Favras, he declares that the King has but the cue to give to be in safety in Peronne this blessed night."

Turning sharply on his brother, the King said as he fixed his eyes on him:

"Are you coming if I go?"

"I" said the other, turning pale and trembling. "I have not been notified, and I have made no preparations."

"You know nothing about it, and yet you found the money for Favras?"

exclaimed the monarch. "You not notified, and the moves in the game have been reported to you hour by hour?"

"The game?" faltered the prince.

"The plot; for it is one of those plots for which, if discovered, Favras will be tried and doomed to death—unless by money and other means we save him as we did Bezenval."

"Then you will save Favras."

"No; for I might not be able to do as much for him. Besides, Bezenval was my liege as Favras is yours. Let each save his own man, and both of us shall have done our duty."

He rose, but the Queen retained him by the skirt of the coat.

"Sire, whether you accept or refuse, you owe the marquis an answer. What is Viscount Charny to answer for the King?"

"That the King does not allow himself to be spirited away like a slave for the Louisiana plantations." He disengaged his coat.

"This means," said Provence, "that the King will not allow of the abduction but if it be executed in spite of his permission, it will be welcome. In politics success condones the crime and blunderers deserve double punishment."

"Viscount," said the Queen, "tell the marquis what you heard and let him act as he thinks it points. Go."

The King had gone over to where the younger men were so hilariously chatting; but the deepest silence fell at his approach.

"Is the King so unhappy that he casts melancholy around him?" he demanded.

"Sire!" muttered the gentlemen.

"You were very merry when the Queen and I came in. It is a bad thing for kings when no one dares laugh before them. I may say the converse:

228

'Happy are the kings before whom laughter resounds.'"

"Sire," returned one, "the subject is not one for a comic opera."

"Of what were you talking?"

"Sire, I yield the guilty one to your Majesty," said another, stepping forward.

"Oh, it is you, Editor Suleau," said the King. "I have read the last number of your journal the Acts of the Apostles. Take care that you do not offend Master Populus."

"I only said that our Revolution is going so slowly that it has to help on that in Brabant. We are lamenting the dulness of the session of the Assembly where they had to take up the motion of Dr. Guillotin upon—of all things—a new machine for public executions."

"Are you making fun of Dr. Guillotin—a philanthropist? remember that I am one myself."

"There are various kinds; the sort I approve of has a representative at the head of the French Nation—the one who abolished torture before trial: we venerate, nay, we love him."

The hearers bowed with the same impulse.

"But," proceeded Suleau, "there are others who try to find means to kill the hale while they had a thousand to send the ailing out of this life. I beg your Majesty to let me deal with them?"

"What would you do? decapitate them painlessly, or at least merely give a slight coolness round the neck?" inquired the King, quoting Dr. Guillotin's recommendation of his invention.

"Sire, I should like all of these inventors to have the first experiment tried on themselves. I do not complain that Marigny was hanged on the Gibbet of Montfaucon which he built. I am not asking, I am not even a judge; the probability is that I shall have to take my revenge on Dr. Guillotin in the columns of my paper. I will give him a whole number and propose that the machine shall bear his name for eternity, the Guillotine!"

"Ha, ha, the Guillotine!" exclaimed the men, without waiting for express permission to laugh.

"I shall assert, also, that life is divided not extinguished by this process," continued Suleau; "why may not the sufferer feel pain in the head and the trunk after being cut in two?"

"This is a question for medical men. Did none of us here witness the experiment this very morning at Bicetre madhouse?" asked the King.

"No, no, no!" cried many voices.

"Sire, I was there," said one grave voice.

"Oh; it is you? Dr. Gilbert," said the sovereign, turning.

"Yes, Sire."

"And how did the experiment succeed?"

"Perfectly in two instances; but at the third the instrument, though it severed the spine, did not detach the head. They had to finish with a knife."

The young gentlemen listened with frightened eyes and parted lips.

"Three executions this morning?" exclaimed Charles Lameth, who with his brother had not yet turned against the Queen.

"Yes, gentlemen," said the King; "but they were three corpses furnished by the hospitals. What is your opinion of the instrument?"

"An improvement on such machines; but the accident at the third experiment proves that it stands in need of improvement still."

"What is it like?" asked the royal locksmith who had a bias for machines.

Gilbert helped his explanation out by drawing a sketch on a sheet of paper at a table. The King saw how curious the bystanders were and allowed them to come near.

"Who knows," said Suleau obeying, "but that one of us may make the

230

acquaintance of Lady Guillotine?"

Laughing, they pressed round the board where the King, taking the pen from Dr. Gilbert, said:

"No wonder the experience failed, particularly after awhile. The cutting blade is crescent-shaped whereas it ought to be triangular to sever a resisting substance. See here: shape your knife thus, and I wager that you would cut me off twenty-four heads one after another without the edge turning up."

He had scarcely finished the words before a heart-rending scream was heard. The Queen had been attracted to the group of which the King and his corrected sketch were the centre. She beheld the same instrument which had been presented her in its likeness in a glass of water by Balsamo the Magician twenty years before!

At the view she had no strength to do more than scream, and life abandoning her as though she were under the blade, she swooned in the arms of Dr. Gilbert.

It is easily understood that this incident broke up the party.

Gilbert attended to the royal patient who was given the bed of the princess. When the crisis was over, which he rightly attributed to a mental cause, he was going out but she bade him stay.

"Therese," she added to Lady Lamballe, "tell the King that I have come to: and do not let us be interrupted: I must speak with the doctor. Doctor," she pursued when they were alone, "are you not astonished that chance seems to place us face to face in all the crises moral or physical of my life?"

"As I do not know whether to be sorry or to be glad for it, since I read in your mind that the contact is not through your wish or your will."

"That is why I said chance. I like to be frank. But the last time we were in contiguity, you showed true devotion and I thank you and shall never forget it."

He bowed.

"I am also a physiognomist. Do you know that you have said without speaking: 'That is over; let us change the subject.'"

"At least I felt the desire to be put to the test."

"Doctor, what do you think of the recent event?" inquired Marie Antoinette as though this was interlinked with what she had spoken.

"Madam, the daughter of Maria Theresa is not one of the women who faint at trifles."

"Do you believe in forewarnings?"

"Science repels all phenomena tending to upset the prevailing order of things; still, facts offtimes give the lie to science."

"I ought to have said; do you believe in predictions?"

"I believe that the Supreme Being has benevolently covered the future with an impenetrable veil. Still," he went on as if making an effort over himself to meet questions which he wished relegated into doubt, "I know a man who sometimes confounds all the arguments of my intelligence by irrefutable facts. I dare not name him before your Majesty."

"It is your master, the immortal, the all-powerful, the divine Cagliostro, is it not, Dr. Gilbert?"

"Madam, my only master is Nature. Cagliostro is but my saver. Pierced by a bullet in the chest, losing all my blood by a wound which I, a physician, after twenty years study, must pronounce incurable, he cured me in a few days by a salve of which I know not the composition: hence my gratitude to him, I will almost say my admiration."

"And this man makes predictions which are accomplished?"

"Strange and incredible ones; he moves in the present with a certainty which makes one believe in his knowledge of the future."

"So that you would believe if he forecast to you?"

"I should at least act as though it might happen."

"Would you prepare to meet a shameful, terrible and untimely death if he foreshowed it?"

"After having tried to escape it by all manner of means," rejoined Gilbert, looking steadily at her.

"Escape? No, doctor, no! I see that I am doomed," said the Queen. "This revolution is a gulf in which will be swallowed up the throne: this people is a lion to devour me."

"Yet it depends on you to have it couch at your feet like a lamb."

"Doctor, all is broken between the people and me; I am hated and scorned."

"Because you do not really know each other. Cease to be a queen and become a mother to them; forget you are daughter of Maria Theresa, our ancient enemy, the sister of Joseph our false friend. Be French, and you will hear the voices rise to bless you, and see arms held out to fondle you."

"I know all this," she replied contemptuously; "fawning one day, they tear the next."

"Because aware of resistance to their will, and hatred opposed to their love."

"Does this destructive element know whether it loves or hates? it destroys like the wind, the sea and fire, and has womanly caprices."

"Because you see it from on high, like the man in the lighthouse views the ocean. Did you go down in the depths you would see how steady it is. What more obedient than the vast mass to the movement of the tides. You are Queen over the French, madam, and yet you know not what passes in France. Raise your veil instead of keeping it down, and you will admire instead of dreading."

"What would I see so very splendid?"

"The New World blooming over the wreck of the Old; the cradle of Free France floating on a sea wider than the Mediterranean—than the ocean. O

God protect you, little bark—O God shield you, babe of promise, France!"

Little of an enthusiast as Gilbert was he raised his eyes and hands heavenward.

The Queen eyed him with astonishment for she did not understand.

"Fine words," she sneered. "I thought you philosophers had run them down to dust."

"No, great deeds have killed them," returned Gilbert. "Whither tends old France? to the unity of the country. There are no longer provinces, but all French."

"What are you driving at? that your united thirty millions of rebels should form a universal federation against their King and Queen?"

"Do not deceive yourself: it is not the people who are rebels but the rulers who have rebelled against them. If you go to one of the feasts which the people hold, you will see that they hail a little child on an altar—emblem of the new birth of liberty. Italy, Spain, Ireland, Poland, all the down-trodden look towards this child and hold out their enchained hands, saying: 'France, we shall be free because of you.' Madam, if it be still time, take this child and make yourself its mother."

"You forget that I am the mother of others, and I ought not do as you suggest—disinherit them in favor of a stranger."

"If thus it be," replied Gilbert with profound sorrow, "wrap your children up in your royal robe, in the war-cloak of Maria Theresa, and carry them with you far from France; for you spoke the truth in saying that the people will devour you and your offspring with you. But there is no time to lose—make haste!"

"You will not oppose?"

"I will further you in the departure."

"Nothing could fall more timely," said the Queen, "for we have a nobleman ready to act in this escape——"

234

"Do you mean Marquis Favras?" demanded Gilbert, with apprehension.

"Who breathed you his name—who communicated to you his project?"

"Oh, have a care, for a bloody prediction pursued him also."

"Of the same Prophet? what fate awaits him?"

"Untimely, terrible and infamous like that you mentioned."

"Then you speak truly—no time must be lost in giving the lie to this prophet of evil."

"You were going to tell Favras that you accepted his aid?"

"He was advised and I am awaiting his reply."

She had not long to wait, for Isidore Charny was ushered in by the Princess Lamballe.

"I am told that I may speak before Dr. Gilbert," said he. "Then, know that Marquis Favras was arrested an hour ago and imprisoned in the Chatelet."

Bright but despairing and full of ire, the Queen's glance crossed that of the doctor. All her wrath seemed spent in that flash.

"Madam," said Gilbert with deep pity, "if I can be useful in any way, make use of me. I lay at your feet my mind, my life, my devotion."

"Dr. Gilbert," she said in a slow and resigned voice, "is it your opinion that the death given by this dread engine is as sweet as the inventor asserts?"

He sighed and hid his face in his hands.

As the news of Favras' arrest had circulated over the palace in a few seconds, Count Provence went to his brother. His advice was that Favras should be repudiated and the King take the oath to the Constitution.

"But how can I swear fidelity to an incomplete Constitution?"

"The more easily," replied the schemer, with his false squint which came from the darkest sinuosities of his soul.

"I will," said the King: "this does not prevent my writing to Marquis Bouille that our plan is postponed. This will give Charny time to regulate the route."

For his part, Provence acted on part of his own suggestion: he repudiated Favras and received the thanks of the Assembly.

Favras was left alone save for Cagliostro who perhaps felt a little remorse that he had let the bravest in the conspiracy go so far in a mission which he had foredoomed to failure. But Favras would not accept rescue and met his death by hanging with unblemished courage and honor.

The King took the oath, as he had promised his brother, to the Constitution, yet in embryo. If he loved it so dearly already, what would he do when it was in shape?

The ten days following were days of rejoicing; joy in the Assembly; calm in Paris; altars built all over the town for passers to take oath after the royal precedent.

The Assembly commanded a Te Deum to be chanted in the Cathedral, where all gathered to renew the oath in solemnity.

"Why did you not go to the church?" sneered the Queen to her husband.

"Because I do not object to lying for a purpose, but I do not mean to perjure myself," said Louis XVI.

The Queen breathed again for until then she had believed in the monarch's honesty. She felt empowered by this perfidy to take the same path and it was after giving her hand for Mirabeau to kiss that this new leader for the court party vowed that the monarchy was saved.

Her forehead was swathed in a wet bandage, her eyes were wandering and her face flushed with fever. Amongst the incoherent words, the farmer thought he could distinguish the name of Isidore.

"I see that it is good time that I came home," he muttered.

He went forth, and was followed by Pitou, but Dr. Raynal detained the latter.

"I want you my lad," he said, "to help Mother Clement hold the patient while I bleed her for the third time."

"The third time?" cried Mrs. Billet, awaking from her dulness. "Do you hear that, my man, they bleed her for the third time."

"Woman, this would not have happened had you looked after your daughter closer," said the farmer in a stern voice.

He went to his room, from which he had been absent three months while Pitou entered the sick room.

Pitou was astonished but he would have felt more so if he had guessed that the doctor called him in as a moral remedy.

The doctor had noticed two names as used by the girl in her frenzy, Ange Pitou and Isidore Charny, and he soon distinguished that one was a friend's and the other a dearer one. He concluded that Pitou was the lovers' confidant and that there would be no inconvenience in the gallant's friend being there to speak with the patient on the mutual acquaintance.

Everybody knew down here that Valence Charny had been killed at Versailles and that his eldest brother had called away Isidore on the next evening.

That night Pitou found Catherine fainted on the high road. When she revived on the farm, it was to be in a fever, and she raved of some one riding away whom the doctor judged to be Isidore Charny.

The greatest need to a brain-stricken invalid is calm. To learn about her lover would best calm Catherine, and she would ask the news of their friend, Pitou.

On seeing the good effect of the bleeding, the doctor stationed Mother Clement by her side, with the strange recommendation for her to get some sleep, and beckoned Pitou to follow him into the kitchen.

Her forehead was swathed in a wet bandage, her eyes were wandering and her face flushed with fever. Amongst the incoherent words, the farmer thought he could distinguish the name of Isidore.

"I see that it is good time that I came home," he muttered.

He went forth, and was followed by Pitou, but Dr. Raynal detained the latter.

"I want you my lad," he said, "to help Mother Clement hold the patient while I bleed her for the third time."

"The third time?" cried Mrs. Billet, awaking from her dulness. "Do you hear that, my man, they bleed her for the third time."

"Woman, this would not have happened had you looked after your daughter closer," said the farmer in a stern voice.

He went to his room, from which he had been absent three months while Pitou entered the sick room.

Pitou was astonished but he would have felt more so if he had guessed that the doctor called him in as a moral remedy.

The doctor had noticed two names as used by the girl in her frenzy, Ange Pitou and Isidore Charny, and he soon distinguished that one was a friend's and the other a dearer one. He concluded that Pitou was the lovers' confidant and that there would be no inconvenience in the gallant's friend being there to speak with the patient on the mutual acquaintance.

Everybody knew down here that Valence Charny had been killed at Versailles and that his eldest brother had called away Isidore on the next evening.

That night Pitou found Catherine fainted on the high road. When she revived on the farm, it was to be in a fever, and she raved of some one riding away whom the doctor judged to be Isidore Charny.

The greatest need to a brain-stricken invalid is calm. To learn about her lover would best calm Catherine, and she would ask the news of their friend, Pitou.

238

On seeing the good effect of the bleeding, the doctor stationed Mother Clement by her side, with the strange recommendation for her to get some sleep, and beckoned Pitou to follow him into the kitchen.

"Cheer up, mother," said he to Mrs. Billet who was mooning in the chimney corner, "she is going on as well as possible."

"It is very hard that a mother cannot care for her child," said the farmer's wife.

"You are too fragile—we should only have you ill. She will get along finely with Mother Clement and Ange to look after her."

"Ange?"

"Yes, he has a leaning toward medicine and I shall make him my assistant. He is coming over to my place now to get a soothing potion made up. He will bring it back and direct the administration of it. He will remain on duty here, to run over to me with the news of any change."

"You know best, doctor; but give the poor father a word of your hope."

"Where is he?"

"In the next room."

"Useless," said a voice on the threshold, "I have heard all."

As though this was all he wanted, the pale-faced farmer withdrew and offered no opposition to this ruling of the house by the medical adviser.

The latter was not a light of science but he was a keen observer.

He had seen that Pitou would be the best confidant to place before his patient's eyes as soon as they opened to life and reason.

He was able with the first words to reassure her upon Isidore's health. There was no rioting in Paris and the young noble had gone off to Italy as a messenger.

He was sure to write to Catherine, she said, and she authorized him to go to the post for the letter.

As Pitou on the farm ate and drank with his accustomed appetite Billet did not suspect the treacherous part he was playing.

Consoled by the progress the girl made after the receipt of the beloved letter, Pitou was enabled to proceed with his public work.

With the money Gilbert gave him, he equipped the Haramont National Guards with new suits; this was for the ceremony of the Federation of Villers Cotterets and other villages of the canton, to be held on a following Sunday.

At this prospect of uniforms, the Guards assembled with their two minstrels and gave their liberal leader a serenade, interspersed with fire-crackers and cheers, among which was to be heard a voice or two, slightly tipsy, shouting:

"Long live Pitou, the Hero of the People!"

Remembering the impression the Haramont National Guard had created when they had hats alike, you can appreciate the justice in the roar of admiration when they appeared in uniforms, and what a dashing air the captain must have worn, with his little cap cocked over one ear, his gorget shining on his breast, his catspaws, as the epaules were irreverently called, and his sword.

Aunt Angelique could hardly identify her nephew who almost rode her down on his white horse.

But he saluted her with a wave of the sword and left her crushed by the honor.

Recalling that the tailor had boasted of the order which Pitou had paid, she thought he had come home a millionaire.

"I must not quarrel with him," she mumbled: "aunts inherit from nephews."

Alas! he had forgotten her by this time. Among the girls wearing tricolored sashes and carrying green palm boughs, he recognized Catherine.

She was pale, her beauty more delicate, but Raynal had fulfilled his word.

She was happy, for Pitou had managed to find a hollow tree where he deposited letters for her to take them out in a stroll, and that morning one was there.

Pitou came up and saluted her with his sword. He would have only touched his hat for General Lafayette.

"How grand you look in your uniform," she said loudly. "I thank you, my dear Pitou," she added in a voice for him alone; "how good you are. I love you!"

She took his hand and pressed it in hers. Giddiness passed into poor Pitou's head; he dropped his hat from the free hand, and would have fallen at her feet like the hat only for a great tumult with menacing sounds being heard towards Soissons.

Whatever the cause, he profited by it to get out of the awkward situation.

He disengaged his hand from Catherine's, picked up his hat and put it on as he ran to the head of his thirty-three men, shouting:

"To arms!"

It was an old enemy of his who was causing a block to the festivities.

Father Fortier had been designated to perform the office of celebrating the Federation Mass on the Altar of the Country, for which the holy vessels were to be carried from the church. The mayor, Longpre, was to superintend the transfer. Like everybody he knew the schoolmaster's temper and thought he would not bear him good will for the part he took in the turning over the muskets.

So, rather than face him, he had sent him an order in writing to be present for the mass at ten.

At half past nine he sent his secretary to see how things looked. The gentleman brought bad news. The church was locked up. The church officials were all laid up with various complaints. It had the air of a conspiracy.

At ten the crowd gathered and talked of beating in the church doors and taking out the church plate.

As a conciliator, Longpre quieted them as well as he could and went to knock at Fortier's housedoor.

In the meantime he sent for the armed forces. The gendarmes officers came up. They were attended by additions to the mob.

As they had no catapult to force the door, they summoned the locksmith. But when he was going to insert a picklock, the door opened and Abbé Fortier appeared, with fiery eye and hair bristling.

"Back," he cried with a threatening gesture, "back, heretics, impious relapsers! avaunt ye from the sill of the man of God!"

The murmur receiving his outburst was not flattering to him.

"Excuse me," said the unctuous mayor, "but we only wanted to know whether you would serve the mass on the altar of the country, or not?"

"Sanction revolt, rebellion and ingratitude," yelled the holy man in one of the fits of passion habitual to him: "curse virtue and bless sin? you cannot have hoped it, mayor. I will not say your sacrilegous mass!"

"Very well; this is a free country now—you need not unless you like."

"Free? ha, ha, ha!" and with a most exasperating laugh he was going to slam the door in their faces when a man burst through the throng, pushed the door nearly open again and all but overturned Fortier though he was a stout man.

It was Billet.

There was profound silence as all divined that not two mere men, but two forces were opposing each other.

Though Billet had displayed so much strength to open the door, he spoke in a calm voice:

"Pardon me, mayor, but I think I heard you say that the father might say the mass or not, at his pleasure? this is an error and it is no longer the time when errors are allowed to flourish. Every man who is paid to do work is bound to do it. You are paid by the country to say mass and you shall say it."

"Blasphemer, Manichean," roared the priest.

"You ought to set the example of obedience and here you are doing the other thing. If you are a citizen and a Frenchman, obey the nation."

"Bravo, Billet!" cried the multitude. "To the altar, with the priest."

Encouraged by the acclamations, Billet lugged out from his hall the first priest who had given the signal for counter-revolution.

"I am a martyr," groaned the priest, comprehending that resistance was impossible in the farmer's vigorous hands, "I call for martyrdom!" And as he was hurried along he sang "Good Lord, deliver us!"

This crowd conducting him was the cause of the turbulence towards which Pitou was marching his cohort. But on seeing the reason, he and Catherine appealed to the farmer with the same voice.

Untouched, the latter carried the prize up to the altar where he let him fall.

"I proclaim you unworthy to serve at this altar which you disdained," said Billet: "no man should go up these steps unless his head is filled with these feelings, the desire of liberty, devotion to the country and love of mankind. Priest, have you these sentiments? if so, go up boldly and invoke our Maker. But if you do not feel you are the foremost of us all as a citizen, give place to the more worthy, and be off!"

"Madman, you do not know what you are declaring war upon," hissed the priest, retiring with uplifted finger.

"I do know, if they are like you, vipers, foxes, wolves," returned Billet: "all that sneak and poison and tear in the shade. Come at me, then—I can face ye, in the open!" he concluded, smiting his broad chest.

During a silent moment the throng parted to let the priest skulk

243

through, and, closing, remained mute and admiring the vigorous man who offered himself as target to the terrible power to which half the world was enslaved at that era.

There was no longer mayor, town councilmen or gendarmes, only the Hero of the People, Billet.

"But we have no priest now," said Mayor Longpre.

"We do not want him," replied Billet who had never been in church but twice, for his wedding and his child's baptism. "We will read the Declaration of the Rights of Man from the altar. That is the Creed of Liberty and the Gospel of the Future."

Billet could not read but he had his manifesto by heart. When he had finished and with a noble movement embraced the Law and the Sword by taking the mayor's and Pitou's hands, the multitude appreciated the grandeur of what they were doing in shouting:

"Long live the Nation!"

It was one of the scenes of which Gilbert had spoken to the Queen without her understanding him.

From that time forward, France became one great family, with one heart and one language.

CHAPTER XXIX. UNDER THE WINDOW.

ON the surface all was calm and almost smiling on the Billet Farm.

As before, Billet, on his strong horse, trotted all over the land keeping his hands up to the mark. But a sharp observer would have noticed that on whatever part he was he tried to get a look at his daughter's room window.

Though his face had a little softened toward her, Catherine felt that paternal distrust hovered over her.

Mother Billet was vegetating as formerly; she did not know that her husband harbored suspicion in his bosom, and her daughter anguish in hers.

Pitou, after his glory as captain of the uniformed National Guards, had fallen back into his habitual state of sweet and kindly melancholy. By the postmark on Isidore's letters he noticed that he had returned to Paris.

He concluded that he would not be long before returning to his estate. Pitou's heart shrank at this prospect.

Under pretence of snaring rabbits to give his friend more succulent food than farm fare, he haunted the wood until he saw Catherine. She was seeking him, too, for she had a word for him.

He need not trouble about her letters as she would not be receiving any for some days.

He guessed that the writer was coming in person to repeat his vows.

"Have you noticed," he said, "how gloomy the master has become of late?"

Catherine turned pale.

"I tell you as a sure thing that whoever is the cause of this change in such a hearty good fellow, will have an unpleasant time with him when he meets him."

"You say, 'him,'" said Catherine; "why may he not have quarrelled with a woman, against whom he nurses this sullen rage?"

"You have seen something? have you any reason to fear?"

"I have to fear all that a girl may fear when she loves above her station and has an irritated father."

"It seems to me that in your place," Pitou ventured to give advice, "I should—no, it nearly killed you to part with him, and to give him up altogether would be your death. Oh, all this is very unfortunate!"

"Hush, speak of something else—here comes father."

Indeed, seeing his daughter with a man, the farmer rode up at speed: but recognizing Pitou, he asked him in to dinner with less gloom on his face.

"Gracious," muttered Catherine at the door, "can he know?"

"What?" whispered Pitou.

"Nothing," replied the girl, going up to her room and closing the shutters.

When she came down, dinner was ready, but she ate little.

"You might tell us what brought you our way to-day," asked the morose farmer of Pitou.

The latter showed some brass wire loops.

"The rabbits over our way are getting shy of me. I am going to lay some snares on your farm, if you do not mind. Yours are so tender from the grain they get."

"I did not know you had so sweet a tooth."

"Oh, not for me but for Miss Catherine."

"Yes, she has no appetite, lately, that is a fact."

At this moment, Pitou felt a touch to his foot. It was Catherine directing his attention to the window past which a man was making for the door where he entered with the farmer's gun on his shoulder.

"Father Clovis," he was hailed by the master.

Clovis was the old soldier who had taught Pitou to drill.

"Yes, Papa Billet, a bargain is a bargain. You paid me to pick out a dozen bullets to suit your rifle and here they are."

He handed the farmer his gun and a bag of bullets. Calm as the veteran was, he inspired terror in Catherine as he sat at table.

"By the way I cast thirteen bullets instead of a dozen so I squandered one on the hare you see. Your gun carries fine."

"Is there a prize for shooting offered anywhere?" asked Pitou simply. "You will win it, I guess like you did that silver cup and the bowl you are drinking of, Miss Catherine. Why, what is the matter?"

"Nothing," replied the girl opening her eyes which she had half closed and leaning back in her chair.

"All I know is," said Billet, "that I am going to lay in wait. It is a wolf, I think."

Clovis turned the bullets out on a plate. Had Pitou looked from them to Catherine he would have seen that she nearly swooned.

"Wolf?" repeated he. "I am astonished that before the snowfalls we should see them here."

"The shepherd says one is prowling round, out Boursonne way."

Pitou looked from the speaker to Catherine.

"Yes, he was spied last year, I was told; but he went off, and it was thought forever; but he has turned up again. I mean to turn him down!"

This was all the girl could endure; she uttered a cry and staggered out of the door. Pitou followed her to offer his arm and found her in the kitchen.

"What ails you?"

"Can you not guess? he knows that Isidore has arrived at Boursonne this morning, and he is going to shoot him."

"I will put him on his guard——"

The voice of Billet interrupted the pair.

"If you are going to lay snares, Master Pitou, it seems to me it is time you were jogging. Father Clovis is going your way."

"I am off," and he went out by the kitchen door, while Catherine went up to her room, where she bolted the door.

The forest was Pitou's kingdom and when he had left Clovis to go home, he felt easy about what he had undertaken to do.

He thought of running to Boursonne and warning Viscount Isidore; but he might not be believed and the warning might not be heeded.

He considered he had better wait.

He had not a doubt that at the windows of Billet's room and of his daughter's, they two were on the alert. All the tragedy or its failure depended on him. If he let the viscount pass within rifle range, he would let him march to his death.

In fact, Billet, sure that the nobleman would not marry a farmer's daughter, had resolved to wipe out the insult done him in blood.

Suddenly Pitou, lying on the ground in a clump of willow, heard the gallop of a horse.

Billet must have heard it also for he came out of the house; and Ange had not a doubt that the willow copse which he had chosen to spy Catherine's window had for the same reason recommended itself to the farmer.

As the latter advanced, he slipped back and slid down into the ditch.

The horse crossed the road at sixty paces, and as a shadow was soon detached from it, the rider must have leaped off, and turned the steed loose. It went on without stopping.

There was ten minutes of dreadful silence.

The night was so black that Pitou, reckoning his eyes better than Billet's, hoped that he alone saw the shadow stealing towards the house.

But at the same moment, as the shadow went up under Catherine's window, Pitou heard the click of a hammer going on full cock on the gun.

The shadow did not notice but rapped three times on the shutter.

Pitou quivered—Catherine would surely blame him for not having passed the warning as he had promised.

But what could he do?

Pitou heard the hammer fall and saw the priming flash; the powder in the touchhole did not catch and the living target received no bullet.

At the same moment Catherine opened her window. She saw all and cried: "Up, it is my father!" she almost dragged Charny in at the casement.

The farmer had his second barrel to fire and he thought:

"He must come out and this time I will not miss him."

Presently the dogs began barking.

"Oh, the jade," he growled, "she has let him out at the back, through the orchard."

He ran round the house to overtake the escaping prey.

"There is hope," thought Pitou: "aim cannot be taken in the night as in the day and the hand is not so steady in firing on a man as at a wolf in the den."

Indeed, Billet had fired on a man whom he saw scaling the orchard wall but he had got away on a horse which came up at his whistle. While Billet was following the pair in vague hope that he had hurt the rider so that he must fall out of the saddle, Ange reached the orchard where he saw Catherine leaning up against a tree with her hand on her heart.

"Let me take you into the house," he said.

"No, I will not live under the roof of the man who shot at my sweetheart."

"But then——"

"Do you refuse to accompany me?"

"No, but——"

"Come."

No one saw them leave the farm and both disappeared in the valley.

God only knew the refuge of Catherine Billet!

All night a dreadful storm raged in the heart of the injured father. Something vital seemed to snap in the mighty frame of the man when he returned emptyhanded to see that his daughter had taken to flight.

When he came home at nine as usual to breakfast, his wife said. "Where is our Catherine?"

"Catherine?" he said with an effort. "The air is bad on the farm and I sent her over to her aunt's in Sologne."

"Good, she wanted a change. Will she make a long stay?"

"Till she gets better."

Drying her tears the good woman went to sit in the chimney corner while her husband rode off into the fields.

Dr. Raynal had passed a restless night also. He was roused by Viscount Charny's lackey pulling at his nightbell and, riding over to Boursonne, found that he had a couple of bullets in his side. Neither wound was dangerous, though one was serious. In three calls he set him up again; but he had to wear a bandage for a time, which did not prevent him riding out. Nobody had an idea of his accident.

It was time for him to be healed—time to return to Paris!

Mirabeau had promised the Queen to save her, and she wrote to her brother on the Austrian throne:

"I follow your counsel. I am making use of Mirabeau but there is nothing of weight in my relations with him."

On the following day, he saw groups on the way to the Assembly and went up to learn the nature of the outcries.

Little newsheets were passing from hand to hand and newsdealers were calling out:

"Buy the Great Treason of Mirabeau!"

"It seems this concerns me," he said, taking a piece of money out. "My friend," he said to one of the venders who had a donkey carrying panniers full of the sheets, "how much is this Great Treason of Mirabeau?"

"Nothing to you, my lord," replied the man, looking him in the eye, "and it is struck off in an edition of one hundred thousand."

The orator went away thoughtful. A lampoon in such an edition and given away by a newsman who knew him!

Still the sheet might be one of those catchpennys which abounded at that epoch, stupid or spiteful. No, it was the list of his debts, accurate, and the note that their 200,000 francs had been paid by the Queen's almoner on a certain date; also the statement that the court paid him six thousand francs per month. Lastly the account of his reception by the Queen.

What mysterious enemy pursued him, or rather pursued the monarchy like a hellhound?

This is what we shall learn, with many another secret which none but Cagliostro the superhuman might divine, in the sequel to this volume entitled "The Royal Lifeguard."

THE END

About Author

His father, General Thomas-Alexandre Dumas Davy de la Pailleterie, was born in the French colony of Saint-Domingue (present-day Haiti) to Alexandre Antoine Davy de la Pailleterie, a French nobleman, and Marie-Cessette Dumas, a black slave. At age 14 Thomas-Alexandre was taken by his father to France, where he was educated in a military academy and entered the military for what became an illustrious career.

Dumas' father's aristocratic rank helped young Alexandre acquire work with Louis-Philippe, Duke of Orléans, then as a writer, finding early success. Decades later, after the election of Louis-Napoléon Bonaparte in 1851, Dumas fell from favour and left France for Belgium, where he stayed for several years, then moved to Russia for a few years before going to Italy. In 1861, he founded and published the newspaper L'Indipendente, which supported Italian unification, before returning to Paris in 1864.

Though married, in the tradition of Frenchmen of higher social class, Dumas had numerous affairs (allegedly as many as forty). In his lifetime, he was known to have at least four illegitimate children; although twentieth-century scholars found that Dumas fathered three other children out of wedlock. He acknowledged and assisted his son, Alexandre Dumas, to become a successful novelist and playwright. They are known as Alexandre Dumas père ('father') and Alexandre Dumas fils ('son'). Among his affairs, in 1866, Dumas had one with Adah Isaacs Menken, an American actress then less than half his age and at the height of her career.

The English playwright Watts Phillips, who knew Dumas in his later life, described him as "the most generous, large-hearted being in the world. He also was the most delightfully amusing and egotistical creature on the face of the earth. His tongue was like a windmill – once set in motion, you never knew when he would stop, especially if the theme was himself."

Early life

Dumas Davy de la Pailleterie (later known as Alexandre Dumas) was born in 1802 in Villers-Cotterêts in the department of Aisne, in Picardy,

France. He had two older sisters, Marie-Alexandrine (born 1794) and Louise-Alexandrine (born 1796, died 1797). Their parents were Marie-Louise Élisabeth Labouret, the daughter of an innkeeper, and Thomas-Alexandre Dumas.

Thomas-Alexandre had been born in the French colony of Saint-Domingue (now Haiti), the mixed-race, natural son of the marquis Alexandre Antoine Davy de la Pailleterie, a French nobleman and général commissaire in the artillery of the colony, and Marie-Cessette Dumas, a slave of Afro-Caribbean ancestry. At the time of Thomas-Alexandre's birth, his father was impoverished. It is not known whether his mother was born in Saint-Domingue or in Africa, nor is it known from which African people her ancestors came.

Brought as a boy to France by his father and legally freed there, Thomas-Alexandre Dumas Davy was educated in a military school and joined the army as a young man. As an adult, Thomas-Alexandre used his mother's name, Dumas, as his surname after a break with his father. Dumas was promoted to general by the age of 31, the first soldier of Afro-Antilles origin to reach that rank in the French army. He served with distinction in the French Revolutionary Wars. He became general-in-chief of the Army of the Pyrenees, the first man of colour to reach that rank. Although a general under Bonaparte in the Italian and Egyptian campaigns, Dumas had fallen out of favour by 1800 and requested leave to return to France. On his return, his ship had to put in at Taranto in the Kingdom of Naples, where he and others were held as prisoners of war.

In 1806, when Alexandre was four years of age, his father, Thomas-Alexandre, died of cancer. His widowed mother, Marie-Louise, could not provide her son with much of an education, but Dumas read everything he could and taught himself Spanish. Although poor, the family had their father's distinguished reputation and aristocratic rank to aid the children's advancement. In 1822, after the restoration of the monarchy, the 20-year-old Alexandre Dumas moved to Paris. He acquired a position at the Palais Royal in the office of Louis-Philippe, Duke of Orléans.

Career

While working for Louis-Philippe, Dumas began writing articles for magazines and plays for the theatre. As an adult, he used his slave grandmother's surname of Dumas, as his father had done as an adult. His first play, Henry III and His Courts, produced in 1829 when he was 27 years old, met with acclaim. The next year, his second play, Christine, was equally popular. These successes gave him sufficient income to write full-time.

In 1830, Dumas participated in the Revolution that ousted Charles X and replaced him with Dumas' former employer, the Duke of Orléans, who ruled as Louis-Philippe, the Citizen King. Until the mid-1830s, life in France remained unsettled, with sporadic riots by disgruntled Republicans and impoverished urban workers seeking change. As life slowly returned to normal, the nation began to industrialise. An improving economy combined with the end of press censorship made the times rewarding for Alexandre Dumas' literary skills.

After writing additional successful plays, Dumas switched to writing novels. Although attracted to an extravagant lifestyle and always spending more than he earned, Dumas proved to be an astute marketer. As newspapers were publishing many serial novels, in 1838, Dumas rewrote one of his plays as his first serial novel, Le Capitaine Paul. He founded a production studio, staffed with writers who turned out hundreds of stories, all subject to his personal direction, editing, and additions.

From 1839 to 1841, Dumas, with the assistance of several friends, compiled Celebrated Crimes, an eight-volume collection of essays on famous criminals and crimes from European history. He featured Beatrice Cenci, Martin Guerre, Cesare and Lucrezia Borgia, as well as more recent events and criminals, including the cases of the alleged murderers Karl Ludwig Sand and Antoine François Desrues, who were executed.

Dumas collaborated with Augustin Grisier, his fencing master, in his 1840 novel, The Fencing Master. The story is written as Grisier's account of how he came to witness the events of the Decembrist revolt in Russia. The novel was eventually banned in Russia by Czar Nicholas I, and Dumas was prohibited from visiting the country until after the Czar's death. Dumas refers to Grisier with great respect in The Count of Monte Cristo, The Corsican

Brothers, and in his memoirs.

Dumas depended on numerous assistants and collaborators, of whom Auguste Maquet was the best known. It was not until the late twentieth century that his role was fully understood. Dumas wrote the short novel Georges (1843), which uses ideas and plots later repeated in The Count of Monte Cristo. Maquet took Dumas to court to try to get authorial recognition and a higher rate of payment for his work. He was successful in getting more money, but not a by-line.

Dumas' novels were so popular that they were soon translated into English and other languages. His writing earned him a great deal of money, but he was frequently insolvent, as he spent lavishly on women and sumptuous living. (Scholars have found that he had a total of 40 mistresses.) In 1846, he had built a country house outside Paris at Le Port-Marly, the large Château de Monte-Cristo, with an additional building for his writing studio. It was often filled with strangers and acquaintances who stayed for lengthy visits and took advantage of his generosity. Two years later, faced with financial difficulties, he sold the entire property.

Dumas wrote in a wide variety of genres and published a total of 100,000 pages in his lifetime. He also made use of his experience, writing travel books after taking journeys, including those motivated by reasons other than pleasure. Dumas traveled to Spain, Italy, Germany, England and French Algeria. After King Louis-Philippe was ousted in a revolt, Louis-Napoléon Bonaparte was elected president. As Bonaparte disapproved of the author, Dumas fled in 1851 to Brussels, Belgium, which was also an effort to escape his creditors. About 1859, he moved to Russia, where French was the second language of the elite and his writings were enormously popular. Dumas spent two years in Russia and visited St. Petersburg, Moscow, Kazan, Astrakhan and Tbilisi, before leaving to seek different adventures. He published travel books about Russia.

In March 1861, the kingdom of Italy was proclaimed, with Victor Emmanuel II as its king. Dumas travelled there and for the next three years participated in the movement for Italian unification. He founded and led a newspaper, Indipendente. While there, he befriended Giuseppe Garibaldi, whom he had long admired and with whom he shared a commitment to liberal republican principles as well as membership within Freemasonry. Returning to Paris in 1864, he published travel books about Italy.

Despite Dumas' aristocratic background and personal success, he had to deal with discrimination related to his mixed-race ancestry. In 1843, he wrote a short novel, Georges, that addressed some of the issues of race and the effects of colonialism. His response to a man who insulted him about his African ancestry has become famous. Dumas said:

My father was a mulatto, my grandfather was a Negro, and my great-grandfather a monkey. You see, Sir, my family starts where yours ends.

Personal life

On 1 February 1840, Dumas married actress Ida Ferrier (born Marguerite-Joséphine Ferrand) (1811–1859). He had numerous liaisons with other women and was known to have fathered at least four children by them:

Alexandre Dumas, fils (1824–1895), son of Marie-Laure-Catherine Labay (1794–1868), a dressmaker. He became a successful novelist and playwright.

Marie-Alexandrine Dumas (5 March 1831 – 1878), the daughter of Belle Krelsamer (1803–1875).

Micaëlla-Clélie-Josepha-Élisabeth Cordier (born 1860), the daughter of Emélie Cordier.

Henry Bauer, the son of a woman whose surname was Bauer.

About 1866, Dumas had an affair with Adah Isaacs Menken, a well-known American actress. She had performed her sensational role in Mazeppa in London. In Paris, she had a sold-out run of Les Pirates de la Savanne and was at the peak of her success.

These women were among Dumas' nearly 40 mistresses found by scholar Claude Schopp, in addition to three natural children.

Death and legacy

At his death in December 1870, Dumas was buried at his birthplace of Villers-Cotterêts in the department of Aisne. His death was overshadowed by the Franco-Prussian War. Changing literary fashions decreased his popularity. In the late twentieth century, scholars such as Reginald Hamel and Claude Schopp have caused a critical reappraisal and new appreciation of his art, as well as finding lost works.

In 1970, the Alexandre Dumas Paris Métro station was named in his honour. His country home outside Paris, the Château de Monte-Cristo, has been restored and is open to the public as a museum.

Researchers have continued to find Dumas works in archives, including the five-act play, The Gold Thieves, found in 2002 by the scholar Réginald Hamel [fr] in the Bibliothèque Nationale de France. It was published in France in 2004 by Honoré-Champion.

Frank Wild Reed (1874–1953), the older brother of Dunedin publisher A. H. Reed, was a busy Whangarei pharmacist who never visited France, yet he amassed the greatest collection of books and manuscripts relating to Dumas outside France. It contains about 3350 volumes, including some 2000 sheets in Dumas' handwriting and dozens of French, Belgian and English first editions. This collection was donated to Auckland Libraries after his death. Reed wrote the most comprehensive bibliography of Dumas.

In 2002, for the bicentennial of Dumas' birth, French President Jacques Chirac had a ceremony honouring the author by having his ashes re-interred at the mausoleum of the Panthéon of Paris, where many French luminaries were buried. The proceedings were televised: the new coffin was draped in a blue velvet cloth and carried on a caisson flanked by four mounted Republican Guards costumed as the four Musketeers. It was transported through Paris to the Panthéon. In his speech, President Chirac said:

With you, we were D'Artagnan, Monte Cristo, or Balsamo, riding along the roads of France, touring battlefields, visiting palaces and castles—with you, we dream.

Chirac acknowledged the racism that had existed in France and said that the re-interment in the Pantheon had been a way of correcting that wrong, as Alexandre Dumas was enshrined alongside fellow great authors Victor Hugo and Émile Zola. Chirac noted that although France has produced many great writers, none has been so widely read as Dumas. His novels have been translated into nearly 100 languages. In addition, they have inspired more than 200 motion pictures.

In June 2005, Dumas' last novel, The Knight of Sainte-Hermine, was published in France featuring the Battle of Trafalgar. Dumas described a fictional character killing Lord Nelson (Nelson was shot and killed by an unknown sniper). Writing and publishing the novel serially in 1869, Dumas had nearly finished it before his death. It was the third part of the Sainte-Hermine trilogy.

Claude Schopp, a Dumas scholar, noticed a letter in an archive in 1990 that led him to discover the unfinished work. It took him years to research it, edit the completed portions, and decide how to treat the unfinished part. Schopp finally wrote the final two-and-a-half chapters, based on the author's notes, to complete the story. Published by Éditions Phébus, it sold 60,000 copies, making it a best seller. Translated into English, it was released in 2006 as The Last Cavalier, and has been translated into other languages.

Schopp has since found additional material related to the Saints-Hermine saga. Schopp combined them to publish the sequel Le Salut de l'Empire in 2008.

Dumas is briefly mentioned in the 1994 film The Shawshank Redemption. The inmate Heywood mispronounces Dumas' last name as "dumbass" as he files books in the prison library.

Dumas is briefly mentioned in the 2012 film Django Unchained. The Southern slaveholder Calvin Candie expressed admiration for Dumas, owning his books in his library and even naming one of his slaves D'Artagnan. He is surprised to learn from another white man that Dumas was black. (Source: Wikipedia)

CPSIA information can be obtained
at www.ICGtesting.com
Printed in the USA
BVHW031105300819
557243BV00008B/88/P